Razor Black

Robert Young Jr

Razor Black

The Dark Years

TATE PUBLISHING & *Enterprises*

This title is also available as a Tate Out Loud product. Visit www.tatepublishing.com for more information.

This novel is a work of fiction. However, several names, descriptions, entities and incidents included in the story are based on the lives of real people.

The opinions expressed by the author are not necessarily those of Tate Publishing, LLC.

Published by Tate Publishing & Enterprises, LLC
127 E. Trade Center Terrace | Mustang, Oklahoma 73064 USA
1.888.361.9473 | www.tatepublishing.com

Tate Publishing is committed to excellence in the publishing industry. The company reflects the philosophy established by the founders, based on Psalm 68:11,
"The Lord gave the word and great was the company of those who published it."

Cover design by Summer Floyd-Harvey
Interior design by Amber Lee

Published in the United States of America

ISBN: 978-1-60696-857-4
1. Fiction: Historical   2. Fiction: Westerns
08.10.30

Dedication

To God, for giving me the skill to write;
To my parents, for the love of writing;
To my wife, for her encouragement, patience, and understanding.

Chapter 1

It's funny the things a man thinks about as he's dying. For dying I surely was, with a bullet hole in my leg and an arrow through my side. My two companions, Riley and Jackson, were already dead out in the brush, and I was severely wounded. Lucky for me it was my day in camp, or I would be one of them. Already dead.

Riley and Jackson had been dropped in the first rush as they were running for camp, and lucky for me those Indians were on foot instead of horses, else they probably would have had me too. As it was, my two partners had given me enough of a warning so I could get ready for a fight as they charged in. I killed two of them outright and drew blood on a third before they figured they were too close. While they were re-grouping and deciding what to do, I reloaded my two rifles and two pistols. Then I took stock of what I was in for.

Our camp was situated on the edge of a small meadow, with a thick stand of timber directly behind us. It was full of blown down trees from some windstorm in the past and almost impossible to get through. So that meant that there was only one way they could approach the camp, and that was straight on. By the same token, that was my only way out too.

So I was more or less stuck here until either they left or killed me. Things weren't looking so good for me anymore, what with eight of them still after my hair and all our camp plunder. Durned Blackfoot! They rank right up there with towns and all the people in them. I don't have much use for either one.

As they tried to put the sneak on me, I shot another one through the arm when he tried to scalp Riley. But he still got away with his rifle and possibles bag before I could get another shot. So now they had a rifle, not just bows and arrows.

Another slow hour passed, and I figured I might as well eat, so I reached out to get the pot of meat by the fire. I couldn't quite reach it, so I scooted a little closer and grabbed it. That's when I felt a white hot pain in my left leg. It took me a minute to realize I had been shot. And with a .54 caliber ball, nonetheless. I cut the bottom off my legging to make a bandage and some fringe off my shirt, tying this together to make a long string. With this I bound up the wound to stop the bleeding, but it didn't do anything for the pain. That red devil was going to pay for that one.

All the rest of the afternoon they tried to put the sneak on me, but I was raised in the mountains back in Virginia. They weren't going to catch me napping. One of the Indians would move towards me slow, hoping to draw my fire, while two others would sneak closer, unseen or heard by me. At least that's what they thought. When the decoy moved in on me, I was watching for the other two, and when they moved, I shot both of them. I took a potshot at the decoy as he was running back to his companions, just to let them know I was still kicking. That ought to slow them down some. And then there were six.

The remaining Indians moved off back in the trees, trying to decide what to do about me. Not for one instant did I think they were gone. There was too much valuable stuff in this camp for them to just to ride off and leave it because they had lost some men. True, they had lost almost half their raiding party, and all they had to show for it was one white-man's rifle. Their medicine was going south on them, but they wouldn't quite be sure. They wanted all the guns in camp, along with the plunder. There wasn't much of that, other than the bales of beaver hides we had trapped last fall and into the winter.

I had hooked up with Tom Riley and Sampson Jackson last summer at Rendezvous, not really wanting to have any more partners but knowing I needed to have someone along to help out, as I was headed up to the Three Forks country. And that meant Blackfoot.

They were free trappers like myself, and we were beholding to no man or company to tell us where we could or couldn't trap. We had our own rules for what we did, and number one was to survive any way we could. The second, and last rule as far as I was concerned, was to watch out for your partners and all make it to the next Rendezvous. Looks like Riley and Jackson weren't going to make this one. I thought I might not either, but I wasn't dead yet.

It was early spring now, and we were trapping our way down to Bear Lake for the annual rendezvous, only the third one, so far. Figured we might as well take what flat tails we could find along the way. That is, until this raiding party of Blackfoot found us and decided they wanted what we had.

Getting close to sundown now. I think they'll try one more head-on rush before nightfall. If I could take a few more of them out of the game, then just maybe the rest of them will realize their medicine is bad and pull out. I'm not too worried about them attacking me in the night. Most Indians believe that if they are killed at night, that their spirit will wander in the afterlife forever. But Blackfoot are a whole different breed of Indian. With them, there's no telling what they'll do, or when.

The sudden clatter of hooves startled me. Looks like they decided to use horses on me this time. Rising up slightly, rifle in hand, I checked to gauge their location and the distance. Doesn't look good. Too close already. My first shot dropped a horse but missed the rider. Instantly, I dropped the now empty rifle and grabbed both pistols. I took one Indian through the throat with my left hand pistol as they charged past me, and I spun around for my last shot.

They had turned and were headed back, and were almost on top of me now. I let go with the second pistol, point blank range, at a big Blackfoot brave. He was so close I could smell the rancid bear grease he had in his hair, and see the blue and black paint he had applied to his face in a zigzag pattern. The ball took him high in the left shoulder and knocked him backwards off his horse, just as his horse jumped over my breastwork of beaver hide bales.

I dropped the empty pistols and reached around behind me for the tomahawk and knife in the back of my belt. Suddenly I felt a sharp pain in my right side, just above my leggin. Taking a quick glance down, I could see the arrow had pierced my flesh right above the hip. It only went part of the way through, so it was sticking out both sides.

As I looked back up, the brave who shot me was notching another arrow to finish me off. Without thinking, I hurled the tomahawk in his general direction as hard as I could, hoping to at least spoil his aim. But my aim was true, and the tomahawk buried itself deep in his chest before he could release the arrow.

Switching the knife to my right hand, I dropped to one knee and picked up the loaded rifle. The three braves that were still on their horses were high-tailing it out of there, back the way they had come. That's when I remembered the big Indian I had shot off his horse. He was only wounded, and he was behind me. I spun around, swinging the rifle in a wide arc in case he was right there.

He was still laying there where he had fallen. He hadn't moved, but he might be playing possum, waiting for a chance to jump me. So I watched him as I tried to figure out what to do with this piece of wood sticking through my hide. The more I watched the brave, the more I was sure he was dead. Just the way he lay—all sprawled out on his back, head twisted off to one side. Probably broke his neck when he fell off his horse.

That made three more down and only three left. If they had any sense they would just keep on riding and leave me alone. I didn't think I could handle another rush. Now that the excitement was over, I was suddenly very tired and weak. Loss of blood and pain will do that to a man I guess.

It was dark now, and I didn't see any fire where the last three Blackfoot braves would be camped. I decided to build a small fire to heat some water to treat my wounds as best as I could, and some coffee sounded like a good idea too.

Crabbing and crawling my way to the fire pit, ever mindful of the arrow in my side, I gathered some bark and shredded it in my hands. Then I added some small slivers of pitchy wood. After that, it was only a matter of getting out my flint and steel to strike a few sparks on the pile. My tiny fire caught, and as it ate up the bark and small wood, I added bigger and bigger pieces until I had a nice blaze going. But not too big. Those red devils might still be out there, waiting for me to make a mistake.

While my water and coffee were heating up on the fire, I decided I better start thinking about how I was going to get this arrow out of my side. I took my knife and slit my buckskin shirt away from the shaft. The arrow, I could see, was through the fatty part of my side. Had it been any higher or lower, I would have been in serious trouble. Lower, it would have lodged in my hipbone, and higher, it would have hit a rib, or something else inside. The Lord was watching out for this 'ol trapper when that one came along.

Back in the mountains of Virginia, my pa had made us use our left hands as much as our right ones. I can still hear him say, "You never know when one of your hands might not be able to do what it's always done. So you teach your other hand to do the same things just as well." I was sure thankful for that advice and teaching right about then. There was no way I could use my right hand to do anything more than steady that arrow shaft.

I took my knife and slowly began to circle the feathered end of the shaft, about six inches away from my skin. When it was cut most of the way through, I snapped it off cleanly. A white-hot pain shot through my whole body, and I started to see blackness closing in on me, so I bit my lower lip as hard as I could to bring myself out of it.

I took a few deep breaths and then poured myself a cup of coffee. While it cooled down, I took a piece of cloth from my possibles bag and dipped it in the water, then washed my side around the arrow. I knew this next part was going to hurt like the devil, but I could see no other way. I had to cut a groove in the top of the arrow shaft, fill it with gun powder, light it, and push the arrow all the way through. Kind of seal the wound up. So that's what I did.

The cold woke me. My fire was down to just a few red eyes glowing at me. I must have passed out when I pushed the arrow through. I tossed some pieces of wood on the fire, and as it flared up, I looked around. Only about two hours had passed, judging by the position of the stars and the different night sounds.

The arrow lay on the ground behind me, and when I looked at the wound, it didn't seem too bad. At least there wasn't a piece of wood stuck in me anymore. I pushed the coffee pot back onto the coals to heat up and moved yesterday's stew closer too. Had to keep up my strength if I was going to get out of this one. I just hoped that arrow didn't have any poison on it. That would be like a Blackfoot. They were such bad shots, they had to poison their arrowheads and lance points to make sure of a kill.

My leg was stiff and sore, but the bleeding had stopped. I tried to take off my makeshift bandage, but the blood had dried to a hard crust, so I had to soak the bandage before it would come off. I didn't need to loose any more blood. The wound itself looked raw and ugly, but it wasn't red around the edges. That would mean it was infected, and that could cost me my leg at the least, my life at the most. Blood poisoning was a nasty bit of business, and I wanted no part of it.

Scooting over to the other side of the fire, I found my rawhide parfletche marked with red and yellow designs. This was my medicine kit, full of things I had picked up over the years for healing and treating various wounds. I opened it, and after some searching, found what I wanted. Since the bleeding in both wounds had stopped, I put the giant puffball back. Instead, I brought out a wad of spider web and a piece of yarrow root.

Laying the spider web to one side, I took the piece of yarrow root and put it in my mouth. It tasted terrible, but it worked, so who was I to complain? Worse yet, who was there to listen to me complain?

Since the wound in my side didn't seem to be infected, I decided to leave it uncovered. I had nothing to cover it up with anyway, and the fresh mountain air would help in the healing process. While the yarrow root was softening in my mouth, I packed both sides of my leg wound with spider webbing, leaving enough room for the yarrow root to sit just inside the two gaping holes. I rinsed the coffee grounds out of my cup with fresh water and then spit the root and my saliva into the cup. The saliva I poured into the wounds, then gently packed the root in.

After binding up the wound with the bottom of my other leggin, I crawled back over to my barricade of beaver bales and went to sleep.

Chapter 2

Waking just before daylight, I added some wood to my fire and checked my wounds. I was stiff and sore all over, but there were things that still needed to be done. Out here in the mountains, a person learned mighty quick that if there was something to be done, you better just do it, because there isn't anybody else going to do it for you. It was like a law out here to fend for yourself.

I knew I had to move around so I didn't get completely stove up, so I walked over to the big brave that I had killed yesterday. His neck was definitely broke. Grabbing my skinning knife at the back of my belt, I reached down and twisted my left hand in his greasy hair, lifting his head. Taking the point of my knife, I started just above his left ear and circled his entire head. Then I put my knee on his chest and pulled the scalp loose with an ugly plopping sound. It wasn't the first time I had done this.

Tucking the scalp in my belt, I headed over to the next one. Out here in the mountains, scalping a dead enemy is just a way of life. It shows you aren't afraid of him, and according to their customs, Indians aren't able to get to the Happy Hunting Grounds without their hair.

After I scalped all the dead Blackfoot warriors, I stripped the bodies of anything I could use, which wasn't much. A few knives for trade, some finger rings, and a beaded belt was about all there was. Now I had to go get one of our horses and drag these bodies away from my camp. Didn't want them stinking it up anymore than they already had, and bringing in the wolves. Not that I mind wolves, I just didn't want them in my camp with me. As I was dragging them away, I found the rifle they had taken the day before. That was good news for all the white men out here. One less gun the Blackfoot had to use against us.

I took the bodies of Riley and Jackson, with their scalps still intact, down stream a ways until I found a steep cut-bank. There, I put the bodies up against the bank, then climbed up on top so I could cave the bank onto them. It wasn't the most proper burial I had ever done, but it would do. I'm sure they would understand and would be thankful I didn't just leave their bodies to rot in the sun and become food for a bear or wolves.

After all this was done, I realized I was pretty much worn down to a nubbin, so I headed back to camp. I still needed to move the eleven horses in the pack string to fresh grass and water, but that could wait. I needed to rest and check my wounds again.

Sitting by the fire in camp, I began to look around at all that was there. The three of us had trapped last fall and into the winter up here in the Three Forks country, taking more than our fair share of beaver. While most trappers only trapped part of the winter due to the cold, we had decided to trap all winter long, and we did well. There were fourteen full bales of beaver, at an average of seventy pounds each. And with the ones still drying around camp, at least another half of a bale. That made close to a thousand pounds of credit for me, if I made it to Bear Lake. While it was true that I hadn't trapped all these beaver, I sure wasn't about to leave them here. Riley and Jackson would have done the same thing as I was planning if it were me that was killed. But first, I had to make it to rendezvous.

Sure would be nice to see the boys again. After being up here close to fourteen years, I'd seen them come and go. Some men just aren't right for the mountains, and the mountains have a way of weeding them out. Sometimes it's Indians, sometimes it's the cold, but most times, it's just the loneliness that we go through up here. Either way, they leave the mountains and head back to the settlements, and that was fine with me. More beaver and more country to see for those of us that are left.

Figuring I had lolly gagged around camp long enough, I got up and headed for the pack animals. I needed some fresh meat, and I still needed to check the traps from yesterday. I was hoping they were empty. Time for me to move on out of this country and head down to rendezvous. Besides, I had enough beaver to get me through next year, and then some. But I needed those traps. Some of them were mine, and they weren't cheap to replace.

Gathering up my mule, I headed upstream to where we had been setting our traps, taking my rifle and two pistols with me. Them Blackfoot might just as well have gone back to their main village and gathered more warriors to come back and finish me off. Another good reason to be moving on. So I wanted to be prepared in case they showed up.

After some time spent looking for the traps, I found all but one, and it was probably drug off by a big 'ol beaver. Four of the nine traps that were set yielded beaver for me. More work than I wanted right now, but I wasn't about to throw them back. They were already dead, and it wouldn't be right to waste them. So I skinned them out, rolled them up into a tube and put them on the mule. She was a good-natured animal, not like some of them I've had.

With the traps in my trap bag and the beaver skinned and loaded, I was just about to head back to camp when I saw something in the willows along the creek. Pulling one of my pistols from my belt, I slowly worked my way towards it. As I got closer, I could see it was another dead Blackfoot, with a tomahawk stuck dead center in his chest. Looked like Jackson's tomahawk. At least he got one of them before he went under.

I pulled out my skinning knife again and scalped this one too. As I was doing so, I found a pistol tucked under his body and took it. This one was far enough from camp to leave right there without having to worry about wolves, bears, or the smell. Hopefully though, I wasn't going to be here long enough to have to worry about it.

On the way back to camp, I stopped long enough to cut me some willow sticks so I could stretch these beaver. All the ones I had in camp had a hide in them already, and even though I planned on leaving in a day or two, the hides needed time to at least dry a little into the round "beaver dollar" shape. And that's exactly what they looked like, a big round furry dollar.

Back in camp, as I was unloading the mule, I noticed the ears of the horses were up and pointing towards where I had hung the Blackfoot bodies in the trees. Dropping down behind some bales of beaver, I drew my rifles closer and pulled my pistols out, laying them close to hand. Checking the prime on all of them, I realized I had forgotten to reload both pistols. Things like that could get a man killed.

I smelled them before I saw them. Trappers have a smell about them that is unlike anything else. They smell like a half-rotted beaver mixed with sweat and horse. That's what I was smelling now. As they came into sight, I saw there were four in the group, and it looked like they were Canadians.

Now, I don't have anything against Canadians in particular, but some of them are just plain ruthless. They would just as soon kill other trappers for their furs as not. I hoped these men weren't like that. I could sure use the company on the trip to Bear Lake.

"Hello, the camp," shouted one of them.

"Hello, yourselves," I shouted back. "Come on in, but you better be on your best behavior. I've had my fill of trespassers lately."

As they rode into my camp, I noticed one of them taking a real good look around. Was he looking for my companions, or was he checking the camp to see what it contained? Made me really uneasy, and I was in no mood to be fooling around with the likes of these men.

As they drew closer, I stood up so they could see me. I knew what they saw, and it wasn't much. The buckskin hunting shirt I wore was stained with grease, sweat, and blood. There were more than a few holes in it from past fights, too. I had on a blue trade-cloth breechclout and a pair of buckskin leggins, the bottoms having been cut off to make bandages for my wounded leg. All this was covering my stocky frame of average height.

Pulling the coyote skin cap off my head, I revealed a head full of graying hair, pulled into two braids that framed my bearded face. Like I said, I wasn't much to look at. And as I took in the group of four trappers, my green eyes hardened.

"We see what you do to 'trespassers,' as you call it, back in the trees," said one of the trappers. "Why you hang them in the trees upside down and without their clothes?"

"To send the rest of 'em a message that I just wanna be left alone," I replied.

"Look to me like they wounded you some," one of the other men said.

"Just a couple of scratches. I been hurt worse than this fallin' off a horse," I said. No use in letting them know how bad off I really was, especially if they planned on killing me and taking all my furs.

"I seen you down at the rendezvous last year. Ain't you the one they call 'Round-Ball'?" asked their leader.

"Yeah, that be me. But I don't know any of you. Who are you?" I asked.

"I am Vergal, this one here is called Pierre, and beside him is Montour. That one over there calls himself Antoin. He say he only speak French. He came into our camp a few weeks ago, wanting to go to Bear Lake with us. He say all his trapping partners have been killed by the Indians, but I don't trust him. He like to look into our things."

"Know what you mean," I replied. "His eyes ain't stopped movin' since you been here. Better you tell him I said for him to put his eyes back in his head, afore I blow out his candle. I don't take kindly to his shifty kind."

Vergal spoke to Antoin in French, and I guess he told him just what I said, because Antoin glared at me, then jumped off his horse. I stood up and leveled my rifle at him, dragging the hammer back to full cock. He might not understand English, but he sure understood that.

The other three Canadians sat their horses and waited to see what I was going to do. I didn't know what they would do for sure, beings as how they were all Canadians, and I was an American. Would they back their countryman, or was it like Vergal said, that they didn't trust him either? Either way, if I was going to go out, I was going to take this skunk with me.

Vergal said something in French, and Antoin hesitated where he was. Then Vergal spoke harshly to him and he got back on his horse, turning away. As he did so, he turned around to glare at me again, dragging his finger across his throat and smiling. I should have shot him right then and there, but I didn't.

"Hope you fellas don't think bad of me, but I don't like him," I said to the three Canadians. "If you're willin' to empty your hands, climb on down. I was just about to make some fresh coffee."

Chapter 3

Over some coffee I learned that the three Canadians had spent the winter trapping up near the border of America and Canada. They had some brushes with the Blackfoot early on in the fall, but as winter moved in, the trappers dug in for the cold weather, and the Indians moved on to their winter camps. It was much the same for me and my former partners.

At length, Vergal asked what had happened and where my trapping partners were. It was obvious from the amount of furs I had in my camp that there was more than one man trapping. As I laid it out for them, I could see them nodding their heads in understanding. They waited until I was done talking before they asked their questions.

"So you kill all of them, by yourself?" asked the one called Pierre.

"I don't recollect that I had much choice," I answered. "It was either them or me, and I'm kind of partial to my hair being on my head instead of on some Blackfoot warrior's belt. But no, I didn't kill all of 'em. One of my partners got one along the stream where they were jumped, and three of 'em rode off like their tails was on fire."

"That is still quite a few Indians for one man to kill all by himself," put in Montour. "Not that I am calling you a liar," he added quickly, "but the Blackfoot are ver' mean."

"Well, that's the way it happened. I don't much care if you believe it or not." I was beginning to get irritated with all this talk, and my side felt as if it were on fire. That right there told me that an infection had set in, and I better take care of it soon.

Pulling up my buckskin shirt, I looked down at my side. It was all red and inflamed. Vergal took one look at it and said something in French to Pierre, who proceeded to get up and go over to one of their packhorses. When he came back to the fire, he had a small buckskin bag in his hands.

"Let me look at it," said Vergal. "It is getting bad, no?" he asked, taking the bag from Pierre.

"Thought I had it under control," I answered, leaning back.

After some gentle probing with his thick fingers, Vergal shook his head, always a bad sign with an injury. Handing my camp pot to Montour, he told him to go get some fresh water. He added some wood to the fire and sent Pierre out for more, as my supply was just about gone.

"It is full of the pus," he stated. "But do not worry, my friend. I have had some experience with this sort of thing before. I studied medicine in Montreal before I decided to become a trapper."

There was a story behind that, and when I asked him how he went from studying medicine to becoming a trapper, he said, "It is simple enough. I was bored with my studies, and there was an expedition going out from Montreal that needed a doctor along. After telling the bourgeois that I was studying medicine, but I was bored with it, he only asked me if I could patch bullet wounds. I told him I could, and now here I am fixing you."

While the water was heating on the fire, we talked about where all we had trapped over the years, and we mentioned names to each other to see if we knew the same people. There were a few men we both knew, but not as many as you would think. He had only been in the mountains for three winters, where as I had been here close to fourteen years now.

When the water was heated, Vergal took a cloth from his bag and, after dipping it in the hot water, gently started to wash at the wound on my side. It hurt like the devil, but there was nothing I could do about it. The scabs on the holes made by the arrow had to come off so the pus could drain and get rid of the infection. Sounded easy enough, but it sure hurt. I laid my head back and tried not to think about the pain.

When Vergal pulled the first scab off, I thought he was stabbing me with a red-hot knife, it hurt so bad. I must have dozed off while he was softening the scab, and it was a good thing for him that Pierre and Montour were standing on either side of me, because I came up swinging, ready to do battle with whoever was hurting me. As they held me, Vergal lightly pressed all around the wound, working the pus out. And there was plenty of it.

Somewhere along the way, I must have passed out, for when my eyes opened again, it was dusk. The Canadians were still there, only two of them in sight, and my rifle was right by my side. That told me enough that they could be trusted. If they were out to kill me and take my plunder, they could have done so while I was passed out. Suddenly, I wondered where that other Canadian, Antoin, was. He had threatened to kill me, and here I was, helpless as a newborn beaver kit.

Pierre was the one who noticed I was awake again, and he smiled down at me, nodding his head. Vergal came over with a stick full of meat and asked me if I was hungry. I was still a little groggy, more than likely from the fever that had been starting to work its way through my body.

Shaking my head no, I managed to sit up. I was thirsty though and reached for the pot of water near the fire. After taking a long drink, I set the pot back down and turned to Vergal.

"Thanks," I said. "I guess I ain't as young as I used to be. This old body's startin' to feel worn out."

Squatting down beside me, Vergal started to laugh. "My friend, if you are starting to feel worn out, I would like to have seen you when you were younger. It was all these two could do to hold you down when I pulled the other plug off your back. Montour is down by the stream, soaking his leg from where you bit him. You took a big chunk out of his leg, my friend. He will be sore for a few days, but he will heal."

"Didn't mean to hurt him. I don't even recall doing it, and I hope he doesn't hold it against me," I said.

I was starting to get hungry now, and when I said so, Vergal gave me the stick of meat. It was some fresh venison they had killed the day before, and it sure tasted good.

As I ate I asked Vergal what he thought about me throwing in with them for the trip down to rendezvous. He said that was fine with him, but the others would have to speak for themselves. Pierre agreed, and Montour was still at the stream, but Vergal thought it would be fine with him as well. And as for Antoin, I was going to be keeping an eye on that one.

Thinking of him, I asked Vergal where he was.

"He is back in the trees, near where you hang the Blackfoot. I tell him he better stay away from you, or you kill him. My friend, we all know who you are now. You have been up here in the mountains longer than anyone. Even the Blackfoot know about Round-Ball. They sing songs of your bravery and how slowly they kill you, if they ever catch you. How you have survived this long is a story I want to hear."

"Not much to tell, really. I just came to the mountains years ago an' never left. I like being up here, where there ain't nobody to tell me I can or can't do somethin.' I've been back to the settlements a time or two. For the life of me, I can't figure out how all them people can stand to live like that, all bunched up together. It just ain't natural." There was more to the story, much more, but I wasn't willing to talk about that right now. Maybe not ever.

Suddenly, we all heard something thrashing around in the brush, followed by a grunt and a thump. Vergal and Pierre grabbed up their rifles and headed to where it was coming from, while I pulled my rifle into my lap, cradling it like a baby. Flipping open the pan, I checked the priming. It was good to go, and cocking it, I waited.

Glancing to the right at my horses, everything seemed to be in order. All of a sudden, the ears on my mule stood up, twitched, and she turned to look off to my left. This was the opposite direction Vergal and Pierre had gone. Whatever it was, there was more than one if they were chasing something down by the stream.

The figure of a man suddenly leapt up on my left, right at the corner of my vision. I tried to swing my rifle in that direction, but it was knocked out of my hands, and I went sprawling across the fire.

Screaming in agony at the pain in my wounded side, I turned around on my hands and knees searching for a weapon. A heavy body slammed into me, and I saw the glint of steel reflected from the firelight. Twisting onto my good side, I tried to throw my antagonist off, but he was too strong, and I was still pretty weak.

I found myself on my back with him on top of me. Suddenly, I just relaxed my body. It had the effect that I wanted, forcing my opponent to change his grip for a new one. And as he raised the knife in his right hand, I started kicking at his back with both knees, momentarily throwing him off balance. It was all I needed.

Rolling to my right, I came to rest up against the packs I had removed from my mule earlier. Reaching inside, I found one of the knives I had taken from the dead Blackfoot that morning. I turned just as he was leaping at me, and holding the knife in both hands, I thrust them into the air in front of me. Too late, he realized his mistake. But he couldn't stop the momentum and he impaled himself on the knife. As he landed on top of me, I rolled over, jerking the knife sideways, tearing the stomach cavity open.

Feeling the warm blood gush out on my hands, I pulled the knife free and kicked the body away. I heard running feet headed my way, and dove over to catch up my rifle. But it was only Vergal, with Pierre following close behind.

Pierre walked over to the body and flipped him over with his foot.

"Antoin," was all he said.

So that's who it was.

Glad that it was over, I looked around for Montour, but didn't see him. I looked over at Vergal, with the question on my face, and he shook his head.

"Antoin kill Montour down to the stream. That is what we heard. I think he do it on purpose to draw us away from you. He not like you ver' much. I also think he try to kill us all so he can take all our furs for himself." Vergal said something in French to Pierre, who immediately pulled his knife out and scalped Antoin.

Shocked at this sudden fury from Pierre, I turned to Vergal.

"What's that all about?" I asked.

"Montour and Pierre were brothers. They not always get along, but they still brothers. Since you kill Antoin, Pierre have no one to take revenge on. Please, my friend, let him have the scalp. He need to send it to his family so they know that revenge was taken."

Waving my hand, I said it was alright. I had taken enough scalps lately.

As I lay there in my sleeping robes by the fire later that night, I began to think of what I had done with my life and what I had been through since leaving Virginia all those years ago.

I had some guns and some horses, along with a bag of scalps I had taken over the years. It didn't add up to much by most people's standards, but I was happy enough with what I had done with my life.

Chapter 4

When I heard the slight skritching sounds, my first instinct was to throw off my sleeping robes, and come up shooting. But after fifteen years of living in these mountains, I had learned that sometimes that's not always the best way. I slowly opened my eyes, and looked around our camp, not moving my head.

The first thing I saw was Pierre, squatting by the fire, holding something in his hands. When I saw the dull reflection of the knife, I knew he was scraping the scalp he had removed so unceremoniously from Antoin's head the night before. That was the skritching noise I had heard.

Glancing up at the star-lit sky, I saw that it was close to dawn and time to be moving. I threw off my robes and sat up, almost forgetting about the two holes in my side. I must have made a small moaning sound, for all of a sudden, Vergal threw back his robes and sprang up, pistol in hand. When he saw it was only Pierre and myself there, he relaxed and shook his head.

"Time to leave this country," he muttered. "Jumping at shadows say to me I been here too long."

"Know what you mean," I replied. "I just about did the same thing to 'Ol Pierre there. I be thinkin' it's time we head on down to Bear Lake and rendezvous. What you fellas think?"

"You think you side can take riding the horse?" asked Pierre.

"Only one way to find out," I said.

Heading towards the stream, I picked up the pot I had been using for coffee. Some things a man can just plain do without, but coffee wasn't one of them, at least for me. I liked it in the morning as well as at night and the stronger the better. Good thing I was headed to rendezvous though; I was just about out.

When I had returned with the pot of water, Vergal had punched up the fire, and Pierre was dragging the lifeless corpse of Antoin away from camp. I set the pot on the edge of the fire, and got out my meager supply of coffee beans.

One thing I had learned over the years was how to build a good pot of coffee. I had picked up some sacking material a few years ago and made them into small bags, with a drawstring around the top. I pulled one out now and proceeded to put in a good-sized handful of coffee beans. Closing the top of the bag with the drawstring, I grabbed up my camp ax and pounded the beans into a fine powder, using a fairly flat rock underneath for backing.

Vergal was watching me, amusement in his eyes and probably more than a little curious as to why I would do such a thing to perfectly good coffee beans. Most trappers just hit them enough to break the beans to release the flavor. But like I said, I like my coffee strong.

"Bet you never seen anybody make coffee like this afore," I said to him. "But just you wait 'till you had some. Be the best cup you ever had, guaranteed."

"The coffee you make yesterday was good," he said, shrugging his shoulders.

"Yea, but I was in a hurry then. Today, I aim to do it right and proper. You'll see what I mean in a few minutes."

The water was boiling by this time, so I dropped the beans in the pot, bag and all. Pierre came walking up just as I was doing this, and his eyes went from the pot to Vergal. Vergal said something in French to him, and then both of them started laughing.

"I tell him you are a crazy man over the coffee," Vergal told me.

I figured I better tell them that there was definitely a method to my madness, so I said, "By crushing the beans up into a powder, it releases the flavor more. You use less beans, and if the traders down to rendezvous want what they did last year for their coffee beans, you'll be thankin' me for this little advice. And when you leave the beans in the bag like I done, there ain't no grounds in the bottom of your cup. Here, gimme your cups, and I'll show you what I mean."

After drinking some, they both agreed that it was the best cup of coffee they had ever drank. Whether they were being truthful or not, I couldn't say, but they sure finished off the pot in a hurry.

As the sun started making its journey across the sky for another day, we packed up and headed out. I was riding my mule, as usual, and using the horses for packing all the beaver pelts my dead partners and I had trapped. It was hard to find anybody to go up into the Three Forks country to trap, what with that being smack dab in the middle of the Blackfoot Nation. But those two knew what they were in for when we headed out. They had both trapped up there a few years before. One thing we all agreed on, and that was that the plews up in the Three Forks were prime furs.

As we were plodding along, following the Blackfoot River south, Vergal asked me how I came about getting the name 'Round-Ball.'

"Well, when I come out here, back in '13, I heard tell there was so many wild Indians runnin' loose on the prairies and in the mountains that a man had better have him plenty of lead and powder. So every night I would sit by the fire an' melt down my lead, makin' round-balls for my rifle. And when I had melted all my lead, I started in makin' 'em for the other fellas that was along.

"The name just kind of hung on, like a tick suckin' your blood." Remembering this now, I thought back to the trip out here from St. Louis with Pepper. My eyes started to mist a little at the memory, and I angrily drug my arm across my face, not wanting to remember what had happened. It was still too painful.

As we wandered down the Blackfoot River, then the Bear River, Vergal and Pierre set their traps at likely looking streams. When we found a good one that produced the flat-tails, we stayed for a few days, catching as many as we could. I had decided I had more than I needed already, so I was the one to stay in camp, stretching the hides and fleshing them.

My side and leg were healing up nicely, thanks to the almost constant attention of Vergal. Why a man of his talents would choose to live up here was beyond me, but I supposed he had his reasons. I had my reasons when I came out here, too, but they had changed over the years. No longer was it a matter of the money to be made from trapping. No, now it was the freedom, the peacefulness of being able to do what I wanted and go wherever I wanted to go.

By late April, or as near as we could figure, we had dropped down low enough so that the plews were no longer worth taking. We still had a ways to go to make it to Bear Lake, but there was time yet. The traders usually didn't make it until sometime in late June or early July.

Chapter 5

Feeling like beating the stuffing out of the young clerk behind the counter, I decided I had better just come back tomorrow morning, like he suggested. It was close to dark anyhow, and I wanted the light good when he re-graded my plews. It was all part of the game, and I knew it, but it still made me angry to have this youngster grading my winter's work. I gathered my horses and headed back to where we had pitched our camp.

We had arrived at the south end of Bear Lake two days ago, and the traders had arrived only the day before. Setting up our camp next to some other free trappers, I took my furs out and dusted them off from the trail, grading them one more time before I took them over to the trader's tent.

Suddenly, I was startled by a voice beside me.

"That's some, now, ain't it? You been here all of two hours, an' you ain't even bothered to come over and say your howdys."

Turning to look at the newcomer, I was startled to see Daniel Potts standing there, hands on his hips and a big smile on his face.

"Daniel," I shouted, dropping my furs and straightening

up. "I figured Bug's Boys raised your hair last winter. Wasn't you headed up to the Three Forks?" I asked.

"Yep, that's where we went. Ain't that where you was headed too? And it seems I recall you had a couple of fellas with you. Jackson and Riley, weren't it?"

"Yea, that were them. We was trappin' early on this spring, when some of them stinkin' Blackfoot jumped us. Killed both of 'em slick as a whistle. Almost did me in too, but lucky for me, a couple of Canadians happened along and patched me up." We ended up talking about our winter experiences for the remainder of the day, and he invited me over to his camp for supper later, saying he wanted to talk some more.

Early the next morning, as I was headed over to the trader's tent with my furs, I could feel the eyes of several men on me. Turning around to look, I saw four men, following me and muttering amongst themselves. They didn't have any furs with them, so I figured they were up to no good. I reached the trader, stopped, and turned to face them.

"You want somethin'?" I demanded.

"We want to know where you got all them furs, old man," said one of them.

"Where I got them furs ain't none of your business," I snapped back at him.

"Seems like an awful lot of furs for one man to have. You take all them flat-tails by yourself?"

"Like I said afore, how and where I got 'em ain't none of your business. But since you wanna push, I stole them."

The leader of the four smiled at his companions.

"See," he said. "Ain't that what I told you boys? I figure this here old man killed some unlucky trappers he found. He's too old to be up here trappin.' He can't do his own trappin' no more. I think we ought to take them furs away from him, show him how we treat thieves."

"I heard enough out of you, boy," I said, walking towards them. When I got close enough, I just reached out with the butt end of my rifle and planted it right in the middle of his face. As the blood poured out of his nose and mouth, he fell like a sack of rocks. Immediately, I turned on the rest of them.

"Anybody else think I stole them pelts?" I shouted.

"What in tarnation's going on here?" a new voice broke in.

Looking over, I saw Davy Jackson and Billy Sublette had come walking up.

"Ol Round-Ball, you picking on these youngsters?" asked Sublette.

"Naw," I answered. "Just settlin' a little question as to who's too old to be up here trappin,' and who's too wet behind the ears not to know when to keep his mouth shut."

"That *is* an awful lot of pelts you got," said Jackson. "Did you really steal 'em, like you said?"

"You should know me better than that by now, Dave. But yea, I did steal 'em. I stole 'em, one at a time, right from under the nose of the Blackfoot, up to the Three Forks. The other two what was with me got themselves killed some time back, and I wasn't about to just up and leave their plews there. So I brung 'em down here, figured you might want 'em."

"Yes, we want them," replied Davy Jackson.

"And as for you three," Sublette said, pointing at the three troublemakers. "You best pick up your friend and make tracks. You're lucky this 'old man' here didn't kill you and take your worthless scalps. Do you have any idea who you was jumpin'?"

"We-we do now," stuttered one of them. "Sorry mister, we didn't realize who you was," he said to me. Picking up their fallen comrade, they quickly left.

"Ain't it nice havin' a reputation as a mean, cantankerous, 'ol hivernant?" asked Billy. "Seems like you get worse and worse every year, Round-Ball."

"You would too, if you had to put up with all these young pups, tryin' to prove to themselves how tough and mean they is. So, how bad are you fellas gonna rob me this year?" I asked.

"You know it ain't like that, Round-Ball. We gotta make a livin' too," said Billy. "'Sides, you got enough plews there to outfit a whole brigade. Don't know as we got enough goods to trade to you though, beings as how you don't never buy no whiskey. You truly are one of a kind, Round-Ball. Probably the only trapper out here what don't drink. One of a kind," he said shaking his head and walking away.

Heading back over to the counter, I noticed the young clerk had an ashen color to his face. Probably his first trip to the mountains, I thought. As I handed him the first of the bundles of fur, his hands were shaking.

"No need to be scared of me, sonny," I said. "That is unless you don't give me what these plews are worth."

"Yes-yes sir," he stammered.

One of the other fur graders came over and tried to take over for the youngster, but he would have none of it.

"Got me my job to do," he says, adding, "and Mr. Sublette was the one that trained me, so if you have a problem with the way I grade your furs, take it up with him."

Well, well, I thought. This youngster just might have the makings of a trapper, what with an attitude like that. Put me right in my place, he did.

The tally showed I had two hundred and fifty-two beaver pelts, of which one hundred and ninety-six were prime, at three dollars and seventy-five cents to the pound, weighing three hundred forty-three pounds. The other fifty-six were good quality, at two dollars and fifty cents to the pound, weighing eighty-four pounds. Came out to $1307.25, more than I ever had in my life, all at once.

"What do you mean, I gotta give you my name?" I asked the man.

"We need to keep track of it, sir," he said.

"Keep track of it? What for? You got all my pelts already, so what do you need my given name for?"

"For record keeping, sir," came the reply.

"You heard Sublette call me 'Round-Ball.' Ain't that good enough?"

"No, sir. We need a proper name."

"Aw, alright. My proper name be Razor Black. Yea, like the color, and don't be makin' fun of it, neither," I said when he gave me a strange look.

"It isn't that at all, sir," he said. "It's just that—"

"Well, spit it out boy. I ain't got all day to be standin' here jawin' with you. I got me things to do."

"Yes, sir. It's just that I was wondering if you were related to someone I came in with, on the pack train. His name is Black too. Kind of looks like you, only he's older and a little taller."

Reaching across the makeshift counter, I grabbed him by the front of his shirt, half way dragging him over it.

"And where might I find this fella what has the same last name as me? Do you recall his first name?" I asked.

He pointed over to where the animals from the pack train were picketed. I let go of him, and as he sagged back across to his side of the counter, I asked him for the name.

"Said his name was Samuel, Samuel Black. Honest, mister. I wouldn't lie to you. That's what he said."

"Thanks," I replied. "Now gimme my paper what says I got $1307.25 coming. I'll be back to do my tradin' later, and if you was lyin' to me, I'll beat the tar outta you!"

After all these years! I couldn't believe it! My own brother, coming out here to the mountains. Last time I saw Samuel was back in '11. Him and another brother, Jonathon, had left for the frontier back in 1806. Samuel had met us in Richmond in 1811, said he was on a business trip, but he wouldn't say what kind of business. Pa had thought maybe it was something on the wrong side of the law, but Samuel swore up and down it was on the level. He was still in Richmond when we left, and that was the last time I ever saw him. Until now.

Chapter 6

Leading my now empty horses, I headed over to the group of men gathered near the horse herd. My mind was swimming with the things I wanted to tell my brother, all that I had been through, and where I had been for the last sixteen years. But then I had a thought. Suppose this Samuel Black wasn't my brother? There was bound to be others with the same name, somewhere. I almost turned and headed for my own camp, then stopped. If that was my brother over there, and I didn't go to make sure, then I would never know if it was him or not.

When I reached the group, all talk stopped. I knew they were all from back in the settlements just by the way they were dressed. A man sheds his city clothes out here fairly quick, much like he sheds his city ways, if he wants to survive.

Quickly, I scanned the group of men in front of me, looking for that familiar face of my brother. True, it had been sixteen years since I had last seen him, but I would recognize the scar on his forehead anywhere. I'm the one who gave him that scar, back home in Virginia. He had been tormenting me something fierce one time, and when he thought I was done for, he relaxed. Big mistake on his part. I was in the process of scalping him, I was so mad at him, when pa stopped me. But

I had cut him pretty deep before pa wrenched the knife from my hand.

I didn't see him and started away, when one of the men asked if I was looking for someone.

"Lookin' for a fella what calls hisself 'Black.' The clerk told me he was over here, but I don't see him. Look like I owe him a beatin' for lyin' to me."

I turned away, leading the horses, when one of the men spoke up from the back.

"Hey mister, wait a minute. Last time I saw him, he was over to our camp, sleepin' one off, if you know what I mean. But if you wake him, you better watch it. He's poison mean when he wakes up after a night of drinkin.' And I ought to know, beings as how him and me knowed each other for years now. What you want him for anyway?" he asked.

"Just want to see if he's someone I used to know from a long way back," I replied.

"I'll just kind of mosey along with you over there, you know, make sure you don't intend any harm come to my friend," he said.

"Suit yourself," I said, walking off in the direction of their camp.

"That be him, over yonder, under that bower. Just you remember what I said about wakin' him up though. You do that, and you're on your own. Last time I woke him after a night like he just had, he broke my nose and a couple of ribs for me."

"Tell me somethin,'" I said. "Does he have a long scar, on his forehead, about like so?" I asked, pointing to my own forehead.

"Yea, he do at that, mister. How do you know about that scar?"

"Because I'm the one what give it to him," I replied.

Well, I guess that settled it. This Samuel Black *was* my brother. I was glad I had decided to come over here and make sure.

We could hear him snoring lightly, and I guess it was the mean streak in me that made me let out a Ute war cry, scaring everyone within earshot, including my own horses. But when Samuel came flying out from underneath that bower, it was worth it, just seeing the look of terror on his face.

"Now what did you go and do that for, old man?" he asked me.

"Who you callin' old man?" I asked. "You best watch what you say to me, or I'll finish that scalpin' job I started on you years ago."

Startled, he took a step back, and almost fell into the fire pit.

"It can't be," he said, his face suddenly gone pale. "It just can't be."

"It can be, and it is," I replied.

"Razor? That really you?"

"It's really me, Samuel. Who else knows how you got that scar?"

His knees buckled, and he fell backwards into the bower. At first, I thought he had passed out, but then he asked for a drink of whiskey.

"Don't have none," I said. "And looks to me like you don't need anymore anyhow. How you ended up out here is what I want to know."

"Let's go get us some whiskey, and we'll talk about it," Samuel said.

"Told you once already, you don't need no more whiskey. Let's go over to my camp where we can talk. Grab all your truck, and we'll load it on one of my horses. We need to get you sobered up so we can talk."

Taking my older brother back to my camp, I left him with

Vergal, who had returned from visiting with some of his people. Asking him to keep my brother there, I went in search of Billy Sublette and Davy Jackson. We had some more business to discuss regarding my brother.

"So, that troublemaker is your brother?" asked Davy when I finally found them.

"Yea, he's my brother. What I want to know is how did he come to work for you?"

"We needed pack tenders, an' he put in for the job. We didn't have any idea he was your brother, though," added Billy.

"Well, he is. Now, what's it gonna to cost me to keep him? I figure he works for you, and I also know you paid him in advance for his work. Since he ain't goin' to be makin' the return trip with you, what's it gonna cost me to get him out of your debt?"

"We paid him four hundred dollars, in advance. And since he made it here, I figure that covers about half. If you want to keep him here, it's gonna cost you two hundred dollars. Does that seem fair to you?"

"Seems fair enough," I said. "I'll be over to the traders tent tomorrow mornin' to straighten it out on your books. Best you tell that youngster over there what we be doin,' so he don't give me any lip about it."

Sublette assured me he would take care of it, so I returned to my camp to see how Samuel was faring. He had taken to drinking somewhere along the way, but if he was going with me for the fall hunt, he best get it out of his system right now. I wasn't about to have a drunk tagging along with me, brother or not.

"What do you mean, you want me to go with you?" Samuel said to me when I asked him.

"Maybe I don't want to go with you. It just so happens, I

want to go back to St. Louis. Got some friends there I need to see. 'Sides, who made you my keeper all of a sudden?"

Boy, I thought. *He sure ain't the same Samuel I knew sixteen years ago. Why, he acts like we aren't even brothers. Must be all that whiskey he's got in him,* I decided.

"Nobody made me your keeper, Samuel," I said. "I just thought you might want to see how it is up here in these mountains, tag along with me for a season. Then, if you don't like it, you can go back with the pack train when it leaves rendezvous next year. All I'm asking for is a year. It's been nigh onto sixteen years since I seen anybody from my family. And now, when you come along, all you want to do is leave."

I was frustrated at his way of thinking. It just didn't make sense to me. All the years we spent together, I thought I knew my own brother. But this was a whole different person. I guess time has a way of changing a man. Looking back on my own life, I realized I had changed a lot, from the young seventeen-year-old kid I was when I left St. Louis, to the now thirty-year-old man I had become.

"Will you at least think on it?" I asked him.

Groaning, he said, "I guess it won't hurt nothin' but my head to think on it. But if I do go with you, all I got is my rifle and a couple of shirts. I don't own nothin' anymore," he added quietly.

"Just you let me take care of gettin' what you be needin.' I done well last season, better than I thought, so I got me some credit to be playin' with over to the trader's tent. But I gotta know as soon as you make up your mind, so I know what all to get. Now, I got me some friends to go see, then we'll talk more on it."

Waving his hand at me, he crawled back under the bower. Still sleepy, I supposed, after the night he had before. But if he was going to run with me, that was going to have to change.

Chapter 7

After thinking on it all day, Samuel decided he didn't have anything to lose by going with me for the year. He told me he would trap with me for the season, and if he survived, which he thought was next to impossible, he would go back with the traders next year. Vergal and Pierre were thinking of throwing in with us, but I flat told them I had something I was needing to take care of, some unfinished business and didn't want to get them caught up in it. Samuel looked at me, shook his head, and muttered something under his breath.

"If you got somethin' to say to me, better spit it out. There ain't gonna be no hard feelings between us, can't afford 'em. I'm gonna be dependin' on you to watch my back, an' you have to depend on me, 'cause you don't know your way around yet. 'Sides, I kept my hair all these years, right here on my head where it belongs, not on some Indian's lodge pole."

"It's just the way you say you have 'some unfinished business.' Sounds like trouble to me."

"It's nothing to be too concerned about, so stop your worryin,'" I told him.

With Samuel following along, I headed over to get the supplies we would be needing for the following year.

"Now here is where 'Ol Billy Sublette takes me, brother," I said. "We free trappers bust our humps all year long in the up-country, freezin' our feet and hands off, only to get took down here with the prices they charge. But just you watch and see how your little brother does his tradin.' Might come in handy for you someday, if'n you should decide to stay here in the mountains and become a trapper like me."

As we stood in line at the counter of the trader's tent, I was doing come calculating on what all we were gonna need. Since I was buying for two, I thought I might just double my order from the last two seasons. Before that, I had me a partner. Sure do miss 'Ol Pepper. Together, he and I covered a lot of country together over the years.

When it was our turn, we walked up to the counter. I handed the same young clerk from yesterday my paper, with my name and amount of credit I had coming written on it.

"Billy Sublette tell you what we discussed yesterday, boy?" I asked.

He looked at the name on the paper, then at Samuel and me standing there together.

"Yes, he told me Mr. Black," he said. "I see you found the man you were looking for. See, I wasn't lying to you."

"No, boy, you didn't lie to me. And this here fella is my older brother. I thank you, by the way, for tellin' me he was here at rendezvous. Been almost sixteen year since we seen each other, ain't that right, Samuel?"

Samuel just nodded his head, so I turned back to the clerk and started in ordering our supplies.

"What's powder goin' for?" I asked

"Two fifty to the pound," he answered.

"English?"

"Yes, sir."

"Better give me seventy-five pound of the shootin' stuff an' fifteen pound of primin.' Now, how much lead be?"

"Lead is one dollar and fifty cents a pound, and it's Galena."

"Nothin' but the best for us free trappers, I always say. Gimme a hundred and seventy-five pounds of it."

"That's a lot of lead, Razor," put in Samuel. "Do we really need that much?"

"It's plain as the nose on your face, you ain't heard my nickname. 'Cause if you did, you wouldn't be askin' such a question. Now, boy, what's the toll on coffee?"

"And just what is your nickname?" asked Samuel.

"It be 'Ol Round-Ball, now what was the coffee?"

"Two dollar a pound."

"Gimme fifty pound of it and another fifty pound of tobacco."

"I didn't know you smoked tobacco, Razor," Samuel said.

"Don't. It's for tradin' and presents."

"Tradin' and presents for who?" He wanted to know.

"We'll be talkin' 'bout that later. Now, let's see. Why don't you give me three dozen of them butcher knives and three dozen lookin' glasses.

"What kind of flints you got? Got you any of the French ones? Good, we need a gross of 'em. Samuel, pick us out the best ones, would ya?" I asked.

Looking down the counter, I spotted the wipin' sticks and got a dozen of them, along with two dozen awls and a half dozen hand axes.

"What that bring us up to, boy?" I asked.

He added it up and said, "That comes to seven hundred thirteen dollars and fifty cents."

"Good, we be needin' more, and we still got us some left. How much you want for them blankets?"

"The three points are fifteen dollars each, and the two points are ten dollars."

"Five dollar a point?" I asked. "Gettin' so a man can't afford to stay warm come winter time. But why don't you just give me six of them three pointers anyhow. An' throw in half a dozen of them handkerchiefs too."

"Razor, don't you think you better slow down on the spendin'?" asked Samuel. "You sure you got enough credit for all this?"

"He still has plenty left, Samuel," said the clerk.

"That's right. And there ain't nowhere else for me to spend it, so I gotta spend it all. Told you before, this is where 'Ol Billy gets me.

"Is that Chinee vermilion? Let me have ten pounds of it, if the price be right."

"It's six dollar to the pound," said the clerk.

"Six dollar!" I yelled it, turning every head in the place towards us. "Better you just give me half of that then.

"Fire steels? Two dozen of 'em and ten pounds of that brass wire. Gimme ten pounds of them beads too. Samuel, would you get those, and mix them up real good. I want lots of each color."

"That brings you up to nine hundred and one dollar, Mr. Black."

"How much that leave us?" I asked.

He bent over the counter, adjusted the numbers, and straightened back up.

"Right about one hundred and six dollars."

"Alright, let me have a gross of them little brass nails over there and two gross of them finger rings. Throw in five dozen of them bone hair combs, too. What's sugar? Got me a friend what likes sugar."

"The sugar is two dollars a pint."

"Seems kind of steep to me, but throw in about ten pint of it. An' take it from the middle of the barrel. Want the dry stuff, not that what's been sittin' on top all the way out here."

Looking around at what we had purchased so far, I figured we were just about done. Not much credit left now.

"We be needin' another one of them small kettles too. How much? Eighteen dollars? Gotta have it, so throw it on the pile. Pepper?"

"Six dollars a pound," came the reply.

"Three pounds of it then. And that's gonna do it. Have I got anythin' left?"

"Let's see, after I add up this last set, that brings you to nine hundred and ninety dollars and twenty-five cents. That leaves you with exactly seventeen dollars."

"Let me have a new paper what says I got seventeen dollars left to my name, boy. And I thank you kindly for takin' all the money I busted my hump for. Nothin' like gettin' took by a money hungry trader. 'Ol Billy Sublette and Davy Jackson sure were kinder souls when they was just trappers and not traders. And you can tell 'em I said so. Better yet, I think I'll go tell 'em myself.

"Come on Samuel. Let's load these horses up with this little bit of plunder these crooked traders was kind enough to let us have. Gettin' so a man can't even make a decent livin' out here in the mountains."

"Hey, this is a lot of stuff, Razor. But tell me somethin,'" he said as we were leading the horses back to my camp. "I saw that paper of yours, and I ain't forgot my numbers. There was two hundred dollars more on that piece of paper than he said. I say we go back and straighten it out with that clerk. He stole two hundred dollars from you. Are you just gonna let him get away with it?"

"He didn't steal it. I owed it to Sublette and Jackson and Smith," was all I said.

"What did you owe 'em two hundred dollars for? That's an awful lot of money, Razor." Suddenly he stopped. "If it's what I be thinkin' it's for, then I'll just head back with the pack train to St. Louis."

I stopped walking and turned around to face him.

"I paid that money to them blood-suckers, because I wanted you out here with me. I can still remember pa tellin' us that if there's a debt to be paid, then you pay it. There ain't no use in complainin' about it; you just do it. So that's what I done; I paid a debt. Don't matter if it was mine or not; it was a family debt. 'Sides, you'll earn it back; I'll see to that. I'm gonna work you like you ain't never been worked before. But it be worth it, come next summer. You'll see."

Back in camp, we laid out all the things we had bought. It was an awful lot of goods, but I was needing them, for presents, mostly. I went through my own gear, along with that of Jackson and Riley, putting it beside the new stuff.

"Where you get all them guns an' traps, an' other things?" Samuel asked.

"They used to belong to my partners. They was killed this last spring as we was makin' our way here. Bug's Boys."

"Bug's Boys? Who they be?"

"Blackfoot, Samuel. The meanest Indians there is out here. But don't worry none. We ain't goin' near them boys this year. Had me my fill of 'em last two seasons, up to the Three Forks country. Need to give 'em a break from 'Ol Round-Ball."

"Seems like I heard that name used before, back in St. Louis, but try as I might, I can't remember where or how. But it'll come to me."

"Had that name a long time now," I said to him. "It were kind of pinned to me when we was—"

"Now I remember. You was headed out here with that boy from Richmond; what was his name?"

"Pepper," I said, turning away from him. Every time I started to think on him, my eyes started to fill up, and I felt like a lost, lonely man. Then there was the anger that was right behind it. I couldn't take it anymore. That's why we were headed over to the parks, just as soon as we could. I needed to put this thing to rest, once and for all.

"Now what was you tellin' me, 'bout how you got your name?"

"Nothin,'" I mumbled. "Finish that story later. Right now we need to be checkin' all this gear, see what we gotta fix, an' get rid of the stuff I don't want to pack along."

"Alright, alright," he answered. "No need to be so testy 'bout it. You was the one that said there can't be no problems between us. I was just askin.'"

Standing up, I worked the kinks out of my back. Samuel was right. I should tell him what he was in for, and I would. But the time wasn't right. Wait until we were out on the trail, then I would tell him.

After we had everything all laid out, I took stock of what we had. There were twenty-eight beaver traps, five rifles, three pistols, three big powder horns and two smaller ones, and two tomahawks. There was also three small pieces of oiled Russian sheeting for covering the packs, my camp gear, and some odds and ends. Not much to show for a man's lifetime, but this was more than some men had.

"We need all them rifles?" Samuel asked. "We could trade 'em, so I could have me one last drink afore we pull out."

"Yea, we need 'em, every one. And I told you, no more whiskey this trip. I want your head clear when we pull out tomorrow."

"Tomorrow? You just got here. Don't you have no friends you want to see?" he asked.

"Seen 'em already," I said. I didn't have me too many

friends left out here, and the one true friend I did have for all those years was dead and gone. Seemed like every time I got me a friend or a trapping partner, they went under. I was beginning to think these mountains had put a curse on me, trying to make me leave and head back to the settlements.

The thought had crossed my mind several times in the past two years, of doing just that, but this was all I was cut out for. Being a trapper, and a free trapper at that, I was free. Free to go where I wanted, do what I wanted. Back in those settlements, they had them laws and rules that didn't make no sense to me. No, I was just going to stay here, in the mountains. It's where I belonged.

Chapter 8

It was three days later, after we had left the rendezvous on Bear Lake, when Samuel finally asked where we were going. We were sitting in camp, and I was showing him how to make the best cup of coffee in the whole mountains.

"We're headed to some place special," I told him.

"Lots of beaver?" He wanted to know.

"Yea, plenty of beaver. But that's not all that's there," I answered him.

"Well, spit it out. What's there? Indians?"

"Might be some there right now, but there won't be by the time we get there. No, we're gonna go visit an old friend of mine."

"Does he live up there year 'round? Why didn't he come down to rendezvous with you if he's such an old friend?"

Turning to look at him, I had to smile. He was older than me in years, but he didn't have any idea what I had been through in the last fifteen years.

"You're just full of questions, ain't you? But to answer you, I guess you could say he lives there year 'round, beings as how he's buried there. And he was the best friend I ever had."

"Your friend from Richmond, Pepper?"

"That be him," I said.

The silence stretched on for several minutes, and then he blurted it out.

"Well, are you gonna tell me what happened or not?"

"Suppose I ought to. I guess that's one of the reasons I brung you up here."

I sat there for a few minutes, gathering my thoughts, deciding where to begin. The memories were all bunched up in my head, like a thundercloud that only wants to drop its rain and be done with it, and I had to line them out so he could understand it. I had to tell him about my Ute wife too, because she was there when it happened.

"Two years ago, this fall," I began, "we were trappin' in a place we call the Middle Park, this side of the Front Range Mountains. There's three big valleys there, the North Park, the South Park, and the one we was in, the Middle Park.

"We were trappin,' like I said, workin' our way down to the Unita Mountains. That's where my wife was from. We had us a nice little—"

"Wait a minute, wait a minute, now back up a step," he shouted. "Did I just hear you say you had you uh Indian wife? Why ain't you said nothin' 'bout her afore now?" He wanted to know.

"Cause she's dead. Buried up there in the Middle Park with 'Ol Pepper. Now let me finish with the tellin' of this story you was so anxious to hear."

We had been trapping our way back to the Ute camp after spending the summer working our way to rendezvous and back. My wife, me, Pepper, and my five summers old son, Buffalo boy, so named because I was out hunting buffalo with the Ute when he was born. He was a rowdy little youngster, always getting into trouble with his mother, so Pepper took to calling him Rowdy. My wife, of course, blamed it all on me and Pepper for the way he was.

We had been in the Park for almost a full moon, moving around to different beaver streams as we trapped. I spotted some fresh Indian pony tracks down by the stream one day, but I finished laying my traps out before I headed back to camp, not too worried about the tracks. This was Ute country after all, and I had lived with them for a long time, so why worry?

Heading back to camp, I heard the sound of guns shooting, too many shots to be Pepper making meat. There was trouble in our camp, and I kicked my horse into a full run, wanting to get there as soon as I could. But before I got there, the shooting had stopped.

When I reached the camp, all our camp plunder was scattered. Dropping from my still running horse, I couldn't see my wife, Pepper, or my son anywhere. Suddenly, I heard the sound of horses running, a lot of them. Dropping down into a crouch and spinning towards the sound, I realized they were going away from me.

Standing up, I called out for Pepper. There was no answer. Walking out to where I could see the ground was scuffed up, probably from the fight, I saw my wife. She was face down in the grass surrounding the camp, and she had three arrows sticking out of her back.

The scream tore from my throat, and I kept on screaming, until I heard, very faintly, my name being called out.

"Razor. Razor. Over here."

It was coming from some blown down trees, about ten yards away. Cocking my rifle, I held it out in front of me and crept to the edge of the blow down. There, I saw my best friend leaning against the stump of a tree.

He was covered in blood, mostly on his face. He had been scalped while he was still alive, and his stomach was sliced open so that his insides were sitting between his legs with an arrow stuck in the middle of them.

Dropping my rifle, I knelt at his side. He was trying to say something to me, but I could hardly hear him. Bending my head down, I put my ear next to his mouth.

"Rapaho. Took Rowdy with 'em. I couldn't stop 'em; there was too many."

"Don't try and talk, Thomas," I said, starting to cry. I couldn't stop the tears from flowing. Watching the life slip out of him was almost too much to handle, but I knew he would do the same for me. So I sat with him, remembering all the good times we had together over the years. All too soon, he was gone.

Going over to my wife, I was thankful that they hadn't violated or scalped her. That would have been too much for me to bear, and this day had brought me enough grief already. I rummaged through what was left of our camp, finding two blankets the Arapaho had missed. With them, I carefully wrapped the bodies of my wife and Pepper and then placed them in hastily constructed scaffolds in the trees surrounding the camp. Sitting by the now dead fire, I tried to figure out what I was going to do next. I knew I was going after my son. But I was alone; how was I going to get him back from the Arapaho?

I sat by the fire pit all night long, thinking back to all the good times I had been through with 'Ol Pepper, how we had first come to the mountains after what seemed like an eternity of traveling west out of St. Louis. I also thought back on the six years I had been married to my wife, remembering her as a scared little girl the first time I had seen her. And my son. How was I going to get him back? 'Ol Pepper had told me that there was too many of them. That meant there was a lot, as I could remember him taking on at least a dozen Indians, Blackfoot at that, one time up in the Three Forks. He came out of that one, so why hadn't he got through this fight?

As the sun rose, I started getting mad at myself. If I had only been here, they would both be alive, and I would have my son with me right now. Why had I decided to go set traps yesterday? I should have been there for them. I felt like it was all my fault.

I must have dozed off along about dawn, and when I heard the horses walking up, my first thought was that the Arapaho had come back. Scooping my rifle up, I darted behind the nearest tree and waited for them to come. If they wanted it, they were sure going to get it.

As the first rider came abreast of me, I launched myself at him, taking the horse down in a jumble with us. I only had one shot, and I was saving it for when I really needed it, so I had my scalping knife in my hand. Just as I was about to plunge the knife into this stinking, murdering Arapaho, rough hands pulled me off of him. There was excited babbling, and it took me a bit before I realized I understood it. My arms were released, and I looked around at the Ute war party surrounding me."

It didn't take long to tell them what had happened, and they could see for themselves the arrows left behind were Arapaho. They were, in fact, trailing them. Some hunters had spotted them three days ago, invading Ute land. When they got back to the village to report it, a war party was formed.

"I am sorry we were not here sooner, my brother," said the slightly built warrior I had taken off his horse. "You were a good husband to my sister, and I know she is in a better place now."

"Yes, but it does not help the pain," I answered in Ute.

"Where is Buffalo Boy?" He asked.

"They took him. I was just trying to figure out how to get him back when you showed up. I am going to kill every one of these murdering pieces of dog dung that have done this to me. You can come along if you want to, but this is something I must do myself."

The scouts found the trail the retreating Arapaho had taken, and it looked like they weren't worried about anyone following them. They didn't bother to hide the trail at all. I left all the camp gear and traps just as they were as we left on the trail of the Arapaho, thinking that if I survived this vengeance trail, that I would return and pick them up.

They had a full day's lead on us, but they weren't moving as fast as they should have been. We found them the next day, just as they were going into camp for the night. Wing of the Hawk, my brother-in-law, asked me how I wanted to handle it. Still in shock at my loss, and I simply looked at him.

"I am going to kill every one of them and get my son back."

"Where do you want us?" he asked.

"You and these fine brave warriors just stay here. This is something I have to do. If I do not get the job done, you can come in and wipe them from the face of the earth," I said, passing my hand in front of my face to indicate a wiping motion.

Wing of the Hawk handed me a small pouch, and looking down, I saw that it was his personal war paint. I took off my coyote skin cap, and he applied the paint to my forehead, eyes, and nose. With my white-man beard, that was all he could cover, so I took off my buckskin hunting shirt that my wife had made me, and I painted my chest red, with black zigzag patterns on it, trying to make it look as frightening as possible.

They thought they were so safe they hadn't even bothered to post a guard, and I crept to within about ten yards of their camp. I counted nine of them, moving around the camp and saw three more slung over the backs of my horses. At least 'Ol Pepper had gone out fighting.

I located my son on the other side of the camp, but when I saw him, all the life drained out of me. They had beaten him something terrible. His face was all bloody, and it looked like they had drug him behind a horse. He wasn't in very good shape to run away, so they hadn't even tied him.

Seeing the shape my son was in, I lost all thought of taking them one at a time. Jumping up with my rifle in one hand and my pistol in the other, I charged the camp, letting out a Ute war cry.

I must have looked like a strange creature to them, all painted up like I was, and yelling at the top of my lungs, because they stood there and just stared. I shot the closest one in the chest with the pistol, then the one nearest my son with the rifle.

Dropping the pistol, I switched ends with my rifle and waded into them. I smashed the butt plate into the face of the third Indian, spraying his blood all over and driving his nose into his brain, killing him instantly. By now, I was in the middle of their camp, and dropping my rifle, I picked up one lying by the fire. It was 'Ol Pepper's, and I knew it well.

I jabbed the barrel of it into the throat of another brave but didn't pull the trigger, knowing he was out of it. Two of them were trying to make it to the horses, and I dropped the sights of the rifle on the furthest one and shot him in the back. Feeling a sharp pain behind my right shoulder, I looked back at an arrow sticking out.

Pulling my tomahawk from the back of my belt with my left hand, I hurled it at the bowman, spoiling his aim, but not killing him. Following along behind the tomahawk, I was on top of him before he could recover. I slammed my knee into his groin, doubling him over. Before he could straighten back up, I twisted my hands in his hair, lifted his head, and slammed it back down into my rising knee. As he sagged, I pulled the knife from the sheath on his side and slit his throat.

The other four braves that were left had re-grouped and were moving in on me. Suddenly, one of them ran towards my son. *He's going to kill him*, I thought, and I threw the Arapaho knife I still had in my hand at him, taking him through the side of the throat. He went down, tearing at the knife and gurgling blood all over himself.

Turning to face the other three, I pulled my own knife from the back of my belt and charged them. They must have thought I was crazy, for two of them turned and ran towards the horses. Slicing and slashing with the knife, I gutted the one Arapaho that hadn't run, dumping his insides out on the ground at his feet.

Thinking that those two on the horses were going to get away, I glanced around for a weapon of any kind. There was a sudden chorus of Ute war cries in front of them, and they hauled back on the horsehair reins, spun around, and headed back towards me.

I picked up a bow at my feet, notched an arrow, and let it fly at the two charging Arapaho. The one on the right took the arrow in the chest, flinging him backwards off his horse. Only one left.

The last brave pulled his horse to a stop and jumped off. Going to his knees, he started to sing his death song. Notching another arrow, I walked towards him, just as Wing of the Hawk and the rest of the Ute came into the camp.

The pain in my right shoulder was starting to make me light-headed, and I lowered the bow. This Arapaho wasn't going anywhere, and he knew it. Motioning to Wing of the Hawk, I sagged down on one knee. As he came over to me, I gave him a weak smile.

"Let them count coup on him, but do not let them kill him," I told him. I had seen something tied to his belt, but I wanted to make sure.

Buffalo Boy was trying to make his way over to me, and pushing the pain away, I stood up and walked to him. The tears were running down our faces, both of us glad to be alive and together again.

The Ute warriors had surrounded the Arapaho brave and were counting coup on him, but not hurting him too bad, just like I had asked. Picking up my son, we walked over to him, the Ute opening up to let us through.

Setting Buffalo Boy down, I took his hand in mine and together we stood in front of the doomed Indian. Looking down at his waist, I saw the scalp. It was just as I thought earlier. It was 'Ol Pepper's hair, and I jerked it from his belt, tucking it into my own, intent on putting it back where it belonged. This was the one who had done the deed, and he was going to get the same done to him.

Buffalo Boy let go of my hand and kicked out with his foot, catching the Arapaho in the groin, doubling him over. The Ute warriors surrounding us let out whoops of pleasure, telling Buffalo Boy that he had become a warrior of the Ute people by his actions this day.

"This is the one that killed my uncle," said Buffalo Boy. "He scalped him slowly as the others held him, showing that he is not a man at all. He could not do it by himself. My uncle was a brave man, Father, he did not cry out once." Suddenly, Buffalo Boy spit on the Arapaho, and then tried to kick him again, but I pulled him away, not liking the look in the brave's eyes. Instead, I kicked him in the face, sending him sprawling backwards into the dirt.

"What do you want to do with this piece of dung?" Wing of the Hawk asked me.

"Tie him up for now," I said. "I will do to him what he did to my friend."

"Father. I want to do it," came the small voice of my son. "He made me watch as he tortured my uncle. I could do nothing to help him then, but I can at least do this. Please, Father, let me do it. For my uncle."

I was shocked that a five summers old boy would want to do such a thing. This was not something to take lightly, and I didn't think he understood what he was asking of me.

Turning to him, I told him I would think about. But that could wait awhile. Right now, all I wanted was to get the arrow out of my shoulder. It was painful and starting to throb with every beat of my heart.

After Wing of the Hawk had removed the arrow and I had rested, I thought more on my son's request. Talking to some of the other warriors in camp about Buffalo Boy's request, they were of the same mind as me that he didn't understand what he was asking. But Wing of the Hawk, his uncle, wasn't so sure.

The next morning, I decided to see where my son's heart lay, if he still wanted to kill the Arapaho captive. Taking him with me as I was scalping the other eight Arapaho, I watched his reaction. I was surprised to see he was happy about it, and when he asked me if he could scalp one, I agreed.

Handing him my knife, I showed him where to start with the point, above the left ear, and circle the entire head, pulling on the scalp as he cut. As he pulled his first scalp off the head of one of the dead Indians, there was a chorus of trilling and some war cries behind us. The rest of the Ute had come up behind us and were watching. Buffalo Boy swung the scalp in the air, as he had seen me do, flinging the gore and blood off. Then he tucked it into his belt, like a warrior would do.

"He knows and understands what he is doing," came the voice at my elbow. "He has been taught well by you, brother."

"It was not all by me," I replied. "'Ol Pepper had a hand in it as well. I guess I owe it to him, to both of them, to let Buffalo Boy kill that murdering skunk." As we approached the Arapaho Indian tied to a tree, I handed Buffalo Boy the knife again. Seeing what was about to happen, the Arapaho started laughing at my son. But he soon realized he meant business, especially when the knife sliced through the muscles of his stomach, spilling his insides onto the ground in front of him.

Holding the knife in his right hand, Buffalo Boy reached inside the stomach and started pulling out more of his insides, making the Arapaho scream out in pain. This caused the whole Ute war party to smile and laugh. It grew even louder as Buffalo Boy started stomping on the guts that were on the ground.

He stopped suddenly and moved the bloody knife towards the scalp. He hesitated for a second, lowering the knife, and I thought he wasn't going to be able to go through with it. But then he smiled at the Arapaho, bringing the knife up to the corner of his left eye.

When the knife pierced the flesh at the corner of his eye, the Arapaho started to squirm and twist, tearing his own eyeball from the socket. Buffalo Boy took the eye on the point of the knife and thrust it into the open mouth, bringing another hoot from those watching.

He was almost dead, and I wanted him alive while he was scalped, so I told Buffalo Boy that he could finish mutilating him after he scalped him so he made quick work of removing his hair. As he pulled the scalp loose, Buffalo Boy let out his own war cry, full of vigor. I couldn't believe this was my own son. He was just a babe still, and here he was, scalping an enemy."

As I finished telling Samuel the story, I moved over to my sleeping robes and crawled into them.

I wasn't really sleepy and was just lying there, thinking on what I was needing to do, when Samuel sat up.

"What was your wife's name?" he asked it quietly, almost reverently.

Watching his face as I was telling him the story, I could see that it had hit him hard. There were things that this brother of mine was holding back from me, but we had a year to talk about it, and there was nobody else to talk to but me.

Without moving, I answered him. "Prairie Flower was her name. Prairie Flower."

Chapter 9

When we were on the trail the next morning, Samuel asked me about Buffalo Boy, why he wasn't with me.

"I sent him back to the Ute village with Wing of the Hawk after we got him back. I was still nursin' a grudge against the 'Rapaho. They had taken so much away from me, and I wanted to take all that much more away from them. So I sent Rowdy on back to the Ute, not wantin' him along with me on my vengeance trail."

"When was the last time you saw him?" Samuel asked.

"That *was* the last time I saw him," I answered. "And that's 'nother reason we're here. Goin' to spend the winter with the Ute after we trap this fall. Now you know why I bought all them presents. They're for my Ute family an' friends, my way of thankin' 'em for watchin' out for me an' 'Ol Pepper for all them years. An' for takin' care of my son while I been gone."

For the next two months, Samuel and I worked our way over to the Middle Park. It was an early fall, and I wanted to do what needed to be done there, before we started trapping for the season. With such an early fall like this, that told me that it was going to be a long and cold winter. We might just cut our trapping short this season.

I had made up my mind late last spring that I was going to do this, and nothing was going to stop me. Short of an arrow or a rifle ball in the wrong spot, I was on my way to see my son. I couldn't count all the times I had laid awake at night, just thinking on him and wondering what kind of boy he had become. He would be seven years old now, playing mock war games with the other boys his age.

Each night after we had eaten our supper, I would take the time to tell Samuel all I knew about the surrounding country. I had covered most all of it over the years, and once I went through a place, I committed it to my memory. Never knew when I might be coming back that way again, and I wanted to know just where I was at.

He picked up on most of it right away, mostly from the training we had gotten from our pa when we were younger. Only this was a much bigger place out here than it was back home in Virginia. After awhile, I started asking him questions about the country we had passed through several days before, and he remembered it, for the most part.

As we got closer to beaver trapping country, I told him how to make a set and where. We practiced setting some traps around camp, just so he would know how to do it before the time came, and he caught on quick. I told him he would have to mix up his own bait after we had caught some beaver but that he could use mine until then.

"How do you make your own bait?" he asked one night as we sat around the fire.

"Well, first off, you gotta catch some beaver. They got a gland on 'em, just under their tail. You just squeeze the milk out of it an' save it up. Mix it from three or four different beaver, so they don't recognize the smell as comin' from the same pond. Beavers is curious animals, Samuel, an' they want to know whose smell it be on your bait stick. I'll show you how it's done proper, soon as we get to where we're goin.'"

When we reached the Middle Park, it was spitting a light rain, not unusual for this time of year. I felt nervous all of a sudden, like I was returning to the scene of a crime. I guess, in a way, I was. But this crime had been committed against me, not by me.

"Seen some tracks down to the stream," Samuel told me that afternoon, as we were setting up camp. "They look to be a couple of hours old," he added.

Checking my rifles and the two pistols in my belt, I told him to do the same. Could be Arapaho roving around in here, and I knew first hand what they could do. I had given Samuel the pistol I had taken off the dead Blackfoot last spring and one of my extra rifles, so we were both ready for trouble.

We stood watch that night in shifts of three hours each, with me taking the last one at dawn. As we moved closer to where I had placed Pepper and Prairie Flower on their scaffolds in the trees, I saw that the tracks were just as fresh as when Samuel had spotted them.

"Let's lay over for a few days," I told him. "That way, whoever is in front of us will stay that way." We had seen no signs of a camp along the way, so whoever it was in front of us was being cautious. If it was other trappers, and this I doubted, we would have seen it right away. Trappers ain't like the Indians. They want folks to know they been someplace, so they leave traces behind. I was almost certain this was a war party we were following.

After two days of sitting in a damp camp, I was ready to move on. Only time I wanted to sit around was in the middle of the winter, when everything was so frozen and cold, there was nothing else to do but sit by the fire.

When we pulled out the next morning, I told Samuel we should be to the place in two, three days at the most. He was just as anxious to be moving as I was. He wasn't prepared for the cold weather up here in the mountains. We needed to meet up with the Ute we were going to be spending the winter with to get him some proper mountain clothes. Get rid of them city clothes he had on.

"'Sides," I told him, "you're startin' to stink. Ain't no beaver gonna touch your set, what with that smell you got goin' on."

"I don't smell that bad," he protested, raisin' his arm up to smell himself. "But then again, maybe I do," he said with a laugh.

We were getting close to the place two days later, when the ears of my mule went up. Throwing myself off her back, I grabbed her nose and spun her around, not wanting her to bray at them other horses she had smelled. Dragging her behind me, I started trotting back the way we had come, motioning for Samuel to do the same.

"What's got into you?" he asked.

"Shhh. Hush up, now," I told him. "This here mule of mine gotta nose on her that you wouldn't believe. An' she smelled somethin' she don't like. Best we sneak on up there an' see what it be."

Tying all the animals to trees, we advanced on foot. As we moved in closer, I could see where the suckers on the trees had been broken off, meaning someone was out here gathering wood. I also spotted some moccasin prints but didn't have time to study on them to see what tribe they were.

Motioning for Samuel to stay put, I went on by myself. If I started shooting, I knew he would come running. Watching for camp guards as I inched my way forward, I didn't see any. Suddenly, I heard the sound of children laughing.

This was a village on the move, and we had blundered into them! But no, there wasn't enough horses for it to be a village, so it must just be a family unit, out for a fall hunt. As I poked my head around the side of the tree I was behind, the first person I saw was Wing of the Hawk. These were Ute. My people. My family.

Chapter 10

Standing up, I pulled my coyote skin cap back so my face could be seen, and cradling my rifle in my arms, I stepped out of the trees. Heads turned and looked in my direction, but they didn't seem frightened in any way. Striding into their camp, I could see they had been hunting, just like I thought.

As Wing of the Hawk and I met on the edge of the camp, he grasped my forearm when I extended it and pulled me close to him, wearing a huge smile.

"My brother," he said. "It is good to see you again. I was worried that you had left your hair on some warrior's lodge pole. We welcome you to our camp," he finished.

"It is good to be among the people of my heart," I started. "It has been too long. But there were things I needed to do to get rid of the anger and hate for what was done to me."

"And did you rid yourself of the hate?" he asked me.

Looking at my brother-in-law, I shook my head. "I do not know if I have or not, my brother. The hate has grown in me for so long that I wonder if I will ever be rid of it."

Suddenly, there was a shout from the trees. Samuel! I had forgotten about him for the moment, and he was probably scared out of his mind.

"Samuel," I hollered. "Come on in, and bring the horses. It's alright." Turning to Wing of the Hawk, I told him I had a special partner this year.

"I hope you do not mind if I have a guest this winter," I told him in Ute.

As Samuel came through the trees leading the horses, I spotted a tall youngster standing by the side of a brush lean-to. There was something different about him. Then I saw the two scalps hanging on his belt, and I realized who it was. This was my son, the one thing that had kept me going for the last two years.

As I started towards him, he turned and ran off through the trees, not looking back. Spinning back around to face Wing of the Hawk, I couldn't even form the words to ask what that was all about. But he knew; I didn't have to ask.

"He is an angry boy these days." Sweeping his arm around the camp, he continued. "We have come here, my family and I, for the last two years for our fall hunt. I knew, in my heart, that one-day you would return, and this is where you would come to. I have tried to raise your son as part of my family, but he is too much like you, my brother. He thinks in a different way."

Samuel had come up with the horses, but to my surprise, he didn't look a bit scared like I thought he would. Introducing him to Wing of the Hawk, I explained who he was.

"This is my brother," I told him. "He came out from the east with the traders, and I invited him to stay here and learn to trap with me. It has been a long time since he has been in the mountains, and he needs a teacher in the ways of the Ute. Not to mention some proper clothing," I added with a wink.

"He does smell bad," Wing of the Hawk said laughing.

"Should I go try to find Buffalo Boy," I asked, "or will he return on his own?"

"He will come back when he is ready. This is not the first time he has done this. I am happy that you are home, brother, back where you belong," Wing of the Hawk replied.

There was more to the story behind the attitude of my son, and I wanted to find out what it was as soon as possible. It just didn't seem right, that after not seeing each other for two years, he wouldn't have anything to do with me.

"Is your son here?" Samuel asked me as we were unloading our packs and setting up our own camp.

"Yea, he's here," I replied. "But he don't want to talk to me right now. Soon as we're done here, I'll go find him and straighten it out."

"I can finish this up. You go find him and do what you gotta do. Not like I ain't never set up a camp afore."

"Thanks," I said. "It's eatin' at me, an' I need to talk to him."

I found Wing of the Hawk talking with his wife and another woman, probably a second wife, I thought. When he saw me walking towards him, he motioned me over.

"Round-Ball, this is Autumn Sky. And no, she is not my wife. One is enough for this old warrior," he said, winking at his wife. "But Autumn Sky has been keeping your son's lodge."

"My son's lodge?" I asked, somewhat startled. "But he is only a boy; he does not have his own lodge yet."

"No, but you had a lodge in the village when you left. When you sent him back with me two summers ago, he decided to stay in your lodge, by himself.

"It has been hard for him. Now, I do not think it was such a good idea for you to let him kill the Arapaho we found. He has it in his mind that he is a warrior and that he needs no one to care for him. So, I made an agreement with Autumn Sky to look in on him and do what a woman does in a lodge."

Turning to Autumn Sky, I was surprised to see that she was a young woman, not old, like I had first thought. I thanked her for all that she had done for my son and told her that when we got back to the village, I would pay her proper, with presents. She threw up her hands and stormed off in the direction of the meat racks, kicking out at a dog in her path.

"What is that all about? I told her I would pay for all she has done for Buffalo Boy. Now she is angry with me, along with my son. I should have stayed gone, from the look of things."

"No, brother. She has grown fond of Buffalo Boy that is all. She has no children of her own. Her husband was killed during a raid on the Arapaho, not long after they were married. The others say that she is bad luck. I know she is not bad luck, and that is why I approached her to care for Buffalo Boy."

"Well, I am here now, to take care of him. I need to find him so I can talk to him. Do you know where he might be?" I asked.

"The same place he always goes when we are here. To the last camping place where he saw his mother."

Picking up my rifle from our camp, I headed off in the direction Buffalo Boy had gone. It made sense that I would find him there. It was more than a mile to the spot, and I wasn't about to go that far without a gun, but I did walk.

He was sitting under the scaffold I had made, two years ago, when I got there. Not trying to hide myself, I walked into the small meadow where we had camped. All traces had vanished, but I could still see it in my head, just like it was yesterday.

"How are you, son?" I asked in Ute.

"I do not wish to speak to you," he replied, using the formal speech of the Ute. "I am angry with you," he added, still not looking at me.

"Well, then you can just listen then. There are some things I need to tell you, and the first of them is that I am sorry. I am sorry I sent you back to the village that day. Someday, when you are older, I hope you understand why I did what I did.

"My whole world was turned upside down that day. And I know that yours was too. I lost the only woman who ever wanted me for who I was, and I lost my best friend. I did not want to lose you too. It is because I love you that I sent you away.

"I did not want to go on in this life without your mother," I continued. "I was going to hunt down as many Arapaho as I could and kill them for what they had done to me. To us. And that is what I did. In my heart, I thought I wanted them to kill me. But they did not get the job done," I added.

After the Ute war party had left, I went back to our camp and gathered up what was left. Using one of the Arapaho horses for a pack animal, I headed for their villages. I didn't want to live anymore, and I was committing suicide, I knew, by going right to them.

I found the first of the Arapaho villages about a week later. After watching it for two days, I decided I would stalk the hunters they sent out, and kill them, one at a time. And that's what I did, stripping them and hanging them upside down in the trees when I was done. After awhile, they got wise to what I was doing, so I moved on.

I did the same thing at the next two villages I came to, and by now, it was the middle of the winter. I headed back over to the South Park, knowing there would be some trappers wintering there, and there was. I stayed with them through the winter, trapping with them, and we all went into rendezvous that next summer.

Figuring I had pushed my luck with the Arapaho, I decided to head up to the Three Forks and try my luck there. Maybe

'Ol Bug's Boys could get the job done, since the Arapaho had failed to kill me.

I had become a mean, vengeance-filled man, only wanting to kill as many Indians as I could. Each time I killed, it was the same. After scalping them, I would strip the bodies and hang them upside down in the trees. It became my trademark, and every time one of those bodies was found, they knew I was around.

But then, when Jackson and Riley were killed last spring, I couldn't stop thinking of my son.

"And now I'm here for you, Buffalo Boy," I finished. "And I will promise you, here and now, that I will not leave you behind ever again."

He finally turned and looked at me, and I couldn't believe the resemblance he had to his mother. He had her nose and cheekbones, but he had my eyes, a dark green. His long hair was pulled back into two braids, tied on the ends with strips of tanned buckskin. He looked so much older than the seven summers he was, wearing his hair like a warrior.

"Are you ready to head back to camp?" I asked him in English.

"Yes," he answered as he stood.

We hadn't gone far when he asked me what was going to happen to Autumn Sky now that I was back.

"I don't really know, son. Haven't had much time to think on it. What do you think we should do?"

He looked up at me and gave me a sly smile.

"I would like to keep her. She has been a good woman to me," he told me, matter-of-factly.

"Huh! So now you think you're a man? There's more to being a man, son, than just havin' a woman take care of your lodge. And besides, that ain't all we need to be thinkin' 'bout. I brung someone special along with me."

"Another woman?" he wanted to know.

"No, no, nothin' like that. I brung my brother along. He came out from back in the settlements with the traders. And I wanted him to meet you."

"What are 'the settlements'?" he asked.

"I can see right now that you need some teachin' 'bout the ways of the white man. Time's comin' when you might need to know 'bout 'em," I replied.

"But to answer your question, that's where all the white folks live. Kind of like a village, only a lot bigger. We'll talk more on that later, when we're just sittin' by the fire of a cold winter day."

Long before we reached the camp, we smelled the smoke.

Chapter 11

It was a hit-and-run attack; Wing of the Hawk told us when we arrived. Arapaho again. Would we never run out of them red devils, I wondered? There was only one wounded in the camp, and that was Samuel. He had taken an arrow in his left arm, just above his elbow.

"Sure, I go off and leave you for a few minutes, an' you get a hole punched in you by some 'Rapaho," I told him. "Seems like I can't let you outta my sight," I said, shaking my head. He knew I was only joking with him when he saw the smile on my face, then he spotted Buffalo Boy.

"Who you got there, Razor?" he asked.

"Introduce yourself, son. This here is your uncle Samuel."

"I am called Buffalo Boy, uncle," he said slowly, in English.

"Pleased to meet you, Buffalo Boy," Samuel replied as he stuck out his hand.

Buffalo Boy turned to look at me, and I told him to grasp the offered hand and pump it up and down.

"Why?" he asked in Ute.

"It's a white man's custom," I answered. "You do that when you meet someone new or when you have not seen them in a long time."

"Oh," was all he said. But he took Samuel's hand, pumped it up and down a few times and then looked back at me.

"That be good enough, son. You can let go. We need to see about gettin' that arrow out of your uncle's arm now. You remember what my medicines be in?" I asked him.

"Yes, father. The red and yellow painted one."

"Go get it for me then. It's over in our camp."

Squatting on my haunches beside Samuel I asked him what happened.

"I don't know. We was all just sittin' here, an' all of a sudden there was this screamin' noise. Everyone jumped up an' started runnin,' includin' me. We gathered over there, by the lean-to, an' these other Indians come-a-runnin' they're horses into camp like they owned the place.

"That little fella you was talkin' to earlier, he drops down on one, an' shoots him off his horse. I pulled my rifle up to shoot this other one, an' I shot, but I don't think I hit him. Then I pulled out my pistol an' shot one in the chest. I know I killed that one.

"All of a sudden my arm starts stingin,' an' when I looked down, there was this arrow stuck in me. After that, I don't know. I leaned against the lean-to, then somebody pulled me off of it, 'cause it was on fire. I think I set it on fire when I shot that last time."

"Don't worry 'bout it. What with all this rain in the last few days, it didn't burn much. Just stinks up the place," I added, as Buffalo Boy returned with my medicine parfletche.

"Wing of the Hawk," I hollered across the camp. When he looked my way, I waved my arm for him to join us. Turning back to Samuel, I told him we would have this thing out of him in the wink of an eye.

Pulling Buffalo Boy to one side, I asked him to go get some water in one of my kettles back in our camp, and bring it to me right away. He nodded his head once and was gone like a flash of lightening. Man, that boy could run!

"What have you said to him now?" asked Wing of the Hawk as he approached.

"Nothing. I just need some water to wash the wound before we pull the arrow. But he is a fast one isn't he?" I added.

"What do you need me for, brother? I was just getting ready to chase down the last two of those stinking Arapaho dogs. They took some of the horses, and we need them to get all of the meat we took in our hunt. Do you want to join me?"

"Well yes, I do want to go, but I need to tend to my brother," I told him.

"Let one of the women do it. I need your help."

While he went off to get his wife to patch him up, I explained it to Samuel. About the time I finished, Buffalo Boy came back with the water. When I stood up and headed for my camp, he followed me.

"Where are you going, father?"

"Some of the horses were stolen. Wing of the Hawk has asked me to help him get them back," I said over my shoulder.

"Can I come?"

"No, I don't think so," I replied to his question.

"I knew it!" he shouted. "You lied to me! You told me that you would never leave me again. But you are!" He was very upset and turned to run again but collided with Wing of the Hawk's horse. He had come up to the camp while Buffalo Boy was yelling and carrying on.

"If you made a promise to him, brother, then you need to honor it. There are only two of the Arapaho, and like you, he has a great hatred of them. We might need someone to hold the horses, and who better than him? Your white brother cannot go, and I need to leave at least one warrior in camp. But it is your choice. He is your son, not mine," he finished.

Glancing at Buffalo Boy, I could see he was on the verge of tears. I also noticed that his teeth were clenched hard, as well as his hands. There was a lot of anger in this young son of mine, and I felt that it might get him killed someday.

"Come here, son," I directed.

When he got to me, I knelt down in front of him and placed my hands on his shoulders.

"If I decide to let you come with us, you need to promise me one thing."

"What?" he sputtered.

"You will stop acting like a one summers old baby every time you do not get what you want. That is how I see you right now. How can you be trusted to do what you are told in the heat of a battle if you do not listen to me now? You must promise me this, in front of your uncle, before I let you join us."

"Do not vow that you will do this thing, Buffalo Boy, unless you truly mean it," put in Wing of the Hawk.

"I will do what you say from now on, father," he agreed.

"Good. Then go get your horse and let's go get those horses back. You do have a horse, don't you?" I asked.

"I have—I mean *you* have many horses father. Do you not remember leaving them behind when you last left our camp?"

"I guess I forgot about them. But now that we have this thing between us on a straight path, let us be after our horses."

I threw myself onto my horses' back as Buffalo Boy ran off to get his own mount. Looking over at Wing of the Hawk, I shook my head sadly. I could see what he had been through with my son over the last two years. He was a mean-spirited, smart-mouthed, little boy. But he was *my* boy, and I was back in his life now, so I guess it was my problem.

Chapter 12

We made it back to the camp late the next afternoon, with the horses in tow. True to his word, Buffalo Boy had done whatever was asked of him. I could tell it was chaffing on him, but he never complained.

Going over to my own camp, I saw Samuel sitting by the fire, all decked out in a new set of buckskins. They weren't anything fancy, just plain clothes, but he looked good in them. Reminded me of how we used to dress back home in Virginia.

Sitting across the fire from him was Autumn Sky. *Now this is a surprise*, I thought. Wonder what this is all about.

Buffalo Boy came over with a questioning look on his face, and, going over to the woman, they spoke in hushed tones for several minutes. There was something going between those two, and I was about to nip it off, when Autumn Sky got up and left.

"What are you up to, son?" I asked him.

"Nothing father," was all I got in return.

Samuel was watching Autumn Sky walk away, a small smile on his face. Without turning his head, he spoke.

"She sure is a handsome woman, Razor. If you don't want

her, I think I'll have a go at it. Been a long time since I had me a woman."

"What in blue blazes are you talkin' 'bout? There ain't nothin' goin' on 'tween her an' me. And you best get the notion out of your head right now of beddin' down with her. She's lookin' for a husband,' an' she won't stop till she gets one, be it you or me. 'Sides," I added, "if you're intendin' to go back to St Louis next summer, don't get attached. You'll never leave if you do."

"Funny you should say that, Razor. I was just thinkin' that I might stay up here. Reminds me of back in Virginia, when we was boys, growin' up. We sure had us some times back then, didn't we?" he asked.

"Father," broke in Buffalo Boy, "what is this 'Razor' my white uncle calls you?"

I burst out laughing at the question, startling both of them.

"Why, that be my white man name, son," I said between fits of laughter. "Never knew I had 'nother name 'sides Round-Ball, huh?"

"No, that is the only name I ever heard you called."

"Well, you just keep on callin' me 'father,' 'cause that's what I am—your father."

Autumn Sky came back over to our camp, all her camp gear on her back. Going to the brush bower we had set up, she dropped her things with a plop and then scooted underneath. Samuel and I exchanged looks, both of us confused.

As our things started flying out from under the bower, I let out a yelp of anger. Where did this woman get off taking over my camp all of a sudden? When I saw the smile on Buffalo Boy's face, I knew. They were plotting against me the whole time. I should have seen it coming.

"What are you doing, woman?" I yelled at Autumn Sky. "This is my camp, not yours to—"

"I am here to take care of Buffalo Boy, not you," she retorted angrily. "Just because you happen to be here does not make a difference. I have seen how you cook, and I am surprised you still breathe. I have spent the last two years of my life taking care of your son. Why should I stop now? Just because you have returned? You will go away in the spring, and he will still need someone to care for his lodge. And it will be me!"

She said it with such finality that I was shocked. I just stood there and took it. Turning around, I could see Wing of the Hawk and his whole family were watching the show. His wife, Morning Dew, smiled at me, and all of a sudden I knew this was all planned.

I turned to face Buffalo Boy, and he was hiding his face. I could see the corners of his eyes smiling, and, disgusted, I stalked away. Samuel followed along behind me, not knowing what was happening.

"What was that all about?" he wanted to know.

"I guess I just been set up for a marriage."

"That was a marriage? If that's how it starts with these people, I better rethink 'bout what I was gonna do. Don't want to go through that again," he stated.

"Naw, we ain't married. But that woman thinks she has to take care of Buffalo Boy, an' that means she has to take care of me too, 'cause we share the same lodge. I don't want me no wife right now."

"I was married once, back in the settlements," said Samuel. "But she was a mean woman, makin' me work the soil, just like I done when we were kids. I had my fill one day and was fixin' to tell her so, but when I got back to our cabin that night, she was gone. Took everythin' that wasn't nailed down, too. Only thing she left me was a pot on the table to hold down the note she left.

"Said I was a worthless man, an' that I wasn't fit to be a pappy to our two little girls. All I did was work like a mule to put food on the table for 'em, an' she said I was worthless. Never did understand women. An' I see you don't neither."

Chapter 13

Leaving the Ute some three days later, we decided to work our way up into the North Park, on over to the South Park, then head to their camp for the winter. Samuel and I had loaded up the packs onto the horses, when Autumn Sky led her horse over.

"No, no," I told her in Ute. "You are not going with us, and that is the end of it."

"I told you, I am going to take care of the son you left behind. He goes with you, and so do I," she said, stomping her foot on the ground for emphasis.

"We will see about that," I replied in Ute.

Stalking over to Wing of the Hawk, I told him what Autumn Sky had said. He simply threw his hands in the air.

"I do not want to be involved in your dispute, brother. But you should really think about it. She is willing to cook your food and keep your lodge for you. I would let her go along. And who is to say that you will not one day soon have feelings for her?" he threw in, grinning from ear to ear.

"It might be different if it was *my* lodge she was keeping. She keeps telling me it is my son's lodge she is keeping, making me feel like I am not worthy to have my own lodge. And she says it in front of Buffalo Boy, too."

"Maybe she needs to be taught that it is your lodge. A good beating will show her that."

"I have never beat a woman in all my winters, and I am not about to start now. There has got to be a different way."

Thoroughly frustrated at this turn of events, I slowly made my back to where we were all packed and ready to go. Samuel was sitting on his horse, and beside him was Buffalo Boy. I needed to set them all straight on one thing, and that was that I was the head trapper of this bunch. Turning to Autumn Sky, I called out to her.

"Woman, come here."

"Yes? What do you want?" She asked.

"If you insist on traveling with us, there are some things that are going to change between us," I told her. Since I wasn't goin' to get out of bringing her along, I figured I better make the best of it. But she had to know a few things first.

"I am the leader of this group," I started off. "And as the leader, it is *me*, not Buffalo Boy, who owns this lodge. If you go with us, you had better learn that quickly. You will do as I say, when I say, and how I say, or I will leave you. Do you understand?"

"Yes, I understand. It is your lodge. I will do as you say. But—"

"There will be no 'but' about it, woman! Now get on your horse. We have a long way to go today."

"You sure put her in her place, didn't you?" asked Samuel.

"Shut-up and leave me be," I told him flatly.

The days were pleasant, but the nights were starting to get mighty chilly by the time we reached North Park. Not really cold yet, but it was going to be cold before too long.

Finding a good beaver stream wasn't too hard; it was finding the right place to set up camp. I wanted a place that we could defend easily if needed, and one that had plenty of grass for the horses. Such spots just weren't that easy to find.

"Whew-wee," cried Samuel. "What *is* that stuff?"

"That there is the milk that helps us catch beaver," I told him. When we had found the right spot, I had Samuel sort out all our traps and other truck while I was out cutting some poles. He had taken the top off the antler vial I used to hold my beaver bait and took a big sniff.

"Smells like somethin' rotten," he said, stuffing the plug back in the small hole.

"What are them long sticks for?" he wanted to know.

"I'll show you in the mornin.' Tomorrow, your learnin' starts on how to catch these here flat-tails. Now, take them traps an' separate 'em into two piles. One for me, an' one for you. How many we got?"

"There's twenty-seven traps."

"We don't need that many to start. Let's see. Just pull out six for each of us, an' put the rest back. Pick the best ones, the ones we fixed on the way out here from rendezvous. That should get us started."

"How did you make that fancy vial you keep that nasty smellin' stuff in? The beaver bait?"

"Just took me an old deer antler an' boiled it till the insides was soft. Then I scooped it out. We'll make you one as soon as we can, but for now, we make you one out of wood."

Buffalo Boy and Autumn Sky were out gathering wood, so I took the pot down to the stream to get some water for coffee. While I was pounding the beans into a fine powder, Samuel sat there, shaking his head at me.

"My, my, but you sure do like your coffee," he said. "It only be the middle of the afternoon, an' here you are makin' coffee."

"Yea, well I notice you be one to drink half the pot whenever I make it," I said back. "'Sides, there ain't a whole lot left to do till tomorrow mornin.' An' I mean *early mornin.'* Gotta be up before them beaver, have our traps in the water, an' be back here 'round first light. Then we go back out in the early evenin,' empty the traps that's full, an' reset 'em. One big cycle."

With our bellies full, we sat around the fire later that night. I had been teaching Samuel some Ute words and Autumn Sky some English ones every night. They were both slow learners, but give them time, and I figured they would catch on.

Long before daylight the next morning, I woke Samuel. This is what it was all about, getting up early, and trudging up the stream, setting traps as you go.

Taking our rifles, traps, and the long poles I had cut the day before, we headed off into the early morning mist that was rising off the stream. I had seen several beaver lodges within a short distance, and it was near them that I led Samuel.

"Now," I whispered, "I'll show you how to make your first set, then I be goin' on upstream a ways. This here stretch of stream be yours to trap. Keep quiet, an' watch what I do."

Locating a recently used slide, I stopped. As I explained to him what to look for, I reached my hand under the water, right at the edge of the bank.

"You gotta make a shelf for your trap to sit on, so it lays flat," I whispered. "Put it off a little to one side of the slide so they won't set it off with their front feet or belly."

Finishing up the shelf, I told him to stick his hand down there so he could feel it and know how to do it. Satisfied that he knew how to make the shelf, I continued on.

"Next, you take the trap, an' set it up here on the bank. It be too hard to open these jaws under the water." I placed the trap on the ground at my feet and pried the jaws open. Stepping down on both sides of the trap, I locked the pan in place with its catch mechanism.

With the end of the chain thrown over my shoulder, I carefully picked up the trap and gently placed it in the water, moving it up onto the shelf I had made. Taking the chain from my shoulder, I slid the large ring on the other end onto one of the long poles and waded out into the stream, pulling the chain tight as I went. There, I pushed the pole into the soft mud in the bottom, then waded back to the shore on the upstream side of the trap.

"Sometimes the beaver's wary of the new smell we're gonna leave for him, so we need to make sure he heads right for the trap. Take you two of them short sticks I had you make, an' push 'em into the mud on either side of the trap. Now he only has a small space to crawl up to where the bait is."

"Like this?" he asked when he had put the sticks in place.

"Yea, that be fine. Push 'em in a little deeper, though, so there's only about five or six inches stickin' out of the water. That's better. Now for the bait," I told him.

"Go downstream a little, an' cut you some willow branches, say, four feet long. Don't strip the leaves off though, 'cause that's where we gonna put the milk."

When he returned with the willow branches, I showed him how to push one into the bank, so that the tip of it was right over the trap we had placed underwater.

"Beaver's is tall when they stand up, so you gotta put it about three feet above the water. That way he has to stand up to smell it, an' that's when he puts his foot in the trap. Then he tries to swim back to his lodge, but he can't go very far. Them traps is too heavy, an' the pole on the other end won't let him go too deep. In about ten minutes or so he drowns," I finished.

"You think you got it?" I asked him.

"Yea, I think so. How far upstream do you want me to go?"

"Skip every two slides you come to. That way your traps are spread out, an' when they spring, it won't scare the rest of 'em off. I'll be countin' the slides as I move on upstream, so you just set 'em like I showed you. When you set the last one, move back in the brush a ways, an' wait for me. I'll be along directly. Then we can head back to camp."

Moving upstream, I counted the beaver slides as I went. There were several lodges within a short distance of where I had left Samuel but not that many slides. That told me that there were several beaver, all using the same slides. We should be able to catch quite a few, just from this stream.

After I had made my own sets, I started back downstream to meet up with Samuel. I had found a nice little meadow about a mile from our present campsite. That was where I wanted to head next, after we had taken some beaver from this stretch of the stream.

Some trappers worked an area until it was completely trapped out, but I had decided long ago that if there was to be any beaver left, then I wasn't going to do that. Sure, there were flat-tails everywhere right now, but I could already see the drop in size and number from back when I came out here. Too many trappers all wanting to make a fortune. After a few seasons, most realized it wasn't that easy to trap, and they never were going to get rich trapping, so they headed back to the settlements. That was fine by me. Let them go on back to their rules and laws. I didn't have much use for them.

It was almost daylight when I came up on Samuel. He was sitting back in the trees, about ten yards from where he had made his last set. As I approached him, he motioned for me to be quiet.

Dropping down into a crouch, I quickly surveyed the surrounding stream bank, thinking that he had seen or heard something, or somebody. Not seeing or smelling anything, I scooted over to him.

"What?" I whispered.

"Watch that last set I made," came his reply.

Squatting own beside him, I turned my attention toward

the stream. I could see the pole he had placed to hold the trap in place and the bait stick. Looking a little further out, I spotted the slight ripple on the glassy surface of the water. A beaver was working his way over to his trap already.

I had seen all this before, but this was a first for Samuel. Together we watched the beaver glide up close to the set with his nose sticking out of the water. When he got close to the slide and his feet touched the bottom of the stream, he was naturally channeled into place by the guide sticks Samuel had put there.

When the beaver stood up and put his hind foot in the trap, it slammed shut, sending the beaver swimming out to deeper water. Samuel jumped up and started to rush to the trap, but I pulled him back down beside me.

"Have to let him drown first," I reminded him.

"I guess I forgot," he said, somewhat sheepishly.

"Don't worry 'bout it," I replied. "You done real good Samuel. Your first day out, an' already you caught you a beaver. An' it ain't even full light yet!"

I felt like a proud parent, watching the look on his face. He had done this all on his own. All I did was show him how to do it.

After the beaver had drowned, we went to remove it from the trap and reset it in the same place. Moving back from the stream, I showed him how to skin his first beaver, making him do the work as I explained it.

"What do we do with the carcass?" he asked.

"Throw it into the bushes," I replied. "Let the scavengers have it. I learned that if we feed 'em, they won't be as apt to raid our traps or our camp."

Taking the fresh beaver pelt, our first one of the season, we started back to camp. Checking all the other traps Samuel had set, we didn't find anymore beaver. But by late afternoon, I was betting we would have plenty of them. And I was right.

Chapter 14

By the time we reached the South Park, it was downright cold. Near as we could guess, it was sometime in early November. The beaver had been putting on their heavy winter coats for some time now, and they were prime pelts.

"'Ol Billy Sublette sure is gonna like these here skins when we get 'em to rendezvous next summer," Samuel remarked one day. "How much you think they're gonna bring?"

"Don't rightly know," I answered. "Beaver's been goin' up last couple of seasons, but when the price of beaver goes up, 'Ol Billy raises his prices all that much more. Kind of disgustin,' if you was to ask me."

"Razor, I want to thank you for lettin' me tag along with you. Don't think I mentioned it afore. When I seen you back to rendezvous, I guess I was a little rough on you. Things ain't been too good for me the last few years."

"Yea, you done told me 'bout your wife up and leavin' you, takin' your little girls with her. I ain't pushed you afore now to find out why you come to the mountains, but if you want to talk about it, I'll listen."

"Well, after I came back to Virginia to take care of that business, when I seen you an' pa in town, I got myself into a mess of trouble. Me an' Jonathon had a nice little business together, cuttin' timbers for the boats they was makin' on the river. I was in Richmond, on business, like I said. Only it wasn't too pleasant business. There was this one fella we had made a deal with for some timbers. We supplied them to him, only he never paid us. I was there to collect, one way or 'nother.

"He told me he had been robbed on his way to pay us, but I didn't believe him. He said he would pay us in a few weeks, when he had been paid for the last boat he sold. I waited in Richmond for him to pay up, but he slipped out of town. I found him in Petersburg, gamblin' an' spendin' our money.

"When he saw me, he tried to get the law to arrest me. Said I was harassin' him. There was no evidence, so they didn't do anything. I finally found him alone one night, drunk as all get out. We got into a fight, and I accidentally killed him. Now the law had a reason to put me in jail, so I lit out of there, headin' back to where Jonathon an' me had our place."

Samuel stopped talking and stood up, moving around the fire. He had a pained look on his face, but he continued on with his story.

When he got back to the small cabin he and Jonathon shared, the law was waiting for him. They arrested him and threw him in jail. Jonathon did what he could do, but it wasn't enough. The law convicted Samuel, and he was on his way to prison.

Some soldiers had come through trying to gather some men to head north and fight with the British. Jonathon told the commander that if he volunteered, he would have to get Samuel out of prison, and together, they would go fight the British.

After two years of fighting with the volunteers, Jonathon was killed in a sneak attack one night. Samuel deserted, heading back to the frontier. It had been over two years since he had left, and, he figured, if he stayed away from the places where he was known, he would be safe.

"I found myself in St. Louis by 1817, and that's where I met and married my wife. She was always wantin' somethin' more, knew there was someplace better than where we was at. So we packed up and moved west, out to the edge of the frontier.

"By 1820," he continued, "she had left me. I was sick of bein' a farmer, so I sold the land and headed back to St. Louis, only wantin' to try and forget that it was me that caused Jonathon's death. If it weren't for me killin' that man back in Petersburg, then he would still be alive.

"I took to drinkin' soon after I arrived back in St. Louis, an' next thing I knew, I was flat broke with no job, no house, no nothin.' I picked up a paper that was layin' in the street one day, an' saw the advertisement for pack tenders. I applied, and the rest, you know."

I was sorry to hear about Jonathon's death. But since it had been several years since I had seen him, it didn't affect me the way it had Samuel. He was carrying a lot of pain and anguish, all pent up inside himself.

"No wonder you was so set on drinkin' yourself into a grave when I first seen you," I said. "But out here, there's only one thing you need concern yourself with. An' that's keepin' your hair on your head, along with mine."

We continued to trap, moving from stream to stream, for the next two weeks. I was getting tired of having to break through the ice at the edges of the streams to set my traps, and I knew Samuel was too. Finally, I decided it was time to head for the village and take some time off.

Packing up all our plunder, I realized we didn't have near the fur I had hoped to have by now. Seemed that after the first couple of weeks we trapped over in the North Park, the beaver had sloughed off. Just have to make a few trips out this winter, I told myself. Besides, it'll give me some time away from Autumn Sky. That woman sure did wear on a man.

She had been true to her word, doing everything I told her to do, like she had agreed to do. But some things she did, it was almost like she was pushing a thorn in my side, on purpose. She knew that the man of the lodge was always the first one served food, then the other adults, then the children. But no, she had to serve Buffalo Boy first. She knew it made me mad, yet she continued to do it, and that made matters worse between us.

Buffalo Boy, on the other hand, was always willing to go the extra distance to please me. He was always out gathering wood for the fire or cutting willow branches to make the round hoops to put the beaver in, and trying to help flesh the beaver Samuel and I brought in. It was almost as if he were trying to make up for something he had done, but if he was, I couldn't think of anything that it might be.

"What are you gonna do with Autumn Sky when we reach the Ute camp?" Samuel asked me.

We had been on our way to the camp for three days, and I had been trying to figure out the same thing. I couldn't just kick her out. She had grown close to my son, and she never let me forget that he was the only reason she did what I told her to do.

"What do you think I should do with her?" I finally asked Samuel.

"She's a mighty fine lookin' woman, Razor. Was I in your place, I might just think 'bout keepin' her. Don't know how you feel 'bout her, but me, I kind of like havin' her 'round. But this is your deal, not mine. You're the one who has to decide what to do with her."

"Yea, she is a handsome woman, I gotta admit that," I said

back. "But I don't want to have a woman 'round unless she cares for me. I know how she cares for Buffalo Boy; she done told me enough times about that. How she truly feels about me, I couldn't say. I guess I better start thinkin' on it though, 'cause we'll be to their camp in a few more days. Then I have to make a choice, one-way or 'nother."

Chapter 15

It was Buffalo Boy who spotted the blood. We couldn't have been more than a day, day and a half, from the village. At first, I thought it might have been a wounded animal, shot by a hunter from the Ute village. But the only tracks in the fresh-fallen powdery snow were horse and man tracks. And they couldn't be more than a few minutes old.

Stepping down from my mule, I took the beaver fur mitten from my right hand and brought the hammer on my rifle back to full cock. Squatting down onto my haunches, I studied the tracks, looking for a sign that might tell me if it were a wounded Ute or an enemy warrior.

Motioning for the others to dismount and keep close to the packhorses, I called Autumn Sky over. As she approached, I saw the apprehension in her eyes, wondering what I wanted her for. When she drew close enough, I pointed to the moccasin tracks in the snow.

"Someone is leading this horse," I whispered to her, "and it carries a heavy load that is still bleeding. Can you tell me if these moccasin prints are from someone in the village?"

Autumn Sky got down on her hands and knees and peered closely at the prints in the snow. She removed her fur mittens and traced the outline of the track. I could tell the difference in moccasin patterns fair enough on dry ground but not in the snow. Autumn Sky had lived with the Ute her whole life and made countless pairs of moccasins, so she would have a better idea than me if these were Ute or not.

Standing back up, she nodded her head once and went back to where the horses were. As she approached Buffalo Boy, I saw her reach her hand out and grip his arm, then she moved to one of the pack animals and pulled one of my extra rifle loose.

As she handed the rifle to Buffalo Boy she bent her head and whispered something to him, then went around the horse to retrieve the last of my extra rifles. Buffalo Boy trotted over to me and handed the rifle over, but I was watching Autumn Sky as she dug around in the pack for the extra powder horn and bag of ball.

Samuel walked over to me, a questioning look in his eyes.

"Ute," I whispered. "And wounded. Looks to be more than one on the horse, might be children."

"What are we goin' to do?" he asked.

"We're gonna go find 'em," I said. "Best go get your extra rifle."

Going back over to Autumn Sky and Buffalo Boy, I was doing some quick calculating. Here we had a Ute leading a horse that was heavily loaded. Dead animals just don't bleed like that, so that told me it wasn't a hunter out from the camp but that someone was wounded.

Bending down so I could whisper in his ear, I told Buffalo Boy to take Autumn Sky and the pack animals back the way we had come. There was a thick stand of timber we had passed through about a half mile back, and that's where I wanted them to go. Samuel and I were going to go on foot and follow the tracks to where they led, and I prayed that whoever it was that they were still alive when we found them.

As I stood back up, I reached into the belt at my waist

and pulled out one of the big heavy pistols that were there. Handing it to Buffalo Boy, I nodded to him. He would know what to do when the time came; I was sure.

Turning to Autumn Sky, I saw the scared look on her face. She was trying not to let it show for the sake of my son, but I saw it, nonetheless. I had a hunch she knew exactly who it was that we were going to find, and I needed to know. I knew most of the warriors in Wing of the Hawk's camp very well, and if I knew who it was I was trailing, I stood a better chance of helping them.

"You know who it is that left those tracks." I said it as a statement, not as a question, and she caught it. Nodding her head, she turned away, rolling her eyes to show she wanted me to follow her.

"Who is it?" I asked when we were far enough from Buffalo Boy.

"It is your brother, Wing of the Hawk. It is his blood that lies in the snow." She turned her eyes to me, and I could read the plea in them as surely as I could read a beaver stream.

"What?" I asked.

"You will be careful, Round-Ball? Your son has suffered much in the last two years, and I do not want to see him suffer anymore. So please, come back to him. Come back to us," she added, much to my surprise.

Nodding my head to her, I gave a weak smile and turned away. Samuel was waiting for me, and the longer we stood here, the further away Wing of the Hawk got.

We took off at a trot, trying to make up for lost time, following the tracks of the horse. The trail had cut across the one we had been taking down to the village, simply heading through the timber and blow downs. As we followed along, I was searching my mind as to where Wing of the Hawk could he headed.

I had hunted over much of this country before, so I knew it well, but try as I might, I couldn't figure out where he was headed. The longer we followed the trail, it was plain to see that Wing of the Hawk was heading for someplace he knew of.

Then I remembered the cave. It was nothing more than a large hole in the side of a hill, probably a bear cave in the past. I had been out hunting with some of the others from our small band, when a sudden rainstorm had caught up with us. As I was making a run for a stand of timber, I spotted the cave and headed there instead.

Wing of the Hawk and some of the others had been close behind me, and we all gathered in the cave to sit out the storm. That had to be where he was headed, so I changed our course, cutting off to the right of the trail.

"Why aren't we followin' the trail?" Samuel wanted to know.

"'Cause I know where he's headed now, and we can shave off some time by cuttin' cross-country," I said over my shoulder.

"That mean you know who it is?"

"Yea, I know who it is. Wing of the Hawk. And Autumn Sky says it's his blood on the snow, and I think the horse is carryin' some children from the village. So we need to get there as quick as we can."

Suddenly, we both heard the sound of a rifle going off behind us, followed by the lighter popping of a pistol. Buffalo Boy and Autumn Sky. Whoever it was that had shot Wing of the Hawk had found them too. We were close to the cave, and much as I wanted to turn around and go to my son, I knew it would be over before I got there, one way or another. There was another shot from the rifle, so that meant they were still alive.

Skidding to a stop at the edge of the small meadow in front of the cave, we hunched down, looking for signs. We could see the tracks of the horse headed directly to the cave, but I knew better than to just walk up to it. Wing of the Hawk was wounded, and he had no idea we were even around. I didn't want him to mistake us for a raiding party and start shooting at us, so I cupped my hands to my mouth and gave the long, lonely howl of the wolf.

Wing of the Hawk knew that this was my call, not for any other reason than it was the only one I could make. But when he didn't answer it, I called again, adding two yips at the end, letting him know there was two of us. Then Samuel and I stood up and ran across the meadow to the cave.

Slowing as we approached the mouth of the cave, I peered in. The first thing I saw was three sets of large, round eyes staring at me. Looking deeper, I could see Wing of the Hawk. He was leaning against the back wall of the cave, holding his rifle in front of him, and it was pointed right at my chest.

"Brother, do not shoot me," I said, breathless from the running we had done.

"Children," I said in Ute, "get further back into the cave, behind the horse."

Going over to Wing of the Hawk, I took the rifle from his now limp hands, leaning it against the wall of the cave with my two guns. The children, I saw right away, were scared out of their minds. They didn't recognize me for who I was, I had been gone from the camp of Wing of the Hawk for so long.

"Listen to your uncle," Wing of the Hawk said painfully.

The children instantly obeyed, moving to stand cowering behind the one horse they had. Turning back to the front of the cave, I saw Samuel standing guard, watching the meadow in front of us. It was nice to know I could count on him to do what needed to be done without having to say a thing.

"Let me know as soon as you see 'em Samuel," I said dryly. "I need to check his wounds and see if we can make it back to Buffalo Boy and Autumn Sky."

Kneeling down next to Wing of the Hawk, I saw the whole

left side of his hunting shirt was soaked with blood. Gently, I lifted the shirt and saw that he had taken a piece of his saddle blanket and had it tied around the wound. Drawing my knife from the back of my belt, I sliced through the leather thong and removed the blood-soaked cloth.

It was a clean slice, made with a knife, but it was deep and still oozing blood. Tossing the bloody rag to one side, I cut the bottom of my own hunting shirt off, and folded it to make a thick pad. As I placed it on the wound and tied it in place with the same thong I had cut off, I saw that Wing of the Hawk had passed out.

"Samuel, I need to go—"

"Just go see if they're alright," he cut me off. "How is he?" he asked, indicating Wing of the Hawk.

"He's lost a lot of blood, and he passed out, but I think he'll pull through," I said.

Turning to the children, I spoke quickly.

"Children, listen to me. There are others out there who need our help. I am going to help them, but you must stay here. This one," I said, pointin' to Samuel, "is here to help you. Listen to him, and help him if he needs it."

Leaning Wing of the Hawk's rifle next to Samuel, I grabbed my two guns and left the cave, running straight across the meadow. My heart felt like it was lodged in my throat as I ran, and my only hope was that I wasn't too late.

Chapter 16

Not wanting to follow the same trail back, I stayed off to one side of it, but still close enough so that I could see if anyone was following it to the cave. If there was, I would be able to warn Samuel ahead of time and possibly take a few of them out, giving him less to deal with. He was still new to this way of fighting, Indian style, but he was a quick learner.

Sure enough, I hadn't gone too far when I saw them walking their horses through the trees. Looked like there was five of them, and not to my surprise, they were Arapaho. All of them had their heads down, watching the trail, except for the last one. I shot him first, the ball hitting him squarely in the forehead, knocking him backwards.

As the echo of my shot went through the trees, the Arapaho horses started plunging and bucking, scattering the raiders out. Leaning the empty rifle against a tree, I brought the second one to my shoulder. One of the braves finally got his horse under control and charged through the trees towards me, not even knowing I was there. As soon as I pulled the trigger, feeling the heavy buck of the rifle against my shoulder, I dropped to the ground and reloaded both empty rifles.

Hearing the horses running off, I peeked my head over the

downed tree I was behind. The three braves that were left were running down the trail, on towards the cave where Samuel was guarding the children and the wounded Wing of the Hawk. The two I had shot were dead, and I started back to the cave, thinking that this was all that was left of the raiding party.

Suddenly, there was another shot from the stand of timber where I had sent Buffalo Boy and Autumn Sky. They were still alive! Breaking into a hard run, I tore through the trees, branches slapping my face and body. But none of that mattered now. They were still alive and still fighting. I had to get there and fast.

When I got to where we had first seen the blood trail, I cut over a slight rise to the left and headed for the fighting. I could hear an occasional shot from the rifle and pistol I had left with Buffalo Boy and Autumn Sky, along with the high-pitched yipping war cries of the Arapaho. Mixed into all this noise, I distinctly heard my son give his own Ute war cry.

There were several rider-less horses milling around just inside the tree line, and catching one up, I vaulted onto its back. Tucking the horsehair reins under my leg, I cocked both rifles and charged into the midst of the attacking Arapaho.

Screaming my own Ute war cry, I fired the first rifle, then the other into them, taking out two of the six raiders. Dropping the rifle in my left hand, I drew the pistol from my belt and shot at a third one, missing him.

Swinging the rifle like a club, I dropped from the horse. I launched myself into one of the attackers, jabbing at his throat with the heavy barrel of the rifle, tearing it open. He went down in a spray of blood, the force of my momentum ripping the rifle from my grasp.

I dropped the pistol and reached to the back of my belt to take up my knife and tomahawk, the only two weapons I had left to defend myself. There were two sudden shots from the trees, and two of the attacking Arapaho dropped. As the third one was closing in on me, I threw the tomahawk, burying the head of it, clear to the handle, in his chest.

Quickly, I reloaded the pistol, but the barrel of the rifle was too caked in blood and gore to use. Buffalo Boy and Autumn Sky came out of the trees, and that told me that this was the last of the Arapaho.

"I knew you would be back, father," shouted a happy Buffalo Boy. He ran up to me, throwing his arms around my waist and almost taking me off balance.

"I got here as soon as I could," I replied, thankful that I had made it in time.

Smiling, Autumn Sky came up to where Buffalo Boy and I were standing, still gripping her rifle. As she put her hand on Buffalo Boy's shoulder, she looked up at me.

"You should have seen yourself as you charged them," she said. "Had I not known you by the hair on your face, I would have thought you were a Ute warrior, screaming your war cry like you were."

Suddenly she looked around, noticing for the first time that I was alone. Buffalo Boy noticed it at almost the same time.

"Where is my white uncle, father?"

"He is taking care of your other uncle, and we need to go to them," I replied. Autumn Sky looked at me expectantly, and I told her he was alive.

Gathering up our horses, I jumped on the back of my mule and we started towards the cave. I needed my medicines on one of my packhorses to treat Wing of the Hawk's wound and any others they might have received.

Following the now well-worn trail to the cave, we arrived in a short time. We heard no sounds of fighting as we approached, and I stopped long enough to give the cry of the wolf.

It was answered by one of the children in the cave, and all three came out as we came across the meadow. There was fresh blood on the snow, leading off into the trees at a right angle to the cave.

Samuel came to the mouth of the cave, limping. There was a crude bandage wrapped around his head, and I could see there was a little blood on his left legging, just below the arrow that was stuck in his thigh. Jumping from my mule, I ran the last few feet to him, just as he dropped to the snow.

"Find me my medicines, son," I told Buffalo Boy.

Turning back to Samuel, I shook my head at him.

"Gonna have to start callin' you the 'Arrow Catcher' if you keep this up. Two fights you've had now, an' this makes two arrows I've had to pull outta your hide."

"Shut-up an' get this thing out of me," he replied, grinning from ear to ear. "But first, you better see how Wing of the Hawk is doin.' He never woke up at all, an' I don't think he made it."

With a sinking feeling, I went into the cave. Wing of the Hawk was just as I had left him, leaning back against the cave wall. As I approached him, I thought I saw the slight rise and fall of his chest, but it could have been a trick of the poor light in the cave.

Shaking him gently, he suddenly cried out, jumping the way a man would when he's awakened from a deep sleep.

"It is me, Wing of the Hawk, your brother," I said soothingly. "We need to get you out into the sunlight where we can sew you up. Are you ready?" I asked when he nodded.

"Yes," he croaked back, his voice sounding like it came from the bottom of a hole.

Reaching down, I scooped him up in my arms and carried him out into the sunlight. Surprised at how light he was, I began to realize just how much blood he had lost. His face was pale as I laid him down on a buffalo robe Autumn Sky had thrown on the snow for him.

"Buffalo Boy," I called. When he came over to me, I told

him, "Take the children into the cave while Autumn Sky and I do what needs to be done to your uncles. Tell them of your fight with the enemy, that should keep them busy for awhile," I added, not wanting any of them to see how bad off Wing of the Hawk was.

"Take care of him first," Samuel said as I went to him. "He's in far worse shape than me. I don't see how such a small man like him managed to make it this far, let alone live this long. I thought he was dead."

"Close, but as long as he's breathin' he's got a chance," I said.

Autumn Sky had gone through my medicine kit, taking out what she thought we might need. There was a giant puff-ball to help stop the bleeding, some white willow bark powder to help ease his pain and a hank of sinew to stitch him up.

"Do you have one of the steel needles of the white man to sew up the wound?" she asked me.

"Yes, I will get you one. Do you want some water to mix the willow bark in?" I asked of her.

"No, I will put it all around the wound to make the flesh go to sleep. It will work faster, and we do not have the time to build a fire right now."

By the time I had found one of the needles I had packed away, Autumn Sky had removed the bandage I had put on Wing of the Hawk earlier. She handed me an empty birch bark cup and said she needed some water to wash the wound. There was no stream in sight, so I scooped up some snow into the cup and tucked it under my arm to melt it with the heat from my body. We were going to need a fire when night fell, so I went to the mouth of the cave.

"Son, I need you and the children to go get us some wood for a fire. When you have enough, make a small fire, inside the cave. And stake the horses out in the meadow so they are out of the way."

Handing the melted snow to Autumn Sky, I asked her if she needed my help sewing Wing of the Hawk up.

"No, I can do it," she replied to my question. "But you can start on your white brother while I am doing this. Do not remove the arrow, though. From the position of it, I think he will bleed to death if you pull it out."

This wasn't the first wound I had taken care of, yet she seemed to think it was. Fuming inside, I spun on my heel and stormed away, angry that she was treating me this way and after looking at me with those big round eyes earlier. I guess I never will understand women.

"How was it, after I left?" I asked Samuel as I sat beside him. I had slit his pant leg away from the shaft of the arrow and wiped away the little bit of blood that had seeped out.

"Well, those two shots from the trees alerted me, an' I was ready for 'em when they charged into the meadow. I shot the first one, but he stayed on his horse, headin' off to the left, there," he said pointing to some rocks. "He dropped in those rocks, but I ain't had the time to check on him.

"The other two kept comin' at me, so I dropped the first rifle, picked up the second one and pulled the trigger. Only nothin' happened. Wing of the Hawk forgot to reload, I guess. By the time I realized all this, I had an arrow in my leg. As my leg went out from under me, I pulled my pistol and shot another one. That's his trail there, goin' off to the right.

"I almost didn't get the last one; he was so close to the trees. All of a sudden, there was my loaded rifle, bein' pushed into my hands by one of them kids. He seen I couldn't get to it, so he reached out and got it for me. I drew a bead on the last one an' touched her off, blowin' him right over the front of his horse."

"So you got all three of 'em, then?" I asked.

"Only one I ain't too sure of is the one that made it to them rocks, yonder. Might want to check him out, soon as you get the chance. He's wounded, that much I do know."

"Better do it now," I told him. "Don't want him out there gettin' away an' back to his people. I'm gettin tired of these 'Rapaho, always stickin' their noses into my business," I added as I walked towards the rocks.

As I approached the place where Samuel had last seen the Arapaho, I saw a foot sticking out from behind the rocks. I watched it and waited for several minutes, but it didn't move, even when I threw a ball of snow at it. Walking around the rocks, I saw that half the brave's face was shot away. Flipping him over onto his back with my moccasin covered foot, I saw that he was no more than a boy, probably only fifteen or so. Seemed like they kept getting younger and younger. Or maybe it was just me, getting older and older.

Leaving the scalp in place for the time being, I went back to the cave. Buffalo Boy had started a fire, and Autumn Sky was working the arrow out of Samuel's leg. I could see the pain he was in, but he was quiet about it.

"He's dead alright," I said as I squatted down next to his head. "You blew half his face off."

"Where's the scalp?" he asked through clenched teeth.

"You shot him, you scalp him," I replied. "Time you started doin' your own scalpin.' You done good, Samuel. Real good. When we get back to the village, them youngsters there are gonna be tellin' the rest of 'em what a brave warrior you are, an' it will look better to 'em if you do your own scalpin,' wounded or not. But it can wait till the mornin.' They ain't goin nowhere. 'Sides, we'll be here for a couple of days, give Wing of the Hawk time to get some strength back."

"Uungh," he cried as the arrow popped free from his leg, and then he passed out.

Chapter 17

Slowly, over the next three days, we got the story of the attack from a recovering Wing of the Hawk. As he told us, it made it all the more urgent that we get to the camp as soon as possible.

No one had expected the attack when it came, right at dawn of the day we had found him and the children. There were shouts of alarm that the enemy was in camp from the boys guarding the horses. As the Ute warriors erupted from their buffalo hide lodges, there were Arapaho swarming all through the village.

Wing of the Hawk had seen several warriors on both sides go down fighting, the women and children running for the thick stands of timber blanketing the hillside behind the village. Catching up his war pony, he made a dash through the village, seeing many children and elders still there. Spinning his pony around, he was charging back through when an Arapaho brave jumped on him, knocking him from his horse.

"I lost the hold on my rifle when we hit the ground, and before I could rise up to meet him, the knife in his hand flashed out, slicing me open. I went down, and as he was gripping my hair, he suddenly went stiff and fell to the side, an arrow through his throat.

"I managed to get back to my feet and catch up my pony. There were still so many children in the village, and with the Arapaho warriors chasing the others into the timber, I gathered up these three, putting them on my pony."

"And this is where you were headed when we found your tracks in the snow," I finished for him.

"Yes. But we must return to our camp. There were many dead and dying people when we left. I do not know if my own wife and children made it," he said, lowering his head.

I could read the sadness in his voice, and I knew what he was going through, having lost my own wife and nearly loosing my son to the Arapaho.

"We will leave before the sun is in the sky tomorrow," I told him. "And we will do whatever we can to help you find your family," I added thickly.

Samuel was recovering from his leg wound rapidly, the fresh air this high in the mountains helping. The head wound he had received in the fight with the Arapaho was nothing more than a scratch and caused him no worries.

Together, we had scalped all the dead Arapaho warriors, stripping them and hanging them in the trees. If nothing else, it served the purpose of letting the rest of the Arapaho nation know that I was back. They would know as soon as they saw the bodies who had done this.

Of the fourteen dead Arapaho, we had managed to capture seven of their horses, and I figured at least three of these belonged to Samuel. He had killed three braves all by himself. I had enough horses already, but when I tried to give them to Wing of the Hawk, he refused them.

"I did nothing to earn them," he told us. "You were the ones who killed the enemy, so the horses belong to you, as do the scalps."

"Then I will give them to the children, for being brave in

the face of our enemies, the Arapaho," I told them all that night around the fire. Wing of the Hawk nodded his head in approval at my decision, and the three children all wore big smiles.

Buffalo Boy was finally starting to act like the seven summers old boy he was instead of the grown warrior he had thought himself to be. I had taken Autumn Sky to one side after she had finished patching up Samuel, and we talked about him at length.

"He is very proud of his father," she told me. "'He is a great warrior among his people and mine' he said to me."

"And I am proud of him," I said. "When I was charging into the Arapaho, when they had both of you pinned down, I heard his war cry, and my heart soared. I would like to thank you for all that you have done for him in the past, while I was away."

Autumn Sky hung her head and stared at her feet before she spoke again.

"I know," she began, "that you loved your wife very much, and that is why you went on the warpath against those that took her away from you." She slowly raised her head to look into my face, and I was surprised at the emotion I saw behind her eyes.

"Has your heart been healed? Is your revenge over?" she asked.

Taking both of her small, delicate hands in mine, I looked down at her. She was beautiful, even after all she had been through in the past three days, and I felt my heart leaping in my chest as if it were trying to break free from my body.

"I do not truly know if my heart will ever heal, Autumn Sky. But yes, the revenge killings are over. Now I will only fight when I have to, not because I want to. There is nothing left for me to prove to myself."

Chapter 18

Early the next morning, we started back to Wing of the Hawk's camp. What we would find, none of us knew. There were nine lodges in his band, totaling thirty-five people. Eight warriors, eleven women, nine elders, and seven children, all of one extended family. Two of the children belonged to Wing of the Hawk, as did one of the women.

Wing of the Hawk tried to remember who he had seen dead or dying in the snow that fateful morning. All he could remember seeing, though, was two of his warriors, both riddled with arrows, and the three children he had managed to save.

We reached the camp of the Ute in the early afternoon, following the trail Wing of the Hawk had made during his escape. The people were happy to see Wing of the Hawk and the three children alive, some having given them up for dead days ago. I saw a few faces I remembered from two years ago, but not many, and my heart began to sink.

"Where is Bad Leg?" I asked Autumn Sky. I was hoping to see my old friend when we arrived, but he was not there.

"He and his family left our band last summer," she replied. "There were getting to be more people in our band than the land would support, so he and a few of his friends decided to go off on their own. I have not seen him since that time."

At least he hadn't been in this camp. He might still be alive, with his own band. I would have to find out where he would be spending the winter and maybe go see him.

The death toll from the raid was three warriors, one child and one woman. Lucky, I thought, as I looked the camp over. By rights, there should have been more. We had killed fourteen of the Arapaho further up the mountainside, and four had been killed here. Eight Ute against at least eighteen Arapaho warriors was pretty bad odds. And that wasn't counting the ones who got away with the horse herd, either.

After we were settled into my lodge, I went to Wing of the Hawk's lodge to speak with him. He was resting as comfortable as he could with his wound, reclining in front of his fire on a willow backrest.

"Brother," I began, "we need more horses. The ones I have are needed for packing, and when I go away in the spring, I will need to take them with me. But the Arapaho have many horses, most of them ours. I would like to organize a raid on the Arapaho village, and I know where they are.

"You are the leader of this band, and I know there are only five warriors, including you. I would like to take two of your warriors with me, but only if you think you can do without them for several days."

"Our band has been through much in the past days," he said. "Perhaps we should wait a little longer to raid the Arapaho. I want revenge on them, and yes, we do need horses. But now is not the time."

Nodding my head to him, I left. He was the leader of this band, and it was his place to decide on matters like this. He had become the leader not only because he was a great warrior, but also because he was respected. His decisions were made for the whole band, not because of his personal feelings, and I admired him for that.

Returning to my lodge, I was surprised to find only Samuel and Buffalo Boy there.

"Where is Autumn Sky?"

"She said somethin' about going to see someone, but I couldn't catch all of it," Samuel said.

"She went to see one of her sisters, father. The woman who was killed was her other sister," Buffalo Boy told me.

"Well, I guess that means we're on our own for supper."

"No, she said she would be back by dark to feed you," Buffalo Boy said with a smirky smile.

It took me a minute to get what he had said, and when it dawned on me, I turned to them both.

"What are you two smilin' like that for?"

"Seems to me that I'm gonna have to find me another lodge to stay the winter in," Samuel sputtered out between fits of laughter. "Yea, you're pretty much a married man already, an' you don't even know it!"

"What do you expect me to do? I don't reckon I have much choice in the matter anymore. An' you were the one who told me I should keep her around," I told Samuel.

"And you," I said pointing to Buffalo Boy. "Come here, I want to talk to you about this."

"Yes, father?" he asked, giggling out of control.

"You set me up, you little runt! You knew that the more time I spent with that she-cat, the less likely I would be to kick her out, now didn't you?"

Laughing too hard to answer, Buffalo Boy just nodded his head, rolling into a ball on the ground.

When we had all calmed the laughter down, I pulled Buffalo Boy into my lap, tousling his hair.

"It's good to see you laugh, son. It's been awhile, hasn't it?"

Sobering a little, he nodded.

"Yes, it has been a long time," he said. "Since the time of my mother's death, I have not had a reason to laugh. But now you are back where you belong, and I am truly happy again."

"What if Autumn Sky doesn't want to spend the rest of her days with a grouchy old man like me?"

"She talks of nothing else," said Buffalo boy, rolling his eyes. "You would think that you are the only man in the world, the way she talks. It is 'Round-Ball this,' and 'Round-Ball that.'"

"How do you feel about it, son? I won't do this unless you want me to."

"I have been waiting for you to ask her ever since we left the rest of our band in the fall. It has taken you longer than I thought, though. And Autumn Sky, or should I start calling her 'mother,' feels like you do not want her. You need to tell her, father, before she decides to take my white uncle for a husband, instead of you!"

We had been talking in Ute, but when he said this, I turned to look at Samuel.

"You been followin' what we been talkin' about?"

"Some of it, but not all. I can't seem to get my tongue to make all them sounds."

"Well, we been discussin' me marryin' Autumn Sky. And Rowdy here seems to think that if I don't ask her mighty soon, then she's gonna start workin' on you! But I think you're safe, at least where she's concerned."

"She sure is a handsome woman, Razor. But what she wants with such an ornery old man like you, I'll never know!"

"She could do worse, an' pick you," I said, starting to laugh again. 'Sides, she—"

The lodge flap was suddenly thrown back, and in she walked, with her sister right behind her.

"My sister, Little Rabbit. I have invited her to eat with us," Autumn Sky told us.

Looking over at Samuel, I started to tell him that it was just like a woman to ruin my plan to ask her, but then I saw his face. He was staring at the newcomer, mouth hanging open. So I did what any younger brother would do. I reached out and kicked him in his wounded leg.

He let out a yelp, and Buffalo Boy and I started laughing again. Both women stared at us like we were crazy, and Autumn Sky shook her head, smiling.

"Crazy white men," she explained to her sister.

"Yea, we're crazy, alright," I said back. "But these 'crazy white men' are the ones who put the food in your cooking pots all winter, so we must not be that crazy! You had better start treating me nice, or all you will have to eat are old, worn out moccasins!"

I said it with a twinkle in my eyes, and Autumn Sky knew I was only joking, but her sister wasn't too sure about us.

"Come on, 'Arrow Catcher,'" I said to Samuel as I pulled him to his feet. "Let's go check on the horses while these two women fix us our supper."

As we left the lodge, I heard Autumn Sky telling her sister that we were good providers and true warriors. Little Rabbit answered her, but we were out of earshot by then.

"Now that's what I'm talkin' about!" exclaimed Samuel.

"What's that?" I asked.

"Oh come on, Razor! Didn't you see that woman? She's the stuff dreams are made of!"

"Now Samuel, don't go gettin a case on her," I admonished him. "Next thing you know, you'll be stuck out here in the mountains, just like me. An' you with your mind set on goin' back to St. Louis next summer. Don't think that'll go over too well, takin' Little Rabbit back there."

"Well, maybe I changed my mind 'bout going back. You were right when you said these mountains grow on a man. Tell you the truth, I've never been happier than this. Since seein' you at rendezvous, I ain't never looked back. An' now, I don't want to."

"Sounds like I created a monster in you," I stated.

"No, it's not like that at all. It makes me feel like it was when we were youngsters, back in Virginia. The freedom, the quietness. An' except for the 'Rapaho, it ain't been bad at all. Think I'm gonna stay."

"Don't do it just for Little Rabbit. She may not even want you, so don't get your hopes up too high."

"Naw, it's not just her, an' you know it."

We made the rounds of the horses, making sure they were all hobbled, and then we headed back to my lodge and hopefully, to a cooked meal. My belly was starting to groan from lack of food in it.

"How does a man go about gettin' his own lodge like yours?" Samuel asked me along the way.

"In the fall, we generally go on a buffalo hunt. That's where we get the hides. Most of the bands don't like to go down onto the flats to hunt 'em, though. Our band does."

"How come this village is so small? I thought there were big tribes of Indians, all livin' together. Is this all there is of the Ute?"

"No, this ain't all there is," I said. "They all gather up in the late spring, an' hunt and live together as a big tribe, then in the fall, they break into smaller groups, like this one. See, the land can only supply so much of what we need, an' by going off in small groups like this, we don't have to move around so much in the winter."

"You keep sayin' 'we,' like you're part of the tribe."

"That's 'cause I am. I was adopted into the Ute tribe a long time ago, even before I married Buffalo Boy's mother."

"Have to tell me about it sometime," he said.

"Yea, sometime. Right now, all I want is to eat."

Chapter 19

Wing of the Hawk and I were out hunting one day, several weeks later, when I asked him if Autumn Sky's father still lived. It was to him that I must pay the bride price if I was going to marry her.

"Her father was killed many years ago, in a fight with the Cheyenne. All her brothers have been killed as well, but she does have an uncle, living with Bad Leg and his band. Are you finally going to marry her?" he asked.

"Yes, my brother, I am. She has made my son very happy and taken care of him while I was away."

"And how do you feel about her? I do not want you to do something as serious as this, only because you feel you need to repay her. You must do it because it is what is in your heart."

"I do love her, Wing of the Hawk, there is no doubt in my mind about that. She has made me happy again. No longer do I only live for the fighting.

"When Buffalo Boy's mother died, I did not want to live anymore. She was my whole world. Then, she was taken from me. I carried around a great hate for a long time, wanting to die in battle so I could be with her again, in a better place. But then, I started thinking on what I was doing to our only son.

It was not right that I should forget him for the sake of my own feelings."

"And now, you have come home again," he stated.

"Yes, I have come home again," I said. "And the first thing you do to welcome me back is try to marry me off," I said laughing.

"It was not only me," he said defensively. "My wife and the other women of the band thought it would be a good match, and it would seem that we were all right. Otherwise, we would not be having this talk right now."

"It is a good match, brother. And thank you. You have once again proved to me why you are the leader of this band. You are wise beyond your years."

"I am only leader as long as the people wish it. And that brings up a request you have made. I think that now is the time to go on a pony-stealing raid from the Arapaho."

Hesitant at first, and not wanting to sound like I was backing out on the raid, I explained to Wing of the Hawk that now I wanted to wait.

"I wish to be married to Autumn Sky before we leave on the raid. Is it possible to send a runner to Bad Leg? I would do this marriage properly, and since she has only one uncle, I must go through him."

"That seems to be a reasonable request. I will send a runner as soon as we return. And if you do not hit the deer this time, we might have to change your name to 'Poor Hunter'!" he added. We both laughed about it as we headed back to camp.

Wing of the Hawk sent the runner to Bad Leg the next morning, saying it should only take three days there and three days back, depending on the snow. Everything was settled, except for the bride price, but I was sure I could come up with just about anything that was wanted.

It was eight days later when the runner returned, and I

wasn't the only person who was getting nervous about his lateness. I was on my way to see Wing of the Hawk to see if he would allow me to take a few warriors and see what had happened to him, but we didn't need to.

"Well, what did he say?" I asked as the runner rode up.

"He said you are to wait, Round-Ball," the runner responded.

"Wait? Wait for what?" I wanted to know.

"He will be here later today. And he said he would not give you an answer until he has met you." Turning his horse, the runner dashed through the camp, telling everyone to get ready for the visitors.

"Well, what did he say?" Samuel asked when I returned to the lodge.

"Who? Wing of the Hawk or the runner?"

"The runner has returned?" asked Autumn Sky.

"Yes, he has returned," I said quietly.

"And my uncle? What was his answer?" she demanded.

"He said to wait."

"Wait for what?" asked Samuel

"He will be here this very afternoon," I said grinning at them both. "And from the sounds of it, he's bringin' his whole band along with him."

"And this is good news?"

"Yea, Samuel, it's good news. Means he's already agreed to the marriage. I imagine he wants to get the bride presents before somethin' happens to me, though. That's why he wants us to wait, so he can be here for the ceremony."

"That reminds me, Razor. Somethin' I been wantin' to talk to you 'bout."

"So go ahead an' talk. I gotta clean myself up some before I meet this fella, but I can listen."

"Well," he said nervously, "it's just that I, uh, what I mean is that, uh, we—"

"Just spit it out, Samuel. What are you tryin' to say?"

"It's just that I want to ask Little Rabbit to marry me. An' since her an' Autumn Sky are sisters, I guess I better meet this uncle of theirs too. But I don't know what to say to him. What do you think he'll want me to give him for Little Rabbit?"

Shocked, I turned on him.

"What do you mean, you want to marry Little Rabbit? When did all this happen?" Turning to face Autumn Sky, I was glad that Buffalo Boy was out playing.

"Did you know this was going on? And you did not tell me?"

"It is not my place to speak of it, Round-Ball. Your white brother has grown fond of Little Rabbit, and she has no husband to provide for her. She does not like living with our dead sister's husband, as she has been forced to do."

"Razor, don't get mad at her, she was only doin' what I asked her to do."

"Are you sure you know what you're doin,' Samuel? 'Cause if you are, then first you have to become a member of this band, permanent like. You have to have someone adopt you, you have to have a naming ceremony, there's—"

"I know, I know. I already talked to Wing of the Hawk about it. He has offered to adopt me into his family, says it's the least he can do, since I stood over him an' killed them three 'Rapaho braves when he couldn't defend them three kids. An' you already gave me a name. Appears you ain't been payin' too close attention on that one. These people been callin' me 'Arrow Catcher' for some time now."

"So it's all been decided without me? Is that what you two are sayin' to me?"

"Yes," they both answered at the same time.

"An' here all this time, I been thinkin' you need someone to take care of you," I said to Samuel, shakin' my head in mock anger. "But here you are, gettin' ready to be married, an' I don't even know it till it happens!"

"You cannot see everything that goes on in this camp, Round-Ball," Autumn Sky said shyly.

"And I do not think I want to see all that happens in this camp," I replied.

We all laughed about it, and then I decided Samuel needed some cleaning up as well as me.

"You think you can follow along in Ute when I talk to the uncle?" I asked Samuel as we were washing up at the stream. "You have to understand, this is a big ceremony to these people. It's not something they take lightly."

"I think I can," he answered in Ute. "But I will watch you and lean," he added.

"Lean?" I asked. "You need a little more practice, but I think when the uncle sees that you're tryin,' he'll approve of you. 'Specially with the backin' of Wing of the Hawk. He's pretty big among the people. Been the leader of this band for a long time. He's wise in many ways, an' the rest of the Ute respect him. It should go well. For both of us," I added, starting to feel the first flutters of nervousness deep down in the pit of my stomach.

Chapter 20

I had Autumn Sky remove all her personal belongings from my lodge, taking them to her sister's. It wouldn't seem right to show that she had been keeping my lodge before we were properly married, even though Wing of the Hawk said he would explain it if there was any question about my honorable intentions. I just felt that it would look better.

Next, Samuel and I broke out the trade goods we had gotten at rendezvous last summer, but not all of them. If I was to show this uncle everything, he would want it all. I was a rich man by Ute standards, and I was counting on that fact to convince this man to allow this marriage.

Samuel and I also made up a separate bundle for him to do his trading with, using as many different trade items as we could. The one thing we were both short on was horses. And horses went a long way when it came to buying a wife. But since we didn't have them, I guess it didn't matter.

The loud commotion outside let us know that the Bad Leg band had arrived. It sure would be good to see Bad Leg again. It had been too long. But first things first. We had to have a feast and let the travelers rest. Then, tomorrow, we would discuss the marriages.

Samuel was more nervous than I was when we stepped out of my lodge to stand in line with the rest, greeting the newcomers. I was shocked that there was so many of them.

After all had been greeted and made welcome, the feasting started. As I was standing with Wing of the Hawk, watching the visitors, a gruff voice at my shoulder startled me.

"I thought the Arapaho had taken your hair, my son."

Knowing the voice instantly, I dropped the buffalo bone I had been gnawing on, and spun around. The man I now faced was almost as tall as me but was starting to show signs of his age. The slightly protruding belly, the gray in his hair, and the creases in his face, all told the story of a hard life.

"Father!" I cried, unable to control the outburst.

"Yes, it is me. Did you think that I would miss the marriage of my son?"

Gripping my arms tightly, he pulled me to him in a huge bear hug, almost crushing the wind from me. As he stepped back, I was suddenly flooded with emotions from the past. This was the man who had found me, almost frozen to death, fourteen years ago.

Chasing the Storm had come across Pepper and I while he was out hunting one day, in the middle of the winter. We were still new to the mountains, only having spent one winter here, and when he found us, we were both in bad shape.

We had been in a fight with some marauding Arapaho, and we were both wounded. Chasing the Storm took us back to his lodge and treated our wounds. The others in his band thought he was crazy for doing this, but he was their leader at the time, and he did what he thought was best. Lucky for us he did.

Even though his name was Chasing the Storm, most people called him 'The Wolf,' a name he had earned by being relentless in battle, always giving chase to the enemy. He ended up adopting Pepper and I into the Ute tribe, and the others soon accepted us as well.

"It has been too long, father."

"Yes, it has," he answered. "I was told you had left your scalp in the lodge of an Arapaho, two winters ago."

Hanging my head in shame, I told him what had happened to Prairie Flower and Pepper that day and what I had done as a result. He understood it well, as he had done the same thing when his first wife had been killed by some Cheyenne.

"It will get better with time," he told me. "And it will help to have a new woman. She can heal the scars, if you will let her.

"Where is my grandson? Is he well?"

"He is here, somewhere," I replied. "But there is another I wish you to meet. He is my white brother."

Calling Samuel over, I made the introductions. I explained to him that this was my father among the Ute, I ended up telling him how he had found us. It seemed like yesterday, but it had been many years since that day.

As the feasting went on, I pulled The Wolf to one side, where we could talk uninterrupted. I wanted to know what kind of man I was going to have to deal with tomorrow, and the more I knew ahead of time, the better off I would be.

"He is, to put it plainly, like a bear with a bad tooth," The Wolf told me. "He is a poor hunter, and he takes it out on everyone else. I hope you have many horses to trade to him. He only thinks of gaining power and will do whatever he can to attain it."

"Well, then I guess I am in trouble. We have no horses to trade," I said, spreading my hands. "The Arapaho that raided our band took most of them. We are planning on going on a pony raid against them, as soon as Autumn Sky and I are married. Perhaps we should have done that first, before the ceremony."

Now what was I going to do? And what about Samuel and Little Rabbit? How were we going to please this uncle, a man called, of all things, The Beaver.

"How many horses do you think she is worth, Round-Ball?"

"She is worth as many as he wants, father. This woman has taken it upon herself to take care of Buffalo Boy for the two years, while I was on the warpath."

"Now, my son, I know that is not the only reason you want to marry her, is it?" he asked.

"No, father, I truly love her. She has made me smile again, when I thought I never would. And I think she is happy as well. You know I would never take a woman unless she was willing to go with me. I respect the laws of the Ute, and do my best to uphold them, even at the cost to my own feelings."

"Good," he stated. "Then you will have as many horses as you need. I will pay The Beaver from my own horses. "But," he added, "you will consider them a loan? And when you return successfully from the Arapaho, you will repay me?"

"Of course, father, you know I will," I said, pretending my feelings were hurt. I was actually relieved that I was going to be able to afford Autumn Sky. One way or another, I was determined to have her for my wife. Now we just had to come up with a bride price that Samuel could afford.

Just before dawn the next morning, I heard several horses walking outside my lodge. Throwing the sleeping robes off, I struggled into my hunting shirt and moccasins, wondering who could be out so early. As I pushed the lodge flap open, I saw a boy of about twelve or so. He was trotting off into the early morning mist, and I couldn't tell who he was.

Going around the back of the lodge, I saw the cause of the noise. There, staked out, were ten ponies! Walking over to them, I could see that they had all been freshly brushed, their winter coats smooth and sleek. These had to be the best horses that The Wolf owned. And he was giving them to me so I could meet any price The Beaver asked.

Shaking my head in disbelief and amazement, I went back into my lodge. Samuel was starting to stir around some, so I built the fire up and started some coffee.

"Do you have to start so early?" he asked yawning.

"We got a lot to do today. But I been thinkin.'"

"Oh no, here we go," he remarked.

"What do you mean, 'here we go'?"

"Every time you start thinkin,' we end up fightin' with 'Rapaho, movin' camp, or just plain workin.' I thought today we was gonna trade for our wives."

"We are. Or at least I am. I don't think you're ready for marriage yet."

Throwing his sleeping robes off, Samuel sprang to his feet. He was fuming at me, a shocked, hurt look on his face. Kicking the robes out of his way, he stormed over to me.

"What do you mean, I ain't ready yet? Has Little Rabbit changed her mind 'bout me? What are you grinnin' at me like that for?"

"Boy, you're just full of questions this fine mornin,' ain't you?" I said. I was trying real hard not to smile, but it wasn't working. As the grin spread to the rest of my face, I told Samuel to shut-up and sit down, before he fell in the fire.

"What I mean, is, *I'm* gonna trade for a wife today. You can't marry Little Rabbit yet, leastwise till you have your namin' ceremony.

"Way I figure it, I'll do my trade today, we have your namin' ceremony tonight an' tomorrow, you can trade with The Beaver for Little Rabbit."

"But why? Why do we have to do it that way? I was sure set on doin' it today."

"That way, we can have more than one celebration, see? One thing you gotta learn, Samuel, is that winter is a time for restin' an' playin.' Social interaction goes a long way with the Ute. So we drag it out an extra day or two, that's all."

"Now it's a day or two! Are you ever gonna let me marry that gal?"

"Calm down, Samuel. Here, have some coffee an' sit. I'll tell you how it works.

"First, I gotta make the trade with The Beaver. That could take most of the day. Him an' me, we'll argue back an' forth for a while, come to an agreement, then he's gonna want more. Then we have to start all over again. It's just the way it works. Not that I wouldn't give everythin' I own for Autumn Sky, I just don't wanna have to.

"Then, we'll set up to have the weddin' tomorrow. In the mean time, while I'm arguin' with The Beaver, you're gonna be havin' a sweat in the sweat lodge to purify yourself. Wing of the Hawk is gonna make an announcement that he's adoptin' you into the tribe an' havin' a namin' ceremony for you tonight. Then, we'll have 'nother big feast, celebrate, an' have fun."

"I gotta go through all that, just to marry Little Rabbit?" he asked.

"No, you don't gotta go through all that, if you don't want to. But you'll find out that a little courtesy in followin' the ways of the Ute will make you a bigger man to 'em.

"See, to them, you're an outsider right now, even though you're my white brother. I'm one of the tribe already, an' that makes a difference. When you become a member of the tribe, though, you won't be considered an outsider. You'll be part of a family, an' families take care of each other.

"You're gonna be expected to feed an' provide for your new family. Not just Little Rabbit and the children you two are gonna have, but you will also be expected to provide for Wing of the Hawk's family if anythin' happens to him.

"You're bein' given a great gift, here, Samuel. To be adopted into the tribe is big, but to be adopted by a man of standin,' like Wing of the Hawk is, why that's even bigger. He's showin' the rest of the tribe what he thinks of you, an' how he feels 'bout you. This is a big honor to him, an' you, too. So the least you can do is do it right, by their customs."

"But all I did was kill a few 'Rapaho. They was tryin' to kill me too, ya know."

"That's not how he sees it, Samuel. To him, it was the most honorable act of bravery that could be done. You not only saved his life that day, you also saved the life of them three children. Those children are the future of this band. Wing of the Hawk knows that, an' he also knows that you would do it again if you had to.

"He got to be the leader of this band by knowin' how to find the game in the bad times, pickin' good campin' spots, an' leadin' successful raids against the enemies of the Ute. And he can read people as well. I think he read you right, Samuel. You'll make a powerful addition to this band. So don't take this ceremony stuff lightly. In time, you'll come to understand just what I been babblin' 'bout."

Samuel and I sat by the fire, drinking coffee, and talking about things we both remembered from our childhood, waiting for The Beaver to arrive. It was a short wait.

Chapter 21

Seven horses was just too many, along with the rest of the things I had offered The Beaver. My father was right. He was a power-hungry man. I wanted Autumn Sky for my wife, and he knew it, using my love for her against me. Exasperated, I threw my hands into the air and walked from the lodge.

Let him think on it awhile, I thought. Going over to the horses The Wolf had sent to me earlier that morning, I heard the flap of the lodge open and close. As The Beaver approached, I kept my back to him.

"You have ten fine horses, Round-Ball. I do not see why you argue over giving me seven of them. Did you not tell me you were going on a raid against the Arapaho soon? You will have many more horses to replace these when you return. If you are successful," he said, plainly doubting my ability.

"Then you must wait until I return from this raid," I told him flatly. "I do not want to wait and neither does Autumn Sky. But if you want the seven horses, along with the other things we have agreed to, then it must be that way."

"I must think on this more, then," he said. "I was not planning on staying with this band for that long of a time. I will give you an answer by the end of the day."

As The Beaver walked away, I had to smile. It was going the way I wanted, not his way. I would gladly give him the seven horses he wanted, but then there would only be three for Samuel to trade with. I didn't want to ruin his chances, so I did what I had to do.

Samuel noticed that the talks were over, and he came over with Wing of the Hawk. They both knew that things weren't finished, from the look on my face.

"Long face, Razor," Samuel said. "Things didn't go your way? Are you gonna get to marry Autumn Sky?"

"Just a little disagreement, that's all," I told them. "He wants what he wants, and it's more than he needs. He's just greedy, that's all."

"Great," Samuel said. "That's just what I wanted to hear. Means I probably won't be able to marry Little Rabbit." As he said it, Samuel turned and walked away, head hanging in dejection.

"What is wrong with my son?" asked Wing of the Hawk.

"The Beaver," I told him, "wants more and more. My white brother does not think he can afford Little Rabbit for his wife. I will go and try to talk to him while I am waiting for The Beaver to give me his answer about Autumn Sky," I told Wing of the Hawk.

"No, I will go and talk to him. If he is to be my son, then it is my place to be the one to talk to him. Besides," Wing of the Hawk laughed, "he needs to practice talking more."

"Yes," I agreed. "But you must admit, he is doing well for only talking in Ute for such a short time."

Waving his hand to tell me he heard me, Wing of the Hawk walked away, following Samuel. There was a true bond developing between those two, and it made my heart glad to see it. I wouldn't always be around for Samuel, and he needed to have others to count on when that time came.

Wandering around the camp, I soon found myself down

by the stream. With nothing better to do at the moment, I sat down with my back against a tree and watched the water. Soon, my eyes grew heavy, and I dozed. The sound of running footsteps woke me up, and I turned to see Buffalo Boy coming.

"Father," he panted. "What are you doing just sitting here? I thought you would be getting ready for your wedding to Autumn Sky."

"I would be, son, if only The Beaver would give me an answer. He wants a lot for her. And it burns me, because he has done nothing for her since her last husband died. He is using her as a way to become rich, and I, for one, do not like it."

"What does he want?"

As I told Buffalo Boy all that The Beaver wanted and what I had offered, he nodded his head. When I had finished, he scrunched his eyes, deep in thought. Suddenly, they flew open, and he nodded to himself, as if he had just had the most wonderful idea.

"Father," he said quietly. "I have decided to give you my horse to trade for her. I know it is not the best horse, but it is a good one."

Pulling him onto my lap, I hugged him.

"You don't need to do that, Rowdy," I said to him. "If you give me your horse, then what are you gonna ride? I thank you, though. It means a lot to me that you would offer your only horse to me. But it's far beyond that with The Beaver and me. Now, it's a matter of power. He wants it, but doesn't deserve it, an' he thinks I'm just gonna give it to him. But he'll see that I ain't gonna give in to him."

"Does this mean that you are not going to marry Autumn Sky?"

"No, I *will* marry her. It's just a matter of when."

Standing up, we both started back to the camp. The Beaver

should have made his decision by now, and we still had the adoption and naming ceremony for Samuel to prepare for. I hoped that Wing of the Hawk had been able to calm Samuel down as far as his own marriage was concerned.

Chapter 22

The camp was a hive of activity when Buffalo Boy and I returned, people scurrying around everywhere. Wing of the Hawk had made the announcement about the double ceremony that was going to take place that night, and all were making preparations for it. I found Samuel just emerging from the sweat lodge with three of the elders from both bands.

Having gone through this before myself, I knew that they had been instructing Samuel on the ways of the Ute, telling him everything that was required of him as a tribal member. There were other things, specific to the band he chose to live with, but Wing of the Hawk would tell him about those things.

Arriving back at my own lodge, I was not surprised to see The Beaver waiting for me. I did not like the man, but I was forced to deal with him, for the sake of Autumn Sky and our future together.

Nodding to him, I held the flap of the lodge open for him, indicating that I wished him to enter. After we were both seated, I waited patiently for him to begin.

"May I have a cup of the brown water?" he asked.

"Yes," I replied, adding "but it might be strong."

Reaching under a pile of buffalo robes, my hand found a

jar of sugar. As I brought it out, I saw his eyes widen, and a smile formed on his lips. So, I thought, The Beaver has a taste for sugar. Passing him the jar, I knew what I was going to do.

After dumping more sugar than coffee into the tin cup I provided, The Beaver settled back and sipped at it, smacking his lips in satisfaction.

Setting my own cup down beside me, I waited.

"Do you have any more of this?" he asked, pointing to the jar of sugar.

"I have that jar and one more," I said.

"If you give me four horses and the two jars of this, then I will allow you to marry Autumn Sky. Along with the other things we agreed on this morning," he added.

Shaking my head, I told him that this was all I had of the sweet sand.

"Let me think a minute," I told him. I had already decided that this was a small price to pay, but I wanted him to sweat a little before I gave him my answer. It would do him good to think he was getting the best of what I had.

Finally, as he finished the sugar-laden coffee, I agreed.

As The Beaver was gathering up the things I had given him for Autumn Sky, I had a sudden thought. Perhaps I might be able to convince him to take less of a bride price for Little Rabbit, if I was to tell him of my brother's wish.

"Wait," I said as he was leaving. "There is another matter I would discuss with you."

When he was seated once again and had another cup of sugared-down coffee, I asked him about Little Rabbit.

"She is my niece, yes. Do you wish to have her for a wife too? I do not think that is such a good idea, Round-Ball."

"No, I was not thinking of her as a wife for me but for my brother, Arrow Catcher."

"I do not think I know this brother you speak of. Is he in this band?" he asked.

"Yes, he is here. The reason you have not heard of him before is, he has never been here before."

"You are not making sense to me, Round-Ball," he said.

"My brother is the one who is being adopted by Wing of the Hawk tonight. And since I will have Autumn Sky in my lodge, I do not feel it is right to have him here as well."

Smiling and nodding his head, The Beaver had to agree to my reasoning.

"A woman has been the cause of many bloody battles, my friend. You do well in thinking of this before you bring one into your lodge with your brother here. But what exactly is it you want?"

"What would you say to three horses and another jar of the sweet sand, as a bride price for Little Rabbit?" I asked.

"But you told me you do not have anymore of the sweet sand. How are you going to give me what you do not have?"

"I said that *I* did not have anymore. But my brother has one jar. That is all the sweet sand we brought with us this winter. And you would be getting it all, my friend. No one else in this camp has had any," I lied.

"And you would give it to me now?" he asked licking his lips.

"No," I said, slapping my legs and getting to my feet. "My brother must ask you for Little Rabbit's hand in marriage. It is his place, as you know. But he is new in the ways of the Ute. I only ask that you simply tell him what it is that you want for Little Rabbit, three horses and a jar of the sweet sand. Nothing more and nothing less. Either way you get what you want and so do we."

"I am beginning to see that you are a wise man, Round-Ball. So when your brother, Arrow Catcher, comes to see me tomorrow, I will tell him that is what I want. It is agreed," he said.

"It is agreed," I responded back. "And I thank you, Beaver. You have made my family whole again."

The Beaver made the wedding announcement after the ceremony for Samuel, stating that it would take place tomorrow. I pulled Samuel to one side and told him what I had done for him and Little Rabbit.

"I thought you said I would have to be the one to make the deal with him."

"And you do. I just helped him to come up with the bride price, that's all. The way I did it, he thinks it was all his idea. All you have to do tomorrow, before Autumn Sky and I are married, is tell him you want to marry Little Rabbit. We have agreed on the price already. And that reminds me; I need to go hide all the rest of the sugar. That was the trick, lettin' him think he was the only one in both bands that got any. Then, after he's gone, we can bring it back out. I'll leave one jar out for you, though," I said as I headed for the lodge. I wanted to do it right now, before I forgot and it came back to haunt me.

Feeling like a first-time groom again the next day, Autumn Sky and I were married. I had made arrangements for Buffalo Boy to stay with his grandfather, The Wolf, for the next few days. I didn't want any intrusions into our privacy.

Samuel made the deal for Little Rabbit, just as we planned, and they decided to get married at the same time as Autumn Sky and I did. We made arrangements for them to borrow a lodge from one of the warriors who had no wife. Even though it cost me some trinkets I had planned on giving out after Bad Leg and his band left, it was needed.

As the day came to an end, I only had one thing on my mind, and it wasn't the pony raid we were leaving for in three days time. Leading my new wife to my lodge, amid the catcalls and whistles from the two bands, I knew I had once again found true happiness. This time I hoped it would last.

Chapter 23

We found the Arapaho village right about where I figured it would be. Sending a scout ahead to check the layout of the village and locate the pony herd, the rest of us made camp in a small stand of trees just off the trail.

When we left the camp of Wing of the Hawk eight days ago, I promised Autumn Sky that I would return as fast as I could. There was still a lot of trapping Samuel and I needed to do before summer arrived, and I was wishful of getting on with it. But we needed these horses.

The scout returned, telling the four of us in camp that the village was unguarded, but the pony herd was heavily guarded. They must have suspected we were going to raid them back and were prepared for it. Either that or one of their hunters had spotted us and alerted the camp. Smelled like a trap to me, and I usually went with my gut feelings.

Besides Samuel and myself, I had managed to convince Wing of the Hawk to let me take three of the warriors left in our band. We needed more, but Bad Leg and his band had left the day after the marriage ceremonies, and I couldn't leave the band totally defenseless. So it was just the five of us against the whole Arapaho village, if they found us.

Not liking the news the scout brought in, I asked the others what they thought. Two of the warriors from our band were for going ahead with the raid, but the rest of us, myself included, thought it was a trap.

"Here is what we are going to do," I told them.

"We are going to make like we accidentally stumbled into this village, just out hunting. We will turn around and head back to our band, but we will only go a day or so. If the Arapaho dogs follow us, they will think we are returning to our homes.

"Then, we will strike out across the mountain, coming at the village from the other direction. If they are looking for and expecting us from the south, we will hit them from the north. We can then drive their pony herd right through the village, destroying what we can on the way."

We needed those ponies, and we needed them bad. Without them, we didn't have enough to move the village come spring, even if we used all my pack animals. This raid must happen, and we must be successful if we were going to survive.

Breaking camp the next morning before dawn, we made tracks out of there, turning and running away. It galled me to run from a fight, but there was just too many of them, and they were expecting us. It would be different in a few days.

Winding our way south, we made good time for most of the day, putting about twenty-five miles or so between us and the village. I was looking for just the right place where we could take off from this trail without it being too obvious but wasn't having much luck. I finally decided that since we couldn't find a good enough place, we would just have to make one.

When I saw the snow covered rocky outcropping right above the trail, I knew this was the place. Riding past it a short distance, we hung a hard right, going up the hillside. Once on top of the small hill, I had Samuel and one of the warriors go back down to the outcropping I had seen.

What I wanted to do was to have them make a landslide of the snow, blocking the trail, in case the Arapaho were following along behind us as I suspected they were. Not only would it block them from following us any further, it would hide the new trail we were taking. Right back to their village and the horses we so desperately needed.

With only five of us, we couldn't afford a fight, at least not for very long. Samuel and I had our rifles and pistols, but the other three only had bows and arrows. I knew some of the Arapaho had guns, and the odds were just not in our favor of winning a fight. So we had to be sneaky about it.

Having made the small landslide, Samuel had just caught up with us when we spotted the Arapaho. They were following our trail, just like I figured they were. They were still two miles from the slide area, and I knew they would probably stop for the night and camp when they came to it. Then they would probably turn back in the morning. I was counting on that, and that's why I had waited until just before dark to leave the trail.

"We will travel all night," I told the small group. "Our horses will be tired when we get there, but we can use the ponies from the Arapaho to leave."

"What about the raiding party that is following us?" asked one of the younger warriors.

"They will turn back in the morning, I think. And they will go slower, thinking they ran us off. They will take the time to hunt on the way back to the village, giving us more time to make our escape."

"Once we get the horses, which way do we go?" Samuel wanted to know.

"Well, we cannot head directly south, or we will run into the returning braves. I think that once we are away from the village, we will turn east. From there, we can make it into the Middle Park, and then turn south again, heading for home."

"That will take longer than we thought, Round-Ball," said one of the Ute.

"Yes, it will take longer," I told him. "But I would rather be a few days late with many horses and all of you, than try to fight that many Arapaho. I do not think my new wife would be too happy if I did not return," I added.

"You seem to have it all figured out," Samuel said. "But what if them 'Rapaho make it back to the village afore we do? What then?"

"If it comes down to it," I told them all, "and things go wrong, I will give the call of the wolf. If any of you hear that, it is every man for himself. Make it back to our camp as best as you can."

The pony herd was unguarded when we arrived, about an hour before first light. The herd was on the north side of the village and directly above it. The Arapaho had put up a brush fence around the horses, but it didn't amount to much. Still, I wanted to get away with as many horses as we could.

Telling the others I wanted to find the entrance and open it for the horses, I started to creep around the perimeter. Suddenly, there was a hiss behind me. Freezing in place, I waited for Samuel to come up behind me.

"How are we gonna know when you have the gate open?" he whispered.

"Tell the others that I'm gonna open the gate an' catch me a pony. When I do, you should be able to see me. When you see me, the rest of you catch a pony yourselves, an' start runnin' 'em. The horses know where the gate is, so just follow 'em on out," I whispered back.

Finding the gate, I slipped inside, but didn't open it all the way yet. I wanted to be on a horse when I did that. Pulling a hackamore made from horsehair out of my possibles bag, I slowly worked my way over to the closest pony and slipped it on, rubbing his neck to show I was friendly. Then I led my new pony to the gate, and swung it open as I leapt onto his back.

Letting loose a wild Ute war cry, I started the horse herd out of the enclosure. Racing my way to the front of them, I guided them straight towards the sleeping village. I could hear the others behind me, yelling their own cries as we sped through the village, the excited horses knocking down lodges and churning up everything as we went.

About a half a mile south of the village, I turned the herd east, heading for the Middle Park, just as planned. After another two miles, I slowed the pony herd to a walk. I hadn't seen any of the others in my raiding party since leaving the village, but we were still too close to stop.

By the time dawn arrived, cold and feeling like snow was on its way, I found a meadow, and stopped the herd. Circling them, I started back towards the rear. The horses started pawing at the snow to get to the grass underneath, and I wasn't worried about them going too far.

Amazingly, no one was injured, though we lost a few horses in the run through the Arapaho village. I was happy to see everyone was well and decided we could use a rest and let the horses eat before moving on. I was desperate for a cup of coffee but knew we couldn't risk a fire, so I just leaned against a tree and dozed off and on for the next three hours.

The snow was falling heavily when we reached the camp of the Ute ten days later.

Chapter 24

My feet were frozen, the beaver hide outer pair of moccasins I had on over my leggins a solid mass of ice. Samuel and I were back in the South Park, trapping again. It had been three weeks or so since we had returned from the raid on the Arapaho, leading close to two hundred horses into the Ute camp.

Wing of the Hawk held a big feast the night we returned, and all of us on the pony raid took our turn telling of the things we had done. No one had done anything heroic or too dangerous, but we had all managed to survive.

Shortly after that, Samuel and I decided we needed to get back to trapping. We needed to get a lot more beaver before rendezvous in the summer if we were going to have enough to trade for another year in the mountains. I wasn't too worried about it, though. Back when 'Ol Pepper was alive and we were trapping together, we had lost all our furs more than once. But we managed, mostly thanks to our families among the Ute.

"I'm c-c-cold," stammered Samuel as I reached the place where we were to meet.

"Know what you mean," I said back, shivering slightly.

"Let's head back to camp, an' warm up. We both could use some coffee," I added.

Snorting and shaking his head, he agreed.

As we neared our small camp, I slowed down. Out of habit more than anything, I always did this, taking a quick survey of everything. I didn't want any surprises when we returned from setting our traps.

"Sure wish you would've let the women come along on this trip," commented Samuel. "I could sure use some warmth from Little Rabbit 'bout now."

"Yea, I know what kind of warmth you're talkin' about. But there weren't any real need of havin' 'em here. 'Sides, I'm sure you'll make up for it when we get back," I said snickering. "I know I will."

Buffalo Boy had wanted to come along too. I felt bad about telling him 'no,' but I didn't want anything to happen to him, like the last time. I took some of the disappointment away by asking him to stay and watch over his new mother, telling him he was the man of the lodge while I was away. Autumn Sky didn't take too kindly to it though.

Beating the ice from my moccasins, I looked around at the camp. We had taken a lot of beaver in the short time we had been here, but I knew we still needed many more. It wasn't just me anymore. There were five of us in our little family group, at least for now, and that meant Samuel and I had to trap more beaver to trade for the things a group that size needed.

After I had warmed myself by the fire, I moved over to the pile of beaver we had taken from our traps that morning. Lashing them into willow hoop frames, I set them off to the side to be fleshed later in the day. Something was nagging at the back of my mind, and I couldn't place what it was.

Then it hit me. That smell. Pointing my nose in the air, I began to sniff, trying to remember just what it was I had been smelling. As I was reaching for my rifle, Samuel turned to me.

"We got company," he whispered.

Nodding my head to him, I eared back the hammer of my rifle to full cock. Glancing down at the lock, I flipped open the pan, checking the powder. I sure didn't need a misfire.

One of the horses screamed in terror, and my mule started braying out of control. We could hear the sounds of a fight coming from where we had staked our small herd of ponies, branches breaking, and lots of noise. Too much noise to be a pony raid.

"The horses! They're stealin' the horses," yelled Samuel.

"More like tryin' to eat the horses," I said as I got to my feet.

"What? Somethin's tryin' to eat the horses?"

"Bear," I answered.

"We gotta bear in with the horses? What're we gonna do?"

"Kill him, that's what we're gonna do. Grab that extra rifle there. We might have need of it."

As I sprinted towards the animals, I remembered the absolute destruction a bear had caused me in the past, killing all but one of my horses. I didn't like these huge monsters that were so common to these mountains. Grizzly bears, Lewis and Clark had called them. Killing machines is what they were.

Skidding to a stop, I saw one horse was already down, Samuel's riding animal. As the horse kicked and screamed in pain, trying to get back on its feet, the huge bear started towards my mule. Now he went and done it. He was just trying to kill everything he could, not really wanting the meat.

"Wagh, wagh," I roared at the big bruin, trying to get him to stand so I could take my shot. He just looked at me, swinging his front leg, throwing snow and dirt all over the place, growling and carrying on.

"Stay back there Samuel," I yelled. "If he don't drop at the first shot, you're the one that's gotta kill 'em."

As the bear advanced, so did I. At least I had taken his attention away from my mule. Kicking my feet and scattering snow and dirt back towards him, I knew I had to shoot fast, or he would be on top of me before I could.

Throwing my rifle to my shoulder, I put the blade of the front sight right beside his front shoulder. Gently, I squeezed the trigger.

When the ball hit him, he let out a roar of rage and stood on his hind legs, pawing the air around him.

"Shoot him, shoot him," I screamed at Samuel. I dodged to the right to get out of his way, but he had moved to the right as well, and I was in his way, blocking his shot.

"Drop!" he commanded.

Dropping to the ground, I instantly rolled backwards, trying to put as much distance between me and that angry bear as I could. I heard the first shot from Samuel's rifle go off, followed by another enraged roar from the bear. Scrambling to my feet, I started to run for the camp, reloading as I went.

Samuel dropped the empty rifle and was swinging the second one to his shoulder, when suddenly, the bear dropped to all fours, and ran off into the brush. Knowing better than to follow him right away, Samuel picked up the empty rifle and strolled back to camp.

"Looks like we got him. I don't think he'll be back," he said.

"Yea, he'll be back. Reload an' we'll go after 'em."

"Why? He's as good as dead."

"Why? Well for starters, them big 'ol bears is hard to kill. Don't think for one instant that he's dead, leastwise till we see him dead. An' if he ain't dead, he'll be back, even madder than he was. Last, we need the meat an' hide. I'm gettin' tired of eatin' dried meat. I need me some fresh meat."

"Well, since you put it that way, I guess—"

"Here he comes again!" I yelled, cutting him off.

The bear had made a small circle around our camp and

was coming right back at us, only from a different direction this time. Scooping up my extra rifle, I turned to face him.

He was charging right at me. Dropping to one knee, I knew this was it. Him or me.

My first shot hit him in the shoulder, a little too high to do much good. Tossing the empty rifle to one side, I picked up my second one, just as Samuel shot. If he hit it, I couldn't tell. That 'ol bear never slowed as he continued to rush us.

Without time to aim properly, I jerked back on the hammer, pointed the rifle and pulled the trigger, all in one motion. I saw the ball strike him in the side of the neck just as Samuel fired his second shot.

Tumbling sideways, the bear rolled over, and got back on his feet, lowering his head for another charge. Dumbstruck, Samuel could only stare as the bear headed for him.

Dropping my second rifle, I reached for the knife at the back of my belt, but it wasn't there. Must've fallen out somewhere, I thought, as I pulled the tomahawk free instead.

With the tomahawk in one hand and my pistol in the other, I ran at the grizzly, trying to cut him off before he reached Samuel.

We came together in a great crash, the force of my momentum knocking him off his feet. Stuffing the pistol barrel into one ear, I pulled the trigger. Nothing happened, and I realized I had forgot to pull the hammer back.

Raking the back of the pistol across the bears' head, I managed to get it cocked. I was now astride of him, and putting the pistol back into his ear, I shot him. At the same time, I brought the tomahawk down as hard as I could, into the back of his mighty head.

Letting go with both hands, I managed to spring free, just as he fell.

Samuel had come to his senses and was reloading a rifle,

but this 'ol boy was dead. The tomahawk had severed his spinal cord right at the base of his neck, killing him almost at the same time as the ball I had sent to his brain.

Feeling wetness on my right leg, I looked down to see my leggin was in tatters. Somehow, and I never figured out when it had happened, that bear had managed to take a swipe at me with his huge paw, shredding my leggin and opening up three long lines of flesh down my leg.

Limping off to the side, I saw the bear twitch a little. Samuel jumped at the movement, and I started to laugh. It was plain to see that Samuel was scared out of his mind. Trying to take his mind from the close call with the bear, I hobbled over to him.

"Now," I panted, "see what I mean 'bout these here grizzly bears bein' hard to kill?"

Samuel nodded his head, still watching the bear.

My head was starting to spin as the pain hit me, and I needed to sit down and look at my leg.

"Samuel," I said.

When he didn't answer, I said it louder, and a little more urgent.

"Samuel. I need a little help here."

Finally tearing his eyes away from the bear, he gave me a dazed look. Turning sideways, I showed him my torn up leg, the pain now spreading upwards.

"Get me over to the fire so I can sit," I pleaded.

Suddenly snapping out of it, he rushed to my side. Slipping his shoulder under one of my arms, he half carried me to the fire.

Using my rifle as a crutch, I lowered myself to the ground, leaning back in agony as the fire of pain shot through my whole right side. Starting to see stars, I bit down on my lower lip to bring myself out of the blackness that was trying to overcome me.

"Heat some water," I managed through clenched teeth. "You gotta clean it an' sew me back up."

"But I don't know nothin' 'bout sewin,'" he complained.

"Then just wash it an' wrap it tight. I'll sew it up myself, when this pain ain't so bad," I said.

By the time Samuel had heated the water and started to wash my wounded leg, I passed out.

Chapter 25

"This 'ol bear sure tastes nasty," Samuel commented.

"Yea, it do at that," I said. "But it sure is better than goin' hungry."

After Samuel had washed my wounded leg and wrapped it up, he decided to go skin the big grizzly. I was still passed out but had awakened when I smelled the meat cooking.

Looking down at my leg, I saw where he had taken some strips of the bear hide and tied them around not only the wound, but my whole leg. From my crotch to my ankle, it looked out of place, one leg much larger than the other.

"How bad was it?" I asked him.

"The one in the middle was pretty deep, but the other two were no more than scratches. I don't even think you'll have to sew 'em up any."

"I'll take a closer look at it later."

"How much longer you think we need to stay here?" Samuel asked later that afternoon.

"You'll have to check all the traps this evenin,' 'an you might as well go ahead an' bring 'em on in. Since I won't be able to help much for the next few days, I figure we can finish stretchin' an' dryin' the ones we got from this stream. In a few days I should be back on my feet, then we'll pack up an' go find us 'nother stream. What do you think?" I asked.

"Sounds good to me. Give me some time to warm up. I been cold forever seems like."

"Better get used to it, Samuel," I said. "We got 'nother three months or so of good trappin.' After that, we need to start thinkin' 'bout headin' to rendezvous."

"We ain't gonna stay up here for them three months, are we?" he asked.

"Naw, we'll head on back to our wives in 'nother week or so, after we trap the next stream. Stay in camp with the women 'bout three, four days, then head back up here, an' do it some more."

"You gonna let me bring my wife this time?"

"After that run-in we just had with that grizzly, you sure you wanna bring her? I think I would rather have my wife down in the camp, where it's at least a little safer. What do you think would have happened to them women had they been in camp this morning, an' we wasn't here? That bear would have had 'em for a snack, that's what.

"So no, I don't think we should chance it. 'Sides, if you had your wife 'long, I wouldn't get no work outta you! All you'd be wantin' to do is lay in them robes all day, pretendin' you was cold so you could snuggle up to her!"

"Suppose you're right. An' with you nursin' that hurt leg, I'm the one what's gotta do all the work."

"Now, Samuel," I admonished. "You went an' hurt my feelin's. It was your bacon I was savin' when I jumped that bear. You think I did it for fun?"

"No, it ain't like that at all, Razor, an' you well know it. I just miss her, that's all."

"Yea, I know. I miss Autumn Sky too. But you gotta think 'bout it. If we're gonna be able to buy them women all the things they're gonna be wantin' come rendezvous, then you an' me gotta trap. Ain't no other way we can make the money for them things way out here."

"You're right. I just miss her, that's all," he said.

"Well, while you're missin' her, why don't you go check the traps. An' don't forget to keep your eyes peeled. There might be a few 'Rapaho out huntin' here 'bouts. I ain't in good enough shape today to come runnin' after you," I added, trying to snap him out of his homesickness.

After Samuel went to check the traps, I was left by the fire with nothing but my thoughts. And as usual, in times like this, my thoughts always returned to Autumn Sky. That woman was something else! Smiling to myself, I let my thoughts drift back to our wedding night.

It was near dark now, and Samuel should have been back already. I was just rising to my feet, with the aid of my rifle, when I saw him coming through the trees. He was hunched under the weight of what I thought was our traps, but I didn't hear the chains jangling. Thinking he was wounded, I started towards him in a shuffling trot.

"What's the hurry?" he asked when I was close enough.

"You look like you had some trouble," I said.

"Only trouble I had was skinnin' all these beaver. I swear, Razor, every one of your traps was full. I just don't know how you do it," he said as he threw the beaver pelts on the ground at my feet.

"Where's all the traps?" I asked.

"They're still back at the stream. I couldn't very well carry all these beaver, an' the traps too. I'm on my way to get 'em right now," he said, turning around and heading back towards the stream.

"I'll have supper started by the time you get back," I told him.

Picking up the beaver pelts he had thrown at my feet, I ran my fingers through them. They sure were sleek and prime furs! And if all my traps were full, as they had been for the last three sets, then I was doing some thinking.

Maybe, instead of moving on to another stream, why didn't we just move a little further up this one? The beaver were there, that was plain to see from the pile of skins I was now carrying back to camp. It sure would save some time trying to find another stream to trap.

When Samuel trudged into camp under the weight of the fourteen traps we had been using, I told him of my thoughts.

"Now, that's some right smart thinkin,'" he said. "I was gonna ask you if you were sure you wanted to move on."

"Why didn't you say somethin'? Just 'cause I'm the one who's been trappin' all these years, don't mean I make all the right moves. You're startin' to become a real good trapper, an' we're in this together. So if you think there's a better way, or a different place you wanna try, let me know."

"In that case, then I wanna move further up this stream," he said with a smile. "I seen lots more beaver dams on up past your last set tonight, an' I want to try 'em. Just one thing I wanna know, though," he said.

"What's that?"

"How in the world do you do it? You seem to have the best trappin' luck I ever seen. You always catch more than me, an' I feel sort of like I ain't doin' my share."

"You're doin' your share, Samuel, don't you fret none 'bout that. But as far as to how I catch so many beaver, did you look at my sets when you pulled my traps?"

"Yea, I looked at 'em. They look just like mine do. You're the one who taught me how to set 'em, remember?"

"I remember. But luck has nothin' to do with it. I been

doin' this for a long time. An' when I come out here, there weren't nobody to teach me how to trap these beaver. Over the years, I learned by watchin' 'em, an' practicin' different ways to set my traps, till I come up with a system that works."

"I guess I'm gonna have to watch you and learn all over again," he said, acting like a scolded child.

"Don't go gettin' upset over it, Samuel. You only been trappin' less than one season. It took me a lot longer than that to get where I'm at today. You'll be good as me in no time. Trust me," I said with a smile.

Samuel and I had started in on fleshing and graining the beaver that night, but there was so many fresh caught ones, we had to finish the next morning. When we were done, we decided not to wait to move camp, but did it that day.

Moving upstream two miles or so, we found a nice little place. Back from the stream far enough so that we didn't disturb the beaver ponds that seemed to be everywhere, we made camp.

Chapter 26

Samuel and I continued to trap the same stream for the next two weeks, moving further up every two or three days. The beaver were plentiful along this stretch, and we caught an average of fifteen a day. It was a lot of work skinning and graining them, but all the hard work would pay off when we took them down to rendezvous.

We had been gone from the camp of the Ute for close to a month, longer than I had wanted, but when the beaver were taking the bait, we just had to continue trapping. But now, we were gonna have to return.

With the loss of Samuel's riding horse to that bear, we were one packhorse shy. He was going to have to ride a packhorse, and that meant we had to stop trapping and take this set of furs back to the camp. As much as I hated to stop, especially when the beaver were so many, we didn't have a choice.

"We'll finish grainin' these here pelts today, an' tomorrow I think we best head on back," I told Samuel.

"But the beaver are everywhere," he said. "Why do we have to go back now?"

"An' you were the one complainin' 'bout wantin' to see

your wife an' warm up," I said laughin.' "Now all you want to do is stay here an' trap.

"But we need to go back," I continued. "With the loss of your horse, we're one animal short for packin' these here furs. They're gonna be overloaded as it is, so we just gotta stop."

"Will we come back to this stream when we go out next time?"

"Depends on the weather, but yea, I'm thinkin' we'll probably head back here. There's a lot more beaver lodges on up this stream, an' we would be fools not to take what we can. It ain't that far to the camp, so we could be back in less than a week. That is," I said chuckling, "if I can get you back out of your lodge once we're there."

"That ain't fair, Razor," he said. "I can't help it if Little Rabbit won't keep her hands off me. I swear, every time that woman closes the lodge flap, all she wants to do is crawl into the sleepin' robes."

"Yea, an' she probably just wants to sleep," I said with a laugh.

"I don't recall seein' much of you after you an' Autumn Sky was married, little brother. An' don't try to tell me you was sleepin' all that time, neither. I ain't so old I can't read the signs."

"Yea, well, let's just finish grainin' these beaver, an' head back."

"Sounds like I ain't the only one who's been missin' my wife."

"Shut-up, Samuel, an' get to work," I told him.

Two long days later, we got back to our camp with the Ute. It had been an uneventful trip, except for the grizzly we had killed, and I noticed that the snow was melting the lower we went. Wouldn't be much longer, and the band would be leaving for the spring get together.

Every spring, all the bands of the Ute would gather in a pre-arranged place and camp together for the summer. Marriages were arranged, families got together, and the losses were mourned. This year though, Autumn Sky, Little Rabbit, and Buffalo Boy wouldn't be going with the band. They were going with Samuel and me to rendezvous.

While I was staking out the horses after unloading them, Wing of the Hawk noticed I was limping a little still. After telling him about the bear, he became spooked.

"How did you kill the bear?" he almost whispered.

"With a tomahawk in the back of his head, and a pistol in his ear," I told him.

Nodding his head, he told me he had seen a vision shortly after we left. It had left him unsettled for many days afterwards, but now, he thought he understood what it had meant.

"I would hear the whole story of the great bear," he said. "But we will talk after you spend some time with your new wife. She has been lost without you, Round-Ball," he added.

"What do you mean?" I asked.

Grinning, Wing of the Hawk continued.

"Your wife has not been the same since you went to trap the beaver, brother. She cannot keep her mind from wandering. Many times I have seen her looking off into the mountains. She stands there, just looking. I think you have made her a happy woman again."

"And she has made me a happy man again," I told him, slightly confused. What he was talking about, I had no idea, but he was a man who saw things others missed. Maybe he had seen something in Autumn Sky.

Suddenly, Buffalo Boy was at my side, panting from his run across the camp. He wore a huge smile, and I noticed something was different about him. I couldn't put my finger on it though, and together, we walked to my lodge.

Autumn Sky was sitting by the fire, humming a song as she sewed at something. When I threw the flap back, she didn't' look up.

"Buffalo Boy, I told you to go and play," she said.

"I am going to play alright," I answered.

Startled, she threw the sewing to the side and jumped to her feet. Rushing around the fire, she threw her arms around me, almost knocking both of us out of the lodge.

"Husband!" she exclaimed.

"Yes, I am your husband," I said laughing. "Who did you think it would be?"

"I am so happy to see you! You have been gone so long; I thought you were not coming back."

"We were gone longer than we planned, yes, but the beaver were calling to us. We had to stay and talk with them."

Stepping back, she grinned up at me.

"And what did these beaver say to you, husband of mine?"

"They said that they all wanted to come home with me. So I asked them why they wanted to come home with me. Do you know what they said?"

"No, what did they say?"

"They told me they had heard that I had the most beautiful wife in the whole mountains, and they wanted to see her for themselves," I told her, my eyes twinkling.

"Huh," she snorted turning away. "I did not know you had another wife, Round-Ball. You should have told me."

As she went back to her place by the fire, I reached outside the lodge, grabbing a bundle of the beaver we had caught. Holding it up, I caught Autumn Sky's eye.

"See," I said talking to the bundle. "Did I not tell you she was the most beautiful woman in the mountains? Look at the way she just sits there. Does it not make your trip here worth it?"

"You were talking of me?" she asked, shocked.

"Of course I was talking about you, woman. Who else could there be?"

"Oh, just go put your furs away," she stammered.

I could see the smile on her face, spreading to her eyes. It was when I looked into her eyes that I saw the tears, the big drops forming in the corners before starting to trickle down her face.

Throwing the bundle of beaver to one side, I pulled the flap closed and went to the fire. Squatting beside her, I cupped her face in one hand and turned it towards me.

"Why do you cry?" I asked her

"I did not know you thought of me in that way," she blubbered.

"I *do* think of you in that way, and many other ways as well, wife."

Pulling her closer, I hugged her tightly and then released her.

"Would you like to see some other ways in which I think of you?" I asked.

"After you have eaten," she said. "Then, I would like to hear of these other ways, husband. And maybe you can tell the beaver over there as well," she laughed.

"They already know. Who else was there to talk to? Arrow Catcher was having his own talks with the beaver, and my horses would not talk to me. They don't seem to understand the white-man words," I added as I stood up.

"If you would have taken us—"

"What happened to your leg?"

"A bear decided that he was hungry. But after he had one bite of me, he saw that I was just too tough for him. So he spit me out," I said.

"Let me see it. I know you do not know how to take care of yourself. That," she said, "is why you had to marry me. You need someone to take care of you. Now, take the leggin off so I can see it."

"If I take them off right now, will you be able to control yourself?" I asked.

As it dawned on her what I said, she threw her sewing at me, standing up.

"No," she answered, taking me by the hand.

Chapter 27

Wing of the Hawk told us that he was planning on leaving for the gathering of the tribe in another moon. Samuel and I had gone to see him that morning, making plans to leave the next day to go back up to trap some more, and we needed to know when the band was leaving.

We wanted to be back before they left so we didn't have to take all our plunder with us on this trip, and it looked like it was going to work out that way. My plan was to go trap for a moon, come back to see them off, and then pick up our wives. From there, we could trap our way to rendezvous.

"I think we should take five packhorses this time," Samuel suggested. "That way, we won't have to load 'em so heavy this trip."

"You're sure confident we're gonna trap lots of beaver," I commented. "Might just be, them beaver won't come to bait this time. But we'll take that chance," I said. I was hoping we would do as well as last time, or better, on this trip.

"Tell me somethin,' Razor," Samuel said as we were loading the horses. "What in the world am I gonna do with my share of all them horses we stole from them 'Rapaho? We sure don't need to be drawin' attention to ourselves with that many horses."

"You're right, Samuel. I been thinkin' the same thing. I

figure we'll need ten or twelve for packin' our plews, another five for ridin,' an' maybe 'nother four as extras. How many that make?"

"Twenty or twenty-one."

"Let's keep the best twenty of 'em, an' trade the rest off. I sent seven to The Wolf, so how many do we have left?"

"I don't know; I ain't counted 'em."

"We best go see what we got, afore we leave. If we do our tradin' now, less we have to do when we get back."

Dividing the horses after the raid on the Arapaho, each man that went along ended up with forty-three horses. Added to that, the seven I brought with me, plus my mule, and Samuel and me had a total of ninety-four horses. That was a lot of horses.

Picking out the best twenty, we separated them from the rest of our herd. That left seventy-four horses to trade off.

There wasn't much that Autumn Sky and I needed, but Samuel and Little Rabbit needed their own lodge. They had been borrowing the lodge they were in right now, but I was sure the owner would be willing to trade for it. He was one of the braves left in camp when we made the pony raid, so he got none of the horses, and he wasn't married.

"Samuel, let's see if we can trade some of these here ponies for that lodge you been livin' in," I said.

"That's a great idea, Razor. I been wonderin' what me an' Little Rabbit was gonna use for a shelter when we leave the band. I also want to see if I can trade for some more sleepin' robes. The ones we got ain't worth much."

"Yea, I need some new ones too. But let's take care of you first. I'll meet you over there. I gotta go find Rowdy. I want him there so he can learn how this tradin' business is done."

Buffalo Boy was upset at me again. He wanted to go with us on this trip, but I needed him here. He was going to be excited over what I was planning to ask him. At least I thought he would. I just had to find him first.

After finding Buffalo Boy, we met Samuel over by his lodge. Owl, the owner of the lodge was there as well. They were engaged in some serious discussion over the lodge, and I could see Samuel was getting frustrated.

"He wants fifty horses for this thing," he said, slapping the side of the lodge.

"An' what's wrong with that?" I asked him.

"Fifty? Ain't that too much?"

"Where did we get them horses, Samuel?"

"You know where we got 'em. We stole 'em off the—"

"Now you get it," I said. "You didn't have all them horses afore, did you? Yet Owl let you an' Little Rabbit stay here anyway, didn't he? I don't think he's askin' for too many. What are you gonna do with 'em if you don't trade 'em to him?"

"You got a point there, but I don't have fifty horses. They ain't all mine."

"Take 'em. I give 'em to you. You just get you an' Little Rabbit that lodge. But I got plans for the rest, so that's all you can have."

"What're you gonna do with the rest?"

"I'm not gonna do anything with 'em. Rowdy here, he's gonna trade 'em for us," I said.

Both Samuel and Buffalo Boy stared at me like I had lost my mind. I needed to make my son feel useful, and this was a sure-fire way to do it. There were some things we needed still, and with Samuel and me needing to get back up the mountain, I didn't want to take the time to trade right now. That left Buffalo Boy to do our trading for us.

"Here is what I want you to trade for, son," I told him. "We need at least five new sleeping robes, good ones, and a new set of poles for the lodge. If there are any horses left after you get those things, they're yours. You can do what you want with them, as long as you get rid of them."

"Can I not keep the ones I don't trade?" he asked.

"No, we don't need 'em, an' I don't wanna have to drag 'em along to rendezvous. 'Sides, when we need more, we'll just go see the 'Rapaho again.

"That's why I want you to stay here while your white uncle an' me go trap some more beaver. You understand what we need?"

"Yes, father. I understand."

"Good. Now, Samuel, let's go tell the women goodbye an' hit the trail. I wanna be a long way from here by the time the sun goes down."

As we were walking back to our lodges, Samuel was deep in thought.

"Spit it out, Samuel. Somethin' is botherin' you, an' I don't want you actin' like this for the next month. You got anythin' to say to me, best say it now."

"I'm just a little surprised that you're gonna let Rowdy do the tradin' for what we need, that's all. I mean, he is only a boy, yet at times, you treat him like a grown man."

"When you start havin' your own children, you'll understand, Samuel. Bein' the father of an Indian child is a lot different than bein' the father of a white child. Out here, every day is a test of survival. Indian children learn things at an earlier age than white children, mostly 'cause they have to. Their life could depend on it. I'm just tryin' to prepare my son for this kind of life."

"You make it sound like you might not make it back someday."

"I might not, an' you might not either. That's why I treat Rowdy the way I do. He may not act like a seven-year-old white boy, but he acts like a seven-year-old Ute. An' that, brother, is what he is."

Chapter 28

"Is it just me, or are these furs gettin' thicker an' heavier?" I asked Samuel.

We had gone back to the same stream we had worked earlier, going higher up this time. I couldn't believe the amount of beaver here, though. It was as good or better than the Three Forks country, way to the north of us. And it wasn't crawling with Blackfoot, neither.

"They do seem to be a little thicker up here. Maybe it's just 'cause we're higher up in the mountains, I don't know," he said. "You're the one who's been trappin' for so long, you tell me."

"That could be a part of it, but I don't think that's all it is. I think we're in for more snow, an' colder temperatures too."

"There don't seem to be anymore ice in the stream than there was when we was here last time."

"No, an' that's what has me puzzled. With fur this thick though, somethin' is gonna happen. Mark my words. We ain't seen the last of the snow."

"So, what do you want to do? Drop back down the mountain? I say we stay up here, while we can. If it gets too bad, we can always go lower. We know there's beaver lower, but they ain't near this good."

"Maybe I'm just gettin' spooked, I don't know," I replied.

We gathered the beaver we had caught and skinned that morning and headed back to our camp. Something just didn't feel right. It kept nagging at me, and I couldn't concentrate on anything all morning.

"We need some more willow branches to finish lashin' these plews," Samuel interrupted my thoughts. "Since you can't seem to get your mind off whatever's worryin' you, why don't you go cut some," he suggested.

"Yea, I guess I ain't doin' you much good this mornin,' am I?"

Taking up the camp ax and my rifle, I headed downstream to get the willow branches. That's when I realized what had been bothering me.

The birds. There were no birds flittering around and chirping like there had been. It was the silence they left behind that had me worried. I learned long ago to watch and trust the animal world when it came to danger.

Reaching the stream, I cut several dozen willows, thinking on what we were going to have to do. If it started to snow now, there was no way we were going to make it back down in time. We might as well get set and stay right here.

Glancing skyward as I made my way back to camp, I saw we were in serious trouble already. There had been no clouds to speak of all morning, but as I watched, the mountains all around us were slowly starting to disappear, hidden under the thick blanket of clouds. The clouds were dropping on top of us as well, and I broke into a run for camp.

"What's the hurry?" Samuel asked when I ran into camp.

"Look at them clouds. We don't have much time, so here's what we're gonna do."

As I outlined the plan for him, I was busy throwing all the round beaver dollars already lashed and grained into our brush-covered bower. Next, I started in on all the rest of our gear. I wasn't worried about making it neat; I just wanted it under some cover.

I sent Samuel back down to the stream to cut as much willow as he could. If this was going to be as bad as I thought it was going to be, then the horses were going to need food too. Willow bark wasn't the best, but it was all we had.

While he was gathering the willow, I took my tomahawk and started stripping the trees of all the branches I could reach. We needed to make our brush bower as thick as possible and as weather tight as we could. The snow, when it got here, would insulate us inside, but we needed to stop the wind from getting in.

Laying the branches I had cut onto the framework of the bower, it was soon thick and snug. There was no smoke hole in the top, so we couldn't completely block off the front. I partially blocked it, using some small trees with the branches left on.

Knowing it wouldn't take much to heat our small space, I gathered several armloads of wood and piled them inside. As far as the horses were concerned, there was nothing we could do to shelter them. There just wasn't time. But I wanted them as close as possible, so I sent Samuel out to bring them in. We were staking them behind our bower where they would be out of the wind, when the first snowflakes started to fall.

They were slow at first, swirling and twirling in the wind that had brought them here. All too soon, it was a complete whiteout. We couldn't see two feet outside the bower where Samuel and I had retreated to.

The snow continued to fall all around us, giving everything a thick white mantle. Several times a day, either Samuel or myself would venture out to check on the horses and give them some of the willow bark we had peeled for them. They weren't too bad off, but by the third day, we were out of willow. And the snow kept falling.

"What're we gonna do if the horses don't make it?" Samuel asked on the fourth morning. "Their ribs is startin' to show through their hides."

"Not much we can do for 'em, Samuel. But if one of 'em does go down, we need to butcher it fast, or it'll freeze."

"Why would we butcher—You mean we're gonna eat the horses?"

"Only if they go down. I ain't 'bout to turn down fresh meat after four days of eatin' dried meat."

"And if they all die? How are we gonna get back to the Ute camp? What then?"

"If, an' I mean a big if, they all die, then we'll cache all our gear an' walk out. But I don't think we'll lose all of 'em. Maybe only two or three. Don't want to loose any, but the longer this goes on, the greater that chance."

"You don't seem too worried 'bout us, little brother."

"That's 'cause I'm not. We have shelter, food, an' snow to melt for water. So stop worryin.' It ain't worth gettin' upset over. We'll survive this here storm, none the worse for it."

On the fifth day of the storm, we ran out of wood. I went out to see what I could find, hoping for the best, but not really expecting to find much. That's when I heard the horse go down.

Hurrying as fast as I could through the snow, now close to four feet deep, I reached the back of the bower. It was one of the packhorses, and it lay in a heap, eyes staring wide open into the still falling snow.

Going back to the front of the bower, I told Samuel to start skinning the dead horse while I continued to look for wood. Finally, there was some fresh meat, and we didn't have any wood to cook it. Seems like it was the story of my life.

Going towards the stream, I seemed to remember there was some fallen trees there. If I could find them, I could get the wood we needed. After stomping around for several minutes, I located the trees at last, under a thick blanket of snow. They weren't dry by any means, but if we could keep our fire going long enough, they would dry out enough to burn.

Scraping the snow off with my arm, I started to hack away at the first one. Frozen solid. This was going to be a two-man operation, I saw that right away.

One of the first lessons I learned out here was that you couldn't work up a sweat in weather like this. When you started to sweat, then stopped, the sweat froze on your skin. Then you were cold all the time, trying to warm back up. Most men died from exposure when this happened, and I made up my mind, I wasn't going to be one of them. So I took it nice and slow, Samuel taking his turn as well.

When I figured we had enough wood for three days or so, we stopped. When we had hauled it all into our bower, I was in need of some coffee and a nice horse steak.

By the time the blizzard wore itself out, some five days later, we had lost two more horses. The ones we had left were in no shape to carry all our gear back to the Ute camp, so Samuel and I cached what we didn't absolutely need. We just dug a hole, right there in our bower, and buried it.

"We still got traps in the stream," Samuel reminded me. "What're we gonna do 'bout 'em?"

"We need them traps, so I guess that means we go get 'em," I replied.

"Think we'll be able to find 'em in all this snow?"

"If we look for the poles we planted out in the stream, we should be able to find most of 'em. The ones we don't find now, we can pick up when we come back with the women.

"Way I figure, this storm is gonna set Wing of the Hawk

back at least a week from movin' the camp, dependin' on how low it went. We'll know more as we head down. Now let's go get them traps."

We found all but four of the traps, and the ones we did find, all had beaver in them. It was hard to skin the frozen carcasses, and after spending three times as long on the first one as it normally would take, we gave up, tossing the rest of the unskinned beaver into the brush along the stream.

"Such a waste, throwin' all them pelts away," Samuel said.

"I know, but it's just takin' way too long, an' we need to get off this mountain. It might decide to do it to us again, an' I don't wanna be here if it does."

"That makes two of us," he replied.

Chapter 29

When we got to the camp of the Ute, six days later, it was gone. The snow hadn't made it this low, so Wing of the Hawk must have decided to take the people and meet up with Bad Leg and his band.

"How long you make it they been gone?"

"Four, five days. I don't see anythin' that shows there was a fight, so they must've left to join up with Bad Leg an' his band, afore headin' for the spring gatherin.'"

"What 'bout our wives, an' Rowdy? Don't you think they would've waited for us to return?" he asked.

"Naw, Wing of the Hawk knows we'll follow along behind 'em. He probably saw that storm up on the mountain where we was, an' decided we was gonna be late. He wouldn't leave them women here all alone, so he took 'em with the rest. Don't worry, Samuel," I added. "We'll be with 'em again in a few days."

We decided to let the worn out horses rest for the remainder of the day, and leave at first light. They would already be in Bad Leg's camp by now, and I was just hoping they would stay there for a while, giving us time to get there.

Following the trail the Ute band had left, it soon became

apparent that Wing of the Hawk was moving slowly. There were tracks of several people walking when they could have been riding, and early in the afternoon, we found their first night's camp.

"Maybe they just got a late start," Samuel said, when I pointed out the fact that they should have been further along by the end of the day.

"No, I think he's waitin' for us to catch up. Let's move on till dark, that way we can gain on 'em."

Right after first light the next morning, we found their second camp. We were gaining on them, and we should be in Bad Leg's camp by nightfall, so we eased the pace a little.

I was dozing in the saddle, when suddenly my mule stopped in her tracks, ears up. In one fluid movement, I was off her back and crouched behind a tree beside the trail, wide-awake. Glancing at the rest of our horses, I saw that Samuel was nowhere to be seen. Now the rest of the horses had their ears up, all looking in the direction we had been headed.

My mule sidestepped as a brown hand appeared out of nowhere, reaching for her halter. Sighting back along the now exposed arm, I was just about to pull the trigger when I saw the blood on the sleeve of the hunting shirt. That quillwork on the shirt looked familiar, and I held my fire.

Taking a chance, I called out in Ute.

"Stand up and show yourself."

"Round-Ball?" Came a questioning voice filled with pain.

I stood up and advanced cautiously, holding my rifle ready to fire if this was a trick. I didn't think it was, but I didn't want to be taking that chance.

Parting the brush with my rifle barrel where the arm was now laying, I saw it was one of the Ute warriors from Wing of the Hawk's band. He had what looked like a bullet wound high on his chest, and another one in his arm. Turning to call out to Samuel, I saw the warrior was motionless, and I feared he was already dead.

"Is he dead?" Samuel asked as he approached.

"I hope not," I replied. "We need to know what happened. Look at those wounds. They was made by a rifle, not an arrow. There ain't too many 'Rapaho that have guns." I feared it was some white trappers who had hit the band as they made their way to Bad Leg's camp, but I needed to know for sure.

"He's still breathin,' but I don't think he's gonna last long," Samuel told me when I returned from retrieving my medicines. I never went anywhere without my medicines, and I was thankful I insisted on bringing them when we cached everything else after the blizzard.

"Let's get him out here where I can work on him," I told Samuel.

Together, we picked the warrior up and brought him out of the brush where he had been laying beside the trail.

"These wounds are at least a day old, maybe two days," I told Samuel. "Round up some wood an' build us a fire. I don't think it'll do much good, but I gotta try an' save him."

He was in bad shape that was for sure. I needed to ask him what had happened. My mind was going in different directions all at once, wondering what was going on, as I worked on him.

Both wounds were full of dirt and dried blood, and as soon as the water had heated I started cleaning them, being as gentle as I could. The ball had gone all the way through his arm, so I just cleaned it and wrapped it up. The chest wound was another story.

As I broke the crust of blood and dirt off his chest, the Ute let out a cry of pain and his eyes flew open. This might be my only chance to find out what happened, so I stopped cleaning the wound and asked him if he could tell me anything about what happened.

"I had just returned from Bad Leg's camp. Wing of the Hawk had sent me on ahead to tell them we would be there by nightfall. Suddenly, there were shots, and people were yelling and screaming." He winced in pain, and I waited for him to continue with his story.

"I saw Wing of the Hawk fall from his horse as he was trying to get the warriors together to protect the women and children. Then, I was on the ground. All I remember after that was crawling into the brush, trying to get away."

"Were they Arapaho?" I asked.

Looking up at me, he brought my fears to life.

"No, Round-Ball, they were like you. White trappers."

"Not like me," I said with a sigh. I knew what I was going to have to do, had done it before. But it must be done. Those trappers, white or not, had to be stopped.

"Do not waste your time on me, Round-Ball," he said with a shudder. "I am not long for this life, this I know. I was trying to reach you with this news. We knew you were behind us. That is the reason we were going so slow, giving you and Arrow Catcher time to reach us."

Turning his head to the side, he coughed up a thick mass of blood, spat it out, and turned once again to face me.

"You have done well," I told him. "We will sing songs of your bravery around the fires. And do not worry; we will avenge you, brother. All of those who are gone because of this, will be avenged."

With a slight smile on his lips, he died there by the trail. Samuel and I put him on a scaffold in the trees, back from the trail, and then we started on.

"What're we gonna do 'bout them trappers?" Samuel asked me.

"After we get to Bad Leg's camp an' check things out, I'm gonna go hunt 'em down."

"But they're white men, Razor. You can't just go kill 'em."

"No, they ain't white men," I said, my voice full of the hatred I was feeling. "They're nothin' but stinkin' animals. Have you forgotten, brother, that your own wife was with this group?" I asked.

The silence that followed told me, then, suddenly, Samuel slammed his heels to his horse and rushed past me. He was headed to the camp, and I put heels to my mule to follow, leading the empty packhorses as fast as I could.

Chapter 30

Wing of the Hawk was dead, and the whole camp was in turmoil when Samuel and I arrived close to sundown. We rode into the middle of the camp before dismounting, and several warriors rushed us, blood in their eyes.

"Enough!" Came the loud voice of Bad Leg. "These men are a part of us; they are not the ones who have done this."

"Bad Leg," I cried out as two warriors took my rifle and pistols from me.

"We came across one who lived on the way here. He told us what happened before he died. Where is my wife and son?"

Samuel was still struggling with a warrior over his rifle, and I told him to let it go.

"We're outnumbered, and besides, these are our people. We don't fight among ourselves. We'll get this straightened out, so just let 'em have your gun."

"Your wife and the wife of Arrow Catcher are well, brother," Bad Leg said as he came into the circle of warriors ringing us. "But there were some who did not make it."

"My son?" I asked, panic setting in.

"He is wounded, but he will live to fight another day."

"I need two fresh ponies, Bad Leg. I am going after them, and I am leaving right now."

"You cannot leave yet, Round-Ball. We have to decide who will go and who will stay to protect the women and children."

"White men did this, brother," I said through gritted teeth. "I am the one who will kill them, not any Ute warriors. We do not need the rest of the white trappers angry at the Ute."

"I'm comin' too, Razor," put in Samuel.

"No. I don't want you havin' to kill any white men, Samuel."

"It wouldn't be the first time, an' you're gonna need me afore all this is over," he said back. "Do we know how many of 'em there was?"

Turning to ask Bad Leg, he shook his head at the question.

"We do not know for sure, but there were at least four seen. There were probably more in the trees, but we do not know."

Nodding to him, I grabbed Samuel by the arm, leading him away from the angry warriors. Realizing we didn't have our rifles or pistols, I stopped and held out my hand to the warrior who had mine. Reluctantly, he handed them over, but only after getting approval from Bad Leg. Samuel got his guns back, and we headed to our lodges.

"Get your extra rifle, load up on powder, an' fill your bag with lead. This could take a while," I told Samuel.

Throwing the flap of my lodge open, I ducked inside. Buffalo Boy was lying by the fire, covered with a buffalo robe. Autumn Sky was by his side, and when she saw me, she jumped to her feet, rushing to me.

"How bad is he?" I asked Autumn Sky as I went to Buffalo Boy.

"He will live, but—"

"But what?" I asked.

"Do you know who did this?" she asked.

"Yes, I know," I told her.

As I gathered my two extra rifles and extra pistol, I told her what I was going to do.

"Why not let the warriors do this thing?" she asked, starting to cry.

"These are white men," I explained. "Arrow Catcher and I can get close to them. Then we will rub them out for what they have done to our people."

"You would kill them?"

"Every last one of them," I said as I headed for the lodge flap.

"Arrow Catcher feels the same as you?"

"Yes," I answered as I stepped outside. The Wolf was leading four fresh ponies up as I straightened up.

"You have food for your journey?" he asked.

Food was the last thing on my mind right now, but I knew we needed to take some. Shaking my head, I got the saddle off my mule and threw it on the back of one of the horses. Samuel showed up as I was tightening the cinch, his extra rifle tucked under one arm.

"You sure you wanna do this?" he asked.

"I'm sure," I said, turning to face him.

"They shot my son, Samuel. Not only am I gonna kill 'em, I'm gonna scalp 'em too."

"What if you know 'em? You still gonna kill 'em?" he asked.

"If you're comin,' let's go. I ain't got time to sit around here an' argue with you. An' yes, I'm still gonna kill 'em. If you can't handle it, then stay here."

The Wolf came trotting up as we mounted our horses, a buckskin bag clutched in one hand. Handing it up to me, he grasped my hand.

"You will be careful, my son?"

Nodding my head to him, I slammed my heels into the

flanks of my horse, sending him dashing through the gathering crowd of people, my spare horse in tow. Samuel was right behind me, following as fast as he could. I wanted to get this over with as quick as possible, before I lost my nerve.

Killing another trapper was not something I enjoyed doing. I had been forced to kill three of them in the past, back when Pepper and I had first come to the mountains. They had beat Pepper and robbed him when he was on his way to St. Louis, then threw him into the river to die. I helped him even the score when we found them.

Going back to where the ambush had taken place, we found the trail of the trappers. They were making tracks out of that country as fast as they could. We followed the tracks half the night, then stopped to rest the horses and ourselves. I wanted to have some idea of how many we were up against, and the next morning, I studied the tracks.

"Looks to be nine horses. The Ute said they saw at least four men, so that would give 'em five packhorses. Don't seem like enough pack animals for four men. What do you think?" I asked Samuel.

"I think you're right. They must have stashed their extra horses somewhere else an' plan to pick 'em up on the way through. Either that, or they lost all their horses, an' they was tryin' to get more. Some of these tracks don't look to be too deep, like they ain't carryin' a load."

Samuel had seen what I overlooked, and when he mentioned it, I saw he was right. There were probably only the four men, the rest of the animals being used as packhorses. The more we followed and studied the trail, the more I was sure. There were only four.

We found their camp a short time later, and as Samuel checked the campsite over, I studied the tracks some more. Samuel came over to me, a discolored piece of cloth in his hand.

"Pulled this out of the ashes where they had 'em a fire. Looks to be blood on it."

"Good," I replied. "One of 'em is wounded, an' that means he's either gonna die on the trail an' we'll find him, or the others are gonna be takin' care of him. If they are, they're gonna have to go slower, might even stop for a day or so."

"You got a plan yet?"

"Yea. We just go on into their camp, make sure it's them, an' kill 'em."

"Sounds simple enough," he said.

"Yea," I said, already wishing it was over.

Mounting back up, we stayed on their trail the rest of the day. We were gaining on them, but not by much. I wanted to close the gap between us, so Samuel and I switched horses and rode on through the second night. There was a sliver of moon showing, and it cast enough light to reflect off the snow, showing us the trail.

As dawn was breaking, I dozed in the saddle. Samuel was in the lead, guiding us, to give me some time to rest my eyes. Following the trail all night watching for sign, my eyes were worn out, feeling gritty from lack of sleep. Suddenly, Samuel stopped, sniffing the air.

"Smell it?" he whispered.

Smoke. And where there's smoke, there's generally a fire.

Pulling my horse around, I motioned for Samuel to follow. We went back down our trail for a little ways, and I pulled up. I didn't want them to know we were there just yet, and I didn't want our horses to smell each other and start whinnying back and forth.

Creeping back up the trail, we soon spotted their camp. There were two men lying down, a third busy with the fire, but I didn't see the fourth one. Samuel and I settled in to wait for him to show up before we made our move.

He soon appeared, carrying an armload of wood for the fire. When he dropped it, he turned around to put his back to the fire, and I got a good look at him. All the blood must have drained from my face as I looked at Samuel.

"You know any of 'em?" he whispered.

Nodding my head, I told him.

"Yea, I know 'em."

It was my so-called friends from last spring. Vergal and Pierre.

Chapter 31

Creeping back to our own horses, I told Samuel I had to think on this. These men had saved my life last spring when I had been jumped by the Blackfoot, up in the Three Forks. Riley and Jackson, my two partners, had been killed, and I had taken an arrow in my side and a ball in my leg. These men had shown up just as the wound in my side had become infected.

When I finished telling Samuel all about it, he asked the question.

"You still gonna go through with it?"

"I gave my word to Bad Leg an' the rest of 'em that I was gonna do this. If we come back without their scalps, there ain't no tellin' what they're gonna do to us."

"We could always say we couldn't find 'em," he suggested.

"That won't fly, an' you know it. No, we gotta do it. If you don't think you can, probably be best if you stayed back here. Let me go on in an' take care of it."

"I don't know 'em, so it makes no difference to me."

"Looks like they're stayin' here, at least for now. Let's rest up a bit, then go on in later in the day. We go in this early, they're gonna know we been followin' 'em."

"I'll wake you in two hours," he said.

"Thanks, Samuel. I know you're just as tired as me, an' I'll give you at least two hours rest too."

Seemed like I just closed my eyes when Samuel's hand shook me awake. Glancing at the sun, I saw he had let me sleep closer to three hours.

"Why didn't you wake me earlier?" I asked him.

"You looked like you needed it, an' I slept along the way last night when you was in the lead. But my eyes is gettin' heavy now. Just give me an hour or so, then I'll be ready."

While he slept, I was trying to decide the best way to go about this. There was no doubt in my mind that I was going to kill them, it was just a matter of how. We needed to take them off their guard first, and I figured that since Vergal and Pierre knew me, that shouldn't be too hard to do.

I didn't know who the other two men were, and I wasn't even sure one of them was Pierre. But I knew Vergal, and he knew me. That was enough. I hated to do it, but I had made a promise to Bad Leg and the rest of the people. It was something that had to be done, no matter what I felt.

Waking Samuel, I filled him on my plan. We were going to go in to the camp, wait until they let their guard down, then strike. When I gave a slight whistle through my teeth, Samuel was to go to our horses and pull the extra rifles loose. He would cough when he was ready, then I would shoot Vergal. After that, it would only be a matter of shooting before they did. I hoped it would work the way I planned.

Leaving our spare horses there, we mounted up. We decided to approach their camp from a different direction, that way they wouldn't know we had been following them. I just hoped they were still there. I wanted to get back to the camp and see my son.

Thinking of him got me mad all over again, and that was what I needed. I needed to be angry to do this thing. It was not something I took lightly, and I was sure Samuel felt the same as me.

Circling around, we approached from the west, away from the direction they had come from. When we smelled the smoke again, I nodded to Samuel and called out.

"Hello the camp."

"Come in with your hands empty," came the reply. I knew it was Vergal who spoke, from the French accent.

When we rode in, there were three rifles pointed at us. I saw Samuel stiffen in fear, and the sweat that trickled down my back wasn't from the heat of the day.

"That you, Vergal?" I asked, trying to sound innocent.

"Round-Ball, my friend!" Vergal said. He sounded like he was genuinely glad to see me as he strode over.

"It has been a long winter, no?" he asked. "But this time, it is the other way around. Last time, it was you who were wounded. This time, I am sorry to say, it is Pierre."

"What happened?" I asked as we dismounted.

Glancing at the other two before he answered, he told me a pack of lies.

"We were just mindin' our own business, trapping the beaver, when we were attacked by some Indians. I think it was some Ute, but I am not sure. Pierre was wounded, and I do not think he will make it to the rendezvous this time."

Nodding my head, I saw that all of them had set their rifles down. I also saw something else. Tucked into the belt of Vergal, was the scalp of my Ute brother, Wing of the Hawk.

Still carrying my rifle, I went to the fire to check on Pierre. He was as good as dead already. I saw where two arrows had pierced his chest, and Vergal had done all he could for him, using his skills as a trained doctor.

Squatting down by the fire, near Pierre, I lifted the blanket covering him. Letting out a low whistle, I saw Samuel go to the horses. Straightening back up, I pointed to the scalp in Vergal's belt.

"Looks like you killed at least one of 'em," I said.

"Yes, he was their leader. At least I think he was the leader. He was the one in the lead when we were attacked, and I killed him."

Samuel coughed, and I moved a little to the side to get out of his way. Slowly, I brought my rifle to bear on Vergal's mid section. When I brought the hammer back to full cock, I saw his eyes widen in fear.

"You're a liar, Vergal," I said as I pulled the trigger.

I was only ten feet away when I shot him, the force of the ball knocking him back into the man on his right. Samuel shot a split second behind me, his ball hitting the one on the left in the forehead.

Pulling my pistol, I shot the one Vergal had knocked off balance as he crawled frantically for his rifle. Samuel walked over to Pierre, intending on shooting him where he lay, but he was already dead. The arrows had done their work.

While I reloaded my rifle, Samuel walked to Vergal, pulling his skinning knife from the back of his belt. Reaching down, he first pulled the scalp of his adopted father from Vergal's belt, tucking it into his possibles bag, and then he scalped him.

As Samuel walked away, I knew he wasn't in the mood to finish scalping the others, so I did, making quick work of it. As I finished the gristly work, I watched Samuel go back over to Vergal, his tomahawk in his hand.

I watched in utter shock as Samuel hacked Vergal's head from his lifeless body. I continued to stare at my brother as he did the same to the other three bodies, throwing the heads into the fire where they slowly burned.

Without saying a word, he drug the bodies to the trees

surrounding the camp and started to strip them. Cutting some long buckskin strings, I went to help him, and together, we hung the bodies upside down in the trees. This is what I always did to the Indians who attacked me, and when I thought about it, I realized that these men were no different. They were worse than Arapaho. Or Blackfoot, for that matter. They were getting just what they deserved.

Gathering the nine horses the renegade trappers had, we looted the camp of everything of value. The rest we threw into the fire, burning it up with their heads.

As we stood there watching everything burn, I reached out to put a reassuring hand on Samuel's shoulder. The death of Wing of the Hawk had finally sunk in for him. I felt a shudder pass through his body, and then he turned and walked to our horses.

"Let's go home, Round-Ball," he said.

Chapter 32

We rode straight through the night heading back to the Ute camp, switching horses every few hours to give them, and us, a short break. Samuel hadn't said a word the whole time, and I was beginning to worry about him. He was acting just like I had when Pepper and Prairie Flower had been killed. I didn't want him to go through what I had. It hurt too much.

I tried to talk to him, but all I got in return was an occasional grunt. Not knowing for sure if it was the pain of loosing Wing of the Hawk, or the fact that we had been forced to kill other trappers, I decided not to press him. We would talk about it later, if he was willing to, after we got to the camp.

Late the second afternoon, we reached the Ute encampment. The weather was sunny and mild, at least down here, and I was wanting to get back to our trapping. We still had another good month of winter in the high country, perfect for catching the flat tails. It was what Samuel needed, to take his mind off what we had done, and to move on with his life.

Heading directly to Bad Leg's lodge, we were surrounded by people, all asking us questions. As we stiffly dismounted in front of his lodge, Bad Leg came out. He was followed by several old men, The Wolf among them.

"Have you brought us the scalps of those who did this to our people?" Bad Leg asked.

Pulling the three scalps from my belt, I handed them to him. Samuel was slow in pulling Vergal's scalp from his belt, and when he handed it to Bad Leg, he spoke for the first time since leaving the renegade trapper's camp.

"This is the scalp of the one who killed my father. He told us he was the one who did it," he finished, holding the scalp out to Bad Leg.

"That scalp belongs to you, brother," Bad Leg told Samuel. "The loss is great and has affected many. But for you, it is worse."

"I have also brought my father's hair home for him," Samuel said. "I would like to put it back where it belongs."

"Of course," Bad Leg said.

As Samuel turned away from the gathered crowd, Bad Leg called out to him.

"Arrow Catcher."

Samuel came back and faced Bad Leg, not sure what to expect.

Putting both hands on Samuel's shoulders, Bad Leg continued.

"Your father would be proud of you, Arrow Catcher. What you have done was a true act of the love you shared with him."

Dropping his hands from Samuel's shoulders, Bad Leg moved beside him. Placing his left hand on Samuel's right shoulder and holding his right hand high, Bad Leg addressed the people.

"People of the Ute, hear me. I am Bad Leg. Let it be known that from this time on, this man, Arrow Catcher, has proven himself to be one of the people. He has avenged the death of one of us, a great leader among the people, the one he called his father. He is to be treated with the respect and love he has shown us this day."

I saw the tears start in the corners of Samuel's eyes as Bad Leg released his hold on his shoulder. With his head hanging low so those near couldn't see the tears, Samuel walked from the gathering, getting back on his horse.

"You want me to come with you?" I asked him.

"No, I'll do this on my own," he said, reigning away.

"I'll tell Little Rabbit you're back," I called after him.

After I had put the animals in with the rest of our small herd, I went to Samuel's lodge. As I approached, a frantic Little Rabbit burst through the opening, running into me, almost knocking me over.

"What's going on—"

Pressing her hand to her mouth, Little Rabbit disappeared around the back of the lodge. Standing there trying to figure out what was happening, I was surprised when Autumn Sky came out of the lodge.

"What is going on with Little Rabbit?" I asked her.

"Where is her husband, Arrow Catcher?" she asked.

"He is returning his father's hair to him. Now tell me, what is wrong with her," I asked again, pointing to the back of the lodge.

"It is not my place to tell you, Round-Ball. Little Rabbit must speak to her husband first."

"How is my son? Can he walk yet?" I asked her as she walked away.

"He is improving, but he cannot walk on his own yet."

As Autumn Sky and I walked back to our lodge, The Wolf came up to me.

"My son, there has been a council called. It will be later tonight, and Bad Leg has asked that you and Arrow Catcher be there. We wish to hear the details of your raid on the white trappers."

"Yes, I will be there. I cannot speak for my brother, though. He is taking this thing very hard, father. I do not know if he will be able to do what you ask."

"If he cannot, we will not force him, you know that. He needs time to mourn the loss of his father. I will inform Bad Leg of this news. Will you at least ask Arrow Catcher if he is able to share with us?"

"I will ask him, if I see him," I told him.

When I entered my lodge, I saw that Buffalo Boy was awake. Going to his side, I knelt down and smiled at him.

"How are you?" I asked in Ute.

"I have been better, father. I hate lying here, unable to take care of the horses and play with my friends. When do you think I will be able to walk again?" he asked.

"Have you tried to walk yet?"

"No, she will not let me," he answered, pointing to Autumn Sky. "But now that you are back, I will listen to you."

Crossing his arms and nodding his head once, I had to hold back a smile. He was definitely just like his father at this age, and that scared me. I had done some pretty foolish things when I was younger. I had survived them, and I knew Buffalo Boy would survive all the things he would do, but I couldn't have him talking and acting like this to his new mother.

"Now, just hold on there, son," I said. "Your mother knows what she's talkin' 'bout. So if she says you're to stay put, then that's what you're gonna do."

Facing Autumn Sky, I gave her a wide grin.

"But I hope it ain't too long. We're goin' back to our trappin' as soon as you're able to sit a horse. And Bad Leg is wishful of movin' the camp on to the spring gatherin,' so they're gonna be leavin' us."

"Two more days, and he should be healed enough to start walking short distances," Autumn Sky said.

"Well then, wake me in two days. I feel as if I haven't slept for a week."

"Have you forgotten about the council tonight?"

"Oh, yea," I said. My mind was dulled from the lack of sleep, and I had already forgotten.

"Wake me when the sun goes down," I told her as I crawled under my sleeping robes. "And if you see Arrow Catcher, give him the message from The Wolf about tonight," I added.

As tired as I was, sleep just wouldn't come. I tossed and turned, my mind going over the events of the past several days. I was worried about Samuel, mostly. I had to get him back to trapping or else he would sit there and stew about what had happened. Somewhere along the way, I finally fell asleep.

Chapter 33

At the council meeting later that night, I told those gathered about the fight at Vergal's camp. It was not a very long story, but the importance of what Samuel and I had done was not lost on the Ute. There were many white trappers who were friendly to the Ute, and I did not want to make things bad between them. If there were going to be bad feelings, I did not want the Ute to have to be a part of them.

Samuel did not show up to the council, and none were surprised about it. He was going through a rough time right now. Not only did he have to provide for his own family, now he had the added burden of caring for Wing of the Hawk's wife and children. This was going to be awkward, with us leaving the rest of our band until next fall.

The next morning as I was looking our remaining horses over, Samuel joined me.

"I know," he started, "that I'm expected to care for my fathers' wife and children now. But if we're gonna be gone trappin' an' headin' out to the rendezvous, how am I to gonna do that?"

"We can't exactly take 'em along, if that's what you're thinkin.' We ain't caught enough beaver to hardly take care of our wives. I'll talk to The Wolf, an' see if he has any advice on how to go about this," I told him.

"They will not go hungry, Round-Ball," The Wolf told me when I asked him. "Your brother was a well-loved man among his band, and they will see to his family's needs.

"Speaking of those who followed him, they have asked me to talk to you and Arrow Catcher. Can the two of you meet me later so we can discuss this?"

"Of course, father," I answered. "Will you join us for our night meal? We can talk about it then."

"Yes, I will be there," he agreed.

Samuel seemed in a better mood when I found him. I told him about what The Wolf and I had talked about, and that he and Little Rabbit were invited to my lodge for supper.

"I'll be there, but I ain't so sure Little Rabbit will be able to make it. She ain't feelin' so good these days," he said with a smile.

"What's wrong with her? She sick?"

"You might say that, Uncle Razor," he said, still smiling.

"Uncle?" I asked.

"Yea, looks like I'm gonna be a papa again."

Reaching out, I pulled him to me, giving him a big hug. So this is what was wrong with Little Rabbit. And Autumn Sky wouldn't even tell me. I never would understand women.

"Congratulations, Samuel," I said. I was happy for them, but in a way, this complicated things for us. We would have to make some adjustments to accommodate for a little baby, but we would deal with that when the time came.

"I need to go tell Autumn Sky we're havin' guest's for supper, so I'll see you tonight."

Walking away from him, I felt a little jealous. His wife had become pregnant already, while Autumn Sky and I were still trying. She had no children of her own, and even though I had

Buffalo Boy, I wanted more. I enjoyed having small children around me, and I knew Autumn Sky did too.

When I told her I had invited some people to supper, she got an angry look in her eyes and stormed out of the lodge. Shrugging my shoulders at Buffalo Boy, I followed her as she went to the pile of wood near the door.

"What's got into you?" I asked. "All I did was invite some friends to eat with us, and you get angry about it."

"I am not angry with you, husband. I cannot explain it," she said, shaking her head.

"Can't explain what?" I asked her.

"Sometimes, I get angry over nothing, and sometimes I cry. I feel as if I am losing my mind, the way it wanders these days. I just do not feel like myself anymore."

She turned to me, and I could see the tears start to run down her face. She looked like a frightened child, full of confusion and doubt.

"Shhh," I said as I pulled her to me. "It will be alright. I think I know what is wrong. I will go and find one of the old women to come and see you. They will know for sure."

"Am I going to die?" she asked. She sounded so scared, but I couldn't control the laugh that came out.

"No, you are not going to die," I said. "I think you are going to have a baby. But we need a woman to check and see if this is true. As a man, I do not know about these things."

"A baby," she whispered in awe. "Could it be true?"

"Anything is possible," I said. "It is not like we have not been trying."

"But how do you know?" she asked.

"When Buffalo Boy's mother was carrying him, she acted much the same as you."

"But my sister, she does not act like this. Why would she

act one way and I act another, if we are both pregnant? It does not make any sense to me."

"Nor to me," I replied. "But some women are different, that's all."

"A baby," she said again, turning to walk back to the lodge.

"Hey," I hollered. "Aren't you forgetting what you came out here for? The wood for the fire?"

"Oh," she said. "I guess I did forget. But since you are there, you can bring it in."

Still smiling, she ducked inside the lodge.

Autumn Sky's pregnancy was confirmed by the old woman I brought to see her. As payment, I gave her a dozen finger rings and an awl. Samuel and I still had many things left from last year's rendezvous trading, and this seemed like the perfect time to make presents of them. Both our wives were pregnant, and we were going to be leaving our band until next fall.

Samuel and I were dividing our trade goods to be given out as gifts when The Wolf arrived. Little Rabbit was there as well, but she declined to eat, saying it hurt too much when it came back up.

After we had eaten, I filled cups of coffee for The Wolf, Samuel, and myself. Buffalo Boy was moved back from the fire so we men could talk.

"With the loss of your father," The Wolf said to Samuel, "and your brother," he said to me, "there is no leader for his band. The people of your band have asked me to speak to you about this."

Setting his cup down, The Wolf paused before continuing.

"Both of you have proven your loyalty to the Ute, and you are well liked among these two bands. Some are for joining Bad Leg and his band, but there are already too many for the land to support for very long in one place.

"After this was discussed with Bad Leg, many have decided they want you, Round-Ball, to be their leader."

"But I—"

Holding up his hands to stop me, The Wolf went on.

"They know that you are a trapper, and only here for the winters, and that you move on in the spring. Many would like to see this gathering of the white men, and they would be willing to follow you wherever you lead them.

"But, I must caution you. This is a great responsibility, leading so many. I have great faith in your judgment and your abilities to do this thing. So does Bad Leg. But there are some who do not, because you are white men.

"You, my son," he said facing me, "have ceased to be a white man to me. You are a Ute warrior until the day you leave this world for the next one.

"And you," he said to Samuel, "have been accepted as a Ute warrior as well. Even though this is your first winter among the people, you have shown that you are worthy of our love and respect. Not only for saving those three children and your father from the Arapaho dogs, but also by your actions since then. You have shown that you are willing to do what is right in the eyes of the people. No matter the personal cost to you.

"Both of you," he added, "do not think of yourselves first, as so many white men do. You put the needs of those around you first, and that is a sign of a great man, a leader.

"I will let the two of you think and talk on this. Do not make this decision until you are sure of it."

With the talks over, at least for now, The Wolf retired to his own lodge. He had given Samuel and I a lot to think about, especially me. I wasn't so sure I wanted this responsibility, and I didn't think Samuel did either.

"Where do I fit into all this?" Samuel asked when The Wolf was gone. "Sounds more like they want you to be the leader, not me."

"The Wolf an' the rest of 'em, they know I ain't gonna

do nothin' without you. You an' me, we're brothers by blood. That's why they asked us to do this together."

"Do you really want to do this?" he asked.

"I ain't sure. I need some time to think 'bout it."

"Well, let me know what you decide. I'm tired, an' all I wanna do is sleep. But whatever you decide, I'll follow along with it. You've got me this far," he said yawning.

"You're gonna be a big part of this, Samuel, if we decide to do it, so you need to think 'bout it too."

"I will," he said as he left with Little Rabbit.

I was tired myself, and stifling back a yawn, I went over to my sleeping robes. Autumn Sky was there already, but she was not sleeping. She had been, I knew, listening to our talk.

"Are you going to do this, my husband?" she asked.

"I don't know yet," I said to her. "Right now, all I want to do is sleep. I have to think about it more and talk to Arrow Catcher and my father."

"When is Bad Leg planning on leaving this camp to join the others?"

"I forgot to ask. But I will find out in the morning."

The morning came all too soon, and I was not ready to crawl from my robes when Bad Leg showed up.

Making some coffee, I waited to find out the purpose of his visit. Bad Leg, I knew from past experience, never did or went anywhere without a reason. If he had come to my lodge this early, there was a good reason.

"Brother, I do not like to push, but have you and Arrow Catcher had time to make a decision on what The Wolf asked you? I only ask this because it is time to leave for the gathering of the tribe. Some of your band do not want to leave until they know if you will be their leader in the fall."

"I have not had time to talk to my brother," I told him. "I would also like to talk to my father before I make any decision. These past days, I have not had much rest, and I am too weary right now to decide. But, if you would wait, I will have an answer for you in two days time. Is this acceptable?"

"I was hoping to leave tomorrow, but one more day will not hurt, I suppose," he said.

"Good. My brother and I will be giving some presents away later today, and I would like you there. I will send someone for you when it is time."

Nodding his head in agreement, Bad Leg left. They sure weren't giving us much time to decide on such an important matter, and I wasn't going to make a decision until I had time to talk it over with Samuel and The Wolf.

Leaving my lodge, I went to find Samuel. If he was feeling like me, I knew he would still be in his own lodge, probably still sleeping. But he wasn't there.

"Arrow Catcher left early this morning, before it was light," Little Rabbit told me.

"Did he say where he was going?" I asked.

"No, only that he would be back later. I thought he was going to talk to you."

"I have not seen him. When he comes back, tell him to come and see me. We have many things to decide before the day is over."

Going over to our horses, I saw the one Samuel favored was gone. Wherever he went, it required a horse, and suddenly I knew. He was visiting his father's final resting place. I did not want to disturb him, but we had presents to pass out. I had already made a decision on whether or not to be the leader of the band, but I still wanted to talk to Samuel about it.

I went back to my lodge to tell Autumn Sky where I was going, and Buffalo Boy was trying to stand. He was arguing with his mother about it, and I didn't have the time right now to deal with either of them.

"If you think you can walk, then try. But do not over-do it. If you injure yourself worse, we will have to stay here longer and wait for you to heal," I told him.

Catching up a horse instead of my mule, I headed for Wing of the Hawk's burial platform. My mule nickered at me, and I felt bad about not riding her, but she was worn to a frazzle. I was going to need her in good shape by tomorrow, and she needed the extra rest.

When I got close to the burial site, I got off my horse and tied her to a tree. I didn't want to disturb Samuel as he did whatever it was he was doing, but I crept close enough to see him. That way, I would know when he was done.

He was standing in front of the scaffold where Wing of the Hawk had been laid, head bowed. I knew he was talking to him. I could hear the murmur of his voice, but I couldn't hear what he was saying. Nor did I want to. This was between the two of them, and I didn't want to hear.

Settling back against a tree, I waited for him to finish. A long while later, I saw Samuel's shoulders start to shake. I knew he was crying, and all of a sudden, I felt bad about being here. I was just about to leave when he startled me with a sudden scream, the sound tearing from his throat.

As he fell to his knees in anguish, I found myself going forward, towards him. This was too much. I couldn't bear to see him in such pain.

As I approached, he heard my steps. He spun around, still on his knees, his hand on his pistol. I stopped, holding up my hands. When he saw it was me, he dragged the back of his arm across his eyes, and turned away.

"Samuel, I—"

"How long you been here?" he asked, sniffling his nose.

"Not long," I lied. It wouldn't be right to tell him the truth right now.

"I'm just 'bout done here anyway," he said.

Putting my hand on his shoulder, I nodded.

"You know, he was one of the few men who really understood me," Samuel said. "I didn't have long with him, but I learned a great deal in that time."

"I know, Samuel," I told him. "And what Bad Leg told you yesterday was the truth. Your father was very proud of you. And so am I," I added. "You've come a long way since I found you back at the rendezvous."

"Yea," he answered.

"Are you ready to hand out your gifts?"

"I suppose so. How'd you know I was here, anyway?"

"When you weren't in your lodge an' Little Rabbit told me you left early, I figured you were here."

As we mounted up and started back to the camp, I told him about the visit from Bad Leg earlier that morning.

"Have you decided, then?"

"Yea, I think I have, but I wanted to talk to you some more 'bout it before I tell them."

"And?" he asked.

"I don't think either one of us is ready for this kind of responsibility. Not that I don't want to, it's just that I don't think we're the right ones for this job. What do you think?"

"I think you're right, little brother. I too, want the best for our band, and I think they could do better with someone else to lead 'em."

"At least we agree on it. We need to tell Bad Leg and The Wolf of our decision, but first, we need to give away some presents. It should have been done long ago, but things kept gettin' in the way."

"Good," Samuel said. "I'm gettin' tired of packin' all that stuff 'round anyhow."

"Yea, I know what you mean. But remember, that 'stuff'

was part of the price you paid for your wife. Which brings up another touchy subject."

"What's that?"

"Have you decided what you're gonna do about your father's wife and children?"

"I been thinkin' on that, an' I got a plan, if you think it'll work."

"I'm listenin.'"

"I was thinkin' of takin' all them horses we took off them murders an' tradin' 'em to someone to take care of 'em. At least until next fall when we join back up with the band. We are gonna be back, ain't we?" he asked.

"We'll be back. If we don't get our hair lifted afore then, that is," I said with a grin.

"And by then, we'll have two more new members to the tribe."

"That's a fact," I said as we reached the camp. "That's a fact."

Chapter 34

The next day, Bad Leg and the others left. Some of our band were disappointed that I wasn't going to be their leader, but they accepted it. We stayed an extra day, then packed our horses and headed back up to the North Park to trap for the rest of the season. It was coming onto spring down here, but the mountains were still several feet deep in snow, and that's where we were headed.

It was pleasant weather, and I wasn't looking forward to wading in those icy streams again. I'm sure Samuel wasn't either, but this was what we did. It was the only way to catch the beaver we were after, and to me, it was better to do this than work for someone else back in the settlements. I didn't have much use for all their rules and such.

"Where we goin'?" Samuel asked the third day out. "This ain't the way we came down."

"No, this ain't the same way. You remember all the trouble we had on that slope yonder?" I asked, pointing to a long, steep hill.

"Oh, yea, I almost forgot 'bout that one. You gonna find us 'nother way up there?"

"Don't need to find it. I already know where it be."

"I don't get how you know where you're at. All the time, you seem to know just where we are. It kind of scares me, Razor. You one of them people what sees things, ahead of time?"

"No, I ain't one of them kind. I just learned long ago to file the land away in my mind. That way, if I ever come to a place I already been, I don't have to fight my way through it, I already know. You'll catch on. It's easy to do, if you put your mind to it."

"We gonna pick up our traps an' pelts we left behind first, or are we gonna trap a while first?" he asked.

"I think we better go get our truck and plunder we left behind, afore we do any trappin.' I figure we can stay in the bower we already got made, an' trap that stream some more. We only set traps a few times afore we got snowed in, so there ought to be plenty more beaver up there still."

"Then we gonna move further up that stream?"

"Depends on what we find when we get there. Might be somebody else is there too. I ain't one of them trappers what horn in on 'nother man's trappin' area," I told him.

"You mean you ain't the only one who knows 'bout that area?"

"Naw, I ain't the only one. At some time or 'nother, most every trapper finds his way to the Parks. Some like it an' stay, others don't, so they leave."

"You know, I been watchin' you, little brother. An' I gotta say, you sure have changed a lot since you was a kid. The Razor I remember, he was a mean one. Always on the prowl, like he was lookin' for a fight all the time.

"But this new Razor, he ain't like that at all. He's so laid back 'bout most things, it's like watchin' a different person altogether."

"I'm still the same, Samuel. It's just that since then, I learned to control my temper. At least most of the time," I added.

"How'd you do that? I been tryin' to do that for years, an' I can't seem to find a way to do it."

"Havin' Buffalo Boy helped a lot," I said. "But I guess the biggest thing I learned was that there ain't a reason to go lookin' for trouble. Out here, there's trouble everywhere, an' I figured if I was gonna survive, I was gonna have to change my ways. So I stopped lookin' for trouble. But sometimes, it still finds me. An' that's when I lose my temper."

"Well, I hope I don't do nothin' to make you lose that temper on me. I can still feel that knife on my head, from when you tried to scalp me when you was a kid."

"You shouldn't have pushed me so hard, then," I said,

Thinking back on that, I had to laugh, and Samuel stared at me.

"What's so funny?" he asked.

"I was just rememberin' the look on your face when that knife started slicin' your head, that's all. An' the way pa acted! Man, you would of thought it was him I was scalpin' instead of you."

"Yea," Samuel said, joining the laughter. "I thought for sure he was gonna take the hide right off you that day. He was mad, ain't no doubt 'bout that."

"Wonder how the folks are doin," I mused. "Sure been a long time since I seen 'em. When was the last time you saw 'em, Samuel?" I asked.

"That time I saw you an' pa in Richmond. That were the last time. I ain't seen ma since I left with Jonathon, back in '09."

"Ever think of goin' back? Just for a visit?"

"Yea, I thought 'bout it a time or two, but I never did make it back. Now, since I been out here, I don't think I'll ever go back. Not even for a visit," he said.

"I thought on it a time or two myself. But I probably won't ever make it back neither."

"I been wonderin.' Since Ashley didn't start havin' his

annual rendezvous till '24, what did you an' Pepper do with your pelts? Where did you sell 'em?"

"Well, depends on which year it was. Sometimes, we traded down in Taos, to the Mexicans. But it got so they was tryin' to steal our plews from us without payin for 'em. Said we was trappin' in their country, an' since we didn't have us no license to trap there, we was stealin' from 'em. So we quit goin' there.

"A few times, we went to Lisa's forts to trade. But it was too far to do it all the time. I got tired of crossin' that open prairie after a few seasons. But we did make it clear back to St. Louis, one year. That were some trip, I'm here to tell you."

"That wasn't back in '19, by chance, was it?" he asked.

Scratching my whiskers, I had to think back. Runnin' all the years through my mind, I finally nodded.

"Yea, that were the year. Why?"

"Remember when I told you I heard the name 'Round-Ball' somewhere? That was where I heard it, back in St. Louis. There was a big fight, 'tween some locals—"

"An 'Ol Pepper an' me," I finished. "I remember it well. Had me a few busted ribs, so we couldn't leave when we planned. Ended up stayin' almost a month longer than we should have, an' almost missed the fall hunt that year.

"How'd you know 'bout that fight?" I asked him.

"Cause I was there. I wasn't in the fight, I was just watchin' it. You an' Pepper was somethin,' let me tell you. There must've been six or eight of them locals that jumped you. What was it about, anyway?" He wanted to know.

"What else? A woman."

Thinkin' back on it now, me an' Pepper was lucky to make it out of that place with our lives that night.

"There was this pretty little gal servin' drinks in there, an' Pepper had a thing for her. We was just sittin' there, not even drinkin,' an' these fellas started mis-treatin' her, pullin' an' grabbin' on her.

"Well, 'Ol Pepper, he had a bad grouch goin' that night, an' he just waded into 'em, swingin' them big fists of his. But there was too many of 'em for him to take on all by hisself. So I stepped in when two of 'em held him an' the rest started in punchin' him. We sure wore them boys down that night," I said.

"You not only wore 'em down, you just 'bout killed two of 'em with that chair leg."

"You saw that?" I asked, still shocked that he was there.

"It was my chair you took an' hit 'em with," he said.

"Well, what do you know? We was together, an' didn't even know it. So how come you didn't get in on the fight?"

"Wasn't none of my concern. 'Sides, them boys had it comin,' not only for the way they was treatin' that girl, but for other reasons too.

"After it was all over 'an you threw 'em out, I remember Pepper callin' you 'Round-Ball.' I didn't know who you was at the time, what with all that hair on your face an' them braids you was wearin.'

"But I never forgot the name 'Round-Ball.' I decided right then an' there, that I was never gonna cross no trappers. You two fought like a couple of mountain lions."

"Yea, them were the days, that's for sure," I said, missing 'Ol Pepper even more.

Samuel noticed my silence and started to say something, just as I smelled the smoke.

Chapter 35

Jerking my mule to a stop I jumped off. Grabbing her halter, I pulled her off the trail into the trees, Samuel and the others following as quickly as they could.

Pulling one of my extra rifles from a packhorse, I handed it to Autumn Sky. Samuel was doing likewise, handing his extra gun to Little Rabbit. Grabbing the last rifle, I gave it to Buffalo Boy.

"Get the powder an' ball off the packhorse," I whispered to him. "An' keep your head down."

"What is it, father?" he asked.

"Not sure. But we ain't takin' no chances. Right up there, under them trees, is where we cached our goods. Looks like someone found our camp an' moved in."

Motioning to Samuel, we started off in the direction of the smoke smell. I was hoping it wasn't any trappers who had found our old camp, but chances were it was. I just hoped they hadn't found our cache of furs.

When we got close enough to see the camp, it was obvious they had been there for some time. The willow hoops of beaver dotting the camp proved that it was indeed trappers. Only five horses were in sight, two with saddles. Only two men, then.

Watching the camp, Samuel and I had the same thought: our pelts and truck we had left behind. The cache we had dug inside the bower was well hidden, mostly from our stomping on it, packing the dirt hard to prevent anyone from finding it. As we watched, one man came out of the bower and stretched, scratched himself, and walked to the fire.

Henry Fraeb. I would know that walk anywhere.

Smiling to Samuel, I nodded my head.

"You sure do make a nice target, Henry," I yelled.

Fraeb jumped up and dove under the protective cover of the bower. Samuel and I stood up, walking towards him. I was chuckling to myself at Henry's antics and his wild display of fear.

"Well, you gonna shoot us, or offer us some of that coffee I been smellin' for half the day?" I asked as he poked his head out.

"Why you wanna go an' scare me like dat? I almost shoot you, you know," he said in his heavy German accent.

"Now, Henry. We both know you couldn't hit a tree unless you was leanin' on it," I said with a laugh.

"Ya, sure," he said with a laugh. "How you been dis winter, my friend? An' who's dat with you? I ain't seen him before."

"This is my brother, Samuel," I said. "An' Samuel, this here old geezer is known as Henry Fraeb. One of the worst smellin' men I ever had the pleasure of knowin.'"

"I don't smell no worse dan you, Round-Ball," Henry said with a laugh.

"What you boys doin' up here?" he asked us.

"We're trappin,' what do you think we're doin'? Just out for a spring stroll?"

"The beaver are ver' thick up here, you know? We begin to tink there is nobody else in the whole of the mountains but us, this winter. We never see anybody, no trappers, no Indians, no nobody."

"Well, you sure made yourselves comfortable in our camp,

Henry. We built this here bower a couple of months ago, an' we was trappin' here when that blizzard blew in. You get caught in that?" I asked.

"Ya, we get caught in it, dat's for sure. But dare was nobody here when we get here, so we move in. What, now you want it back?"

"Easy, Henry, easy. Don't get all riled up 'bout it," I said.

"No, we'll move on, an' trap somewhere else, away from you. But," I added, "we did leave a few things behind when we lit out of here. You by chance didn't happen to find some traps still in the stream, did you?"

"Ya, we did find some traps. But they so rusted up, we trow dem away. Is dat what you come back for? A few rusty traps?"

"Naw, we left some other things behind too," I told him.

"Dat is all we find when we get here. Maybe somebody else is up here too, an' dey take dem."

Before I said anything more about our plews and other truck we had buried under his feet, I had to know who Henry was trapping with. I didn't want to have to fight over our plews, but we would if we had to. We needed them pelts cached here to make it through another year.

"Who you trappin' with this year, Henry?"

"Gabe. Why?"

I heaved a sigh of relief at hearing the name. Jim Bridger, otherwise known as 'Gabe,' was about as honest as the day was long, at least when it came to other trappers.

"Well, Henry, since it's just the two of you, I guess I can tell you," I said.

"What are you talkin' bout?"

"Henry, you an' Gabe been sleepin' on top of all the furs we took from this stream, an' others, when we was here last. We cached 'em there after that blizzard. Our ponies was too wore out to carry 'em back to the Ute we spent the winter with.

"Speakin' of which, you better go get the women an' the rest of our truck, Samuel. They might just think we ain't comin' back for 'em."

As Samuel went to bring the women in, I asked Henry where Gabe was.

"He checkin' da traps we set. But he be back anytime now."

"You boys won't mind if we get out furs an' other stuff from under your robes, do you?" I asked.

"You not fooling'? You really put dem in dare?"

Nodding my head, I told him yes.

"Den of course, you can have dem back. Me an' Gabe, we do lots of trappin' dis winter, but I not ever see plews like I seen here. Dey are so tick, I don't hardly believe it myself. So you take you furs, we don't need dem."

"Thanks, Henry," I said as Samuel showed up with the rest of our plunder.

"Ahh, you finally decide to marry up, huh Round-Ball? Which one belongs to you?" he asked as they rode into camp.

"That one, there on the right. And the boy is my son, too."

"I never know you have a son. How come you never tell me till now about you wife, huh?"

"It's a long story, Henry. Maybe I'll tell you sometime. Right now, though, all I want to do is get our furs out so we can move on. There's still plenty of winter left to trap 'afore it's time to head to rendezvous."

"Maybe we better wait for Gabe 'afore you start to dig dem up, huh? He come back an' see all dese ponies here, he tink I been rubbed out. He shoot first, talk later, you know what I mean?"

"You got a point there, Henry. I sure don't want 'Ol Gabe shootin' at me. He don't miss too often."

"Dat for sure, dat for sure," he agreed.

We sat around the fire and talked about all sorts of things, waiting for Bridger to get back from checking his traps. By the time he finally arrived, it was close to sundown. He was surprised to see other trappers after not seeing anybody except Henry all winter, and he made us welcome.

"How you been, Round-Ball?" he asked.

"Been a rough winter, Gabe. Lost some friends a little while back. But other than that, ain't been too bad. The usual, you know. Occasional 'Rapaho raidin' party what thinks they're gonna steal my hair."

"I should have known you was here 'bouts somewhere. We seen some of your handiwork late last fall, hangin' upside down in the trees. They been botherin' you much this spring?" he wanted to know.

"Naw, we ain't had no trouble with 'em since last fall. We did steal a bunch of ponies off 'em this winter, but most of them was Ute horses they stole from us first."

"Henry here, he tells me you cached a bunch of furs here where we been sleepin.' That true?"

"Yea, they're right under you. Been there close to a month now. We was plannin' on trappin' up here through the rest of the spring, but since you're here, we'll just dig up our plews an' move on."

"There ain't no need to move far. There's plenty of beaver right here, an' we ain't gonna trap all of 'em. Be kind of nice to have the company, if you know what I mean, just in case them 'Rapaho decide to get an early start on killin' this season."

"Well, we thank you kindly, Gabe, but I think we'll just move on a ways. Maybe head over to the South Park. I ain't decided yet."

"I wouldn't bother with the South Park this year. The trappin' was fair, but when we was there, the plews weren't the best. That was just a month or so ago," Bridger told us.

"Guess that means we head to North Park, then. I was

savin' that for next fall's hunt, but if that's where the beaver is, than that's where we're gonna go," I decided.

"Best of luck to you both, then. I suppose we'll be seein' you down on Bear Lake again this year?"

"We'll be there, if the 'Rapaho don't raise our hair first," I replied. "An' thanks for the information on the South Park. I sure would of been sore if we went there an' the trappin' was as poor as you say. Since we both got wives now, an' both of 'em are expectin' babies, we need more furs for tradin.' You know how it is, Gabe."

"Yea, I know. The higher the price of plews, the more the traders charge us. It don't seem right, do it?" he asked.

"No, it don't, but it sure beats workin' for 'nother man back in the settlements."

"You said that true, Round-Ball."

Chapter 36

We moved on, towards the North Park the next day. Henry and Gabe wanted us to stay, I knew, but I felt like moving on. I liked my privacy when I was trapping. There was a bigger chance of loosing our hair in such a small group, but I felt that Samuel and I could handle most things that came our way.

"How 'bout this stream?" Samuel asked me four days later.

"Good as any, I suppose. Let's find a place to make camp, then we'll scout the stream."

After we had thrown up a bower for ourselves, I thought it would be best if we added another one for all our plunder. With spring almost on top of us, I knew there was bound to be rain. I didn't want all our furs getting ruined, just because I was feeling lazy.

When everything was stowed away, and the women had some food cooking, Samuel went downstream to check for beaver dams. I decided that it was time Buffalo Boy started learning how to find a good trapping area, and so I took him with me, going upstream. He needed to move around on his wounded leg anyway, and this was as good a time as any.

As we followed the meandering stream upwards, I started thinking on my son. He was starting to fill out some, growing taller too. He was going to be eight summers old before too long, and that's when I had bought my first rifle, a .45 caliber Pennsylvania made full stock. He was a little too short for any of the extra rifles we had, but if he wanted to earn it, I was going to buy him his own rifle when we reached rendezvous.

"What do you think 'bout havin' your own rifle, son?" I asked him.

"My very own? Not one of yours?"

"Yea, your very own. An' all the things you'll need for it, too. But there's a catch to it," I told him.

"What do I have to do, father? I would do about anything to have a rifle like yours."

"It's gonna be a lot of work, but I think you're up to it. Do you still remember how to lash the beaver pelts into the willow frames?" When he nodded, I continued. "Then this trip, I'll show you how to grain 'em after they're in the hoops. It's dirty work, an' takes time, but if you do this, then I'll buy you a rifle."

"When can I start?" he asked, full of excitement.

"First, we gotta catch some beaver," I said laughing. "You might not be so excited after a month of stretchin' an' grainin' all the beaver we plan on catchin.'"

"I will do it anyway," he told me. "It will help you and my Uncle, and you can spend more time trapping. The more you trap, the more we can trade for, right?" he asked.

"You catch on fast," I told him.

We saw several beaver ponds, but there wasn't much sign of them. Maybe this spot wasn't going to work for us. Buffalo Boy was feeling worn out, so I decided to send him back to the camp, but I wanted to go further up this stream. There just had to be more beaver than what we had seen, and I had a feeling they were further up.

Scouting the surrounding area as I followed the stream, I didn't spot any evidence of other trappers in the area, nor any

Indian sign. That was fine with me. I had gotten my fill of fighting last fall and into the winter.

The further up I went, the more numerous the beaver dams became. This is where I'm going to set my traps, I told myself. It wasn't too far from our camp, and I figured one man could trap here for a week or so. I hoped Samuel had found some good places to set his traps on the lower end of this stream. If not, we would have to move closer to this spot, and I would go higher.

There was no sign of spring this high up, as of yet, but I knew it would be only a matter of time before all this snow was gone. And when the snow started to go, we would too, following the runoff-swollen streams down into the flats.

It was close to dark by the time I got back to camp. Samuel had found what he thought was a pretty fair place to set his traps downstream. I told him what I had found further up, and so it was decided. He would trap downstream, and I would go upstream, each going his own way.

"You might be able to talk Rowdy into grainin' an' stretchin your plews, Samuel," I told him two weeks later. We had both been successful where we were trapping, but Samuel was getting worn out.

He was setting his traps in the morning, like I was, and then we both went out in the evening to empty them and reset them. But while I turned my day's catch over to Buffalo Boy to take care of, Samuel was stuck doing all his own work.

"I just might have to do that," he said. "Either that, or I'm gonna have to take a day off an' work on all the ones I already got."

"He does good work, but he don't do it for free," I told Samuel.

"What do you mean, he don't do it for free? How much are you givin' him for doin' all your work?"

"He ain't doin' all the work, just the stuff here in camp. An' he's gettin a rifle out of it, if I can find one short enough for him when we get to rendezvous."

"An' what do you think he's gonna charge me for lendin' a hand to his poor old Uncle," he said with a wink.

"Ask him, not me. He's become quite the little trader already. Why, just yesterday, he told me that if I keep catchin' so many beaver, he's gonna have to have more than a rifle to pay for his time an' his experience. Experience, he says! I think I created a little monster, that's what I think!"

Buffalo Boy was sitting between us as we talked, and I saw his face flush with embarrassment. Autumn Sky gave me a cold stare, and I thought I better say something to ease the situation.

"But his work's worth it," I said to Samuel, giving a broad smile to Buffalo Boy. "He's definitely earnin' that rifle," I added.

"Well, what 'bout it, Rowdy? How much you gonna charge your poor old Uncle Samuel to work on his hides?" Samuel asked him.

Squinting his eyes like he always did when he was thinking hard, Buffalo Boy thought for several minutes. The rest of us were waiting for his answer, all watching him. Nodding his head once, he turned to Samuel.

"Uncle, since my father is getting me a rifle and powder horn, I am going to need some powder, some lead for making balls, and a bullet mold. I would also need a new knife. But what I really want is a tomahawk, like yours. Is this a good trade?"

"Let's see. You want some powder, some lead, a mold, an' a knife. That right?" asked Samuel.

"And a tomahawk," reminded Buffalo Boy.

"Oh yea, an' a tomahawk. That seems a little steep to me,

beings as how trappin' season is just 'bout over," Samuel said, turning to wink at me. "But if that's the price, then I guess I gotta go with it. You gotta deal, Rowdy."

"He is not old enough to have any of these things," Autumn Sky said, getting to her feet. "And you," she said pointing to me. "You are only encouraging him in wanting these things. He is only a boy, do not forget."

"Yes, he is only a boy," I told her. "But this 'boy' has already taken several scalps. And you seem to have forgotten that, had it not been for this 'boy,' you would not be here right now."

"So now you are using him against me?" she asked.

"No, Autumn Sky, I am not using him against you. I am only trying to prove to you that he is old enough for these things. He will be a grown warrior before we know it, and I am only trying to help him in these things. Would you have him turn his back on his people and their way of life?"

"I would not have him do that, and you know it," she threw back at me.

"Then let him become what it is he needs to become: a warrior of the Ute people. I do not plan on taking him away from here, back to the settlements of the whites. There, he would only chafe under their rules and laws. He is a Ute. I am only trying to help him now, so that one day, he might be able to help his people."

"You sound very convincing, husband. But I still say he is too young for these things. Other boys his age do not have these things. Why should he? You will only make him an outsider within his own people, by making him into a white man."

"How do you figure it will make him a white man if he has his own rifle?" I asked. "There are several Ute who have these things. Does that make them white? And you use the cooking pots of the whites. Does that make you white as well?"

"You are twisting my words, Round-Ball. That is not what

I meant, and you know it. But you are his father," she said, starting to cry. "And I am only the woman who keeps your lodge and cooks for you."

Turning away, she ran into the bower. I looked at Samuel, my mouth hanging open in surprise.

"Well, that went well," he said sarcastically.

"Shut-up," I said back. "You're gonna be in this same spot someday, an' I'm gonna laugh at you when you are."

"Not me, little brother. My wife knows her place. She knows I make the decisions, not her," he said. Turning to Little Rabbit, he asked "Ain't that right?"

Little Rabbit stood up and threw the sewing she had been working on, hitting Samuel in the face and then stormed after her sister. As Samuel and I watched, our wives threw our sleeping robes out in front of the bower.

"Now look what you went an' did," Samuel wailed. "Thanks to you, I gotta sleep outside."

"You an' me both," I told him. Then, as we watched, Autumn Sky threw Buffalo Boy's robes out as well.

"If he wants to be so much like his father, then he can sleep outside, just like him!"

"Well," I said to Buffalo Boy. "You still think you wanna be like your father and your Uncle? I don't know what's got into either one of them women, but I sure hope they get over it."

Buffalo Boy swallowed hard as he got up and went to retrieve his sleeping robes.

"She is your wife," he said angrily, as he threw his robes down by the fire.

"An' she's also your mother, son. What happens between her an' me is one thing, but I don't ever want to hear you talkin' bad 'bout her. She's the one who took care of you for all that time when I was gone, an' she don't deserve to be treated this way by you."

"But it is alright for you to treat her this way?" he asked from under his robes.

"No, it's not," I answered. "But I don't think right now is the best time to talk to her, do you?"

When he didn't answer me, I went and picked up my own sleeping robes, laying them across the fire from Buffalo Boy. Crawling into them, I heard Samuel snickering as he got his robes.

"What're you laughin' 'bout?" I demanded.

"You sure got the trappin' all figured out, but you ain't got women figured out."

"An' I suppose you do?" I asked.

"Not me," he answered. "But at least I know when to keep my mouth shut an' when to open it. You better learn that, little brother, else you just might find yourself sleepin' out here all the time."

"Oh, just shut-up an' go to sleep," I said, throwing a stick of wood at him.

Rolling over, I snuggled deeper into my sleeping robes, trying to sleep. At least the crying coming from the bower had stopped. I couldn't understand the way Autumn Sky was thinking these days, and I guessed it was because of the baby she was carrying. Either way, I knew I had to straighten this out as soon as possible. I didn't want her mad at me.

Chapter 37

Rising even earlier than normal the next morning, I slipped away from the camp. I hadn't been able to sleep much, thinking on how I was going to patch things up with Autumn Sky. I still had no solution by the time I reached my first set.

Following my sets, emptying them of the beaver they held, I reached the last one. As I was resetting it, I heard a branch snap in the clear morning air. The sky was just starting to turn a light pink, promising another clear day. It was still cold this high up, but spring was on the way.

Wading from the pond created by the beaver, I set the carcass on the bank, moving closer to the rifle that lay there. Acting like nothing was wrong, I checked the priming on my rifle as I started skinning the last beaver, my ears tuned to every sound.

It was only a matter of time, I told myself. We were bound to be found by a hunting party of Arapaho. We were still several days from the village we had raided last winter, but with snow this deep, they would have been forced to hunt in a wider area, away from the village.

Finished with the beaver, I tossed the hide into the pile with the rest, wiping my knife on my leggins. Picking up my rifle as

I slipped the knife back into the sheath, I pulled the hammer back to full cock, waiting. There was someone or something out there, and I didn't want to be taken by surprise.

After several minutes of waiting, I gathered my plews in my left hand and threw them over my shoulder. Making sure my powder and ball was easy to get to, I started back to camp. There was one place along the stream that was very narrow, the trees coming right to the waters edge. That would be the spot for an ambush, I was thinking.

As I got closer to the place I figured they were, I shifted the beaver pelts. Now all I had to do was shrug my shoulder and they would fall off, freeing both arms. I still didn't know if it was Arapaho or not, but I was ready for whatever it was.

The snow suddenly exploded right in front of me as a man materialized. Definitely Arapaho, I saw, as I dropped the beaver, swinging the barrel of my rifle up under his chin.

The warrior let out a scream of pain as the barrel ripped him open, spilling him backwards. I hadn't hit him in the throat as I had planned, only grazing his chin with the front sight of the rifle. As he went down, I heard the loud war cries of at least two more behind me.

Dropping into a crouch, I spun around just as two more Indians broke from the trees. Holding the rifle in front of me, I pulled the trigger, hitting one of them in the stomach. He went down in a heap, and I knew he was out of the fight.

The last Arapaho threw the tomahawk he was charging me with, and I blocked it from hitting me with the empty rifle. Just as I was pulling the pistol from my belt, I felt the sharp pain in my back, sending me forward onto my face in the snow. It probably saved my life, causing the one who threw the tomahawk to sail right over me.

Rolling over as best as I could, I pulled the trigger on the pistol as soon as it lined up on the first one, the one who cut me. The small caliber ball hit him right under the nose, sending out a spray of blood that covered both of us.

Crawling to my knees in pain, I met the charge of the last brave, grabbing his knife hand as he slammed into me. We both tumbled back into the snow, and I ended up on my back, him on top of me.

Holding the knife hand with both of mine, the brave reached for a hold on my throat with his free hand. Tossing my head from side to side, I tried to get away from the hand, but failed to do so. The hand clamped down on my throat, cutting my wind off.

I had to do something fast, or I wasn't going to make it out of this one, so I started kicking at his back with both knees. It made the knife cut in my back hurt so bad, I thought I was going to pass out, but the grip loosened a little on my throat.

Twisting my body, I managed to turn both of us onto our sides, face to face. The warrior's face was contorted in pain as he concentrated on sending his knife into me, the veins standing out on his bare neck. I was starting to get weaker, and the longer this went on, the less chance I had.

Letting the war cry tear from my throat, I dug deep into the pit of my stomach for the extra strength I needed. Seeing the Arapaho's eyes widen in fear, I spit directly into his face, following it up with a knee into his groin.

The hand on my throat fell away, and I slammed my knee into his groin again. As the knife hand loosened, I suddenly pulled him towards me, butting him in the head with my own. Seeing stars, I shook my head to try and clear it. Feeling the blood start to flow from a cut on my forehead from the force of the blow, I let go and rolled away.

The Arapaho warrior was the first one to gain his feet, and he dove for me again. This time, though, I was ready for him. Taking one step to the side, I grabbed his hair as he flew past me, jerking him backward and twisting. It snapped his neck, and I dropped him.

Staggering to the stream, I splashed into it. I dunked my head under the water, sweeping my hand across my face when I came up to get the water from my eyes. The cut on my forehead, from when I had hit the Arapaho, was bleeding badly. The blood was mixing with the water as it rolled off my face, making it seem worse than it really was.

Stumbling out of the water, I went to get my rifle and pistol from where I had dropped them. After reloading both of them, I picked up the beaver I had caught and started back to camp. I was in no shape to scalp these three right now, but I would send Samuel back to do it and find their ponies.

Hunching my back against the pain, I reached camp to find Samuel had already returned from checking his traps. With all of them staring at me, I went to the fire, dropping the beaver beside Buffalo Boy.

"Run into a tree?" Samuel asked me.

"Somethin' like that," I said, dropping down as best as I could.

"Must have been a big tree," Samuel commented, handing me a cup of coffee.

"More like three trees."

Autumn Sky went to the second bower, coming back with my medicines. As she knelt down in front of me, I took her wrist in my hands.

"Please, forgive me for last night. I should have talked to you before I promised him a gun," I told her.

"There is nothing to forgive, husband," she said. "You are his father, and you know what is best, not only for him, but for me as well. I was wrong to question your decisions."

"You better get them wet clothes off, or you're gonna be in trouble," Samuel said as Autumn Sky finished cleaning my head wound.

"You might have to help me," I said. "Think I got a nasty cut on my back, an' my shirt feels like it's already stuck."

Samuel went around behind me to look at the slice in my hunting shirt, opening it as far as he could. Letting out a whistle, he turned to Autumn Sky.

"We better take care of this cut before we take the shirt off," he told her. "It's pretty deep, Razor," he said.

"Let her take care of it," I said indicating Autumn Sky. "I need you to go back up the stream an' scalp them dogs. Hang 'em in the trees like we normally do, then find their ponies. There was only three of 'em, but there could be others nearby we ain't seen yet."

"You want to send the rest of 'em the message not to mess with us, that right?"

"Yea, somethin' like that," I told him. Autumn Sky was trying to pull the shirt free from my back, and it caused me to wince and cry out in pain.

"Easy, woman," I told her. "That hurts."

"Stop acting like a child, Round-Ball. It must be done and you know it," she said, continuing to torture me.

As Samuel went after the scalps and ponies, I called Buffalo Boy over to where I sat.

"Son, I need for you to go get all the extra rifles. Check 'em an' make sure they're loaded. After that, I want you to go bring the horses in closer, but bring my mule right into camp. She can smell them stinkin' 'Rapaho long before I can."

Nodding his head, he was gone. As Autumn Sky finished cleaning the knife wound on my back, I looked around our camp. We were starting to get spread out too much. When she was done sewing me back up, I planned on moving things in closer if Samuel wasn't back by then.

Calling Little Rabbit over, Autumn Sky wanted her to watch as she sewed me back up.

"If your husband is like mine," she told her, "then you will need to learn how to do this. Men cannot help the way they are, always wanting to fight with each other."

"Ouch," I screamed as the needle pierced my back. "You ain't gotta be so rough."

"Stop acting like a baby," she said. "I know it hurts, but it must be done. You are lucky, you know," she added.

"How am I lucky?" I sure didn't feel lucky at that point in time.

"It could be worse. You could have your brother doing this instead of me. At least I have done this before."

She had a point there. Samuel wasn't able to sew my leg up after the run-in we had with that grizzly. He said he didn't know how to sew. He needed to take some lessons from these women on sewing. Might just come in handy one of these days.

Samuel and Buffalo Boy arrived back in camp at the same time, both leading animals. When Samuel took the new ponies over to the rest of our herd, though, our animals started bucking around, not wanting anything to do with them. Must be the stink of them Arapaho, I thought.

"Just tie 'em off on the other side of camp, Samuel." I said to him. "They'll get used to each other afore too long."

As he walked the ponies across to the other side of camp, he had the same thought as me.

"Think we ought to pull our traps an' move on out of here? It don't seem right there was only three of them 'Rapaho. I think there's more here 'bouts we ain't seen, an' when they don't come back—"

"Yea, the rest of 'em are gonna come lookin' for 'em," I finished for him.

"Let's start packin' up all our plunder. I think we should be safe enough here until tomorrow, then we'll move out of here.

It's still a little early to head to Bear Lake, but I would rather lose some time trappin' than my hair."

"Gotta agree with you on that one," Samuel replied as he started moving the piles of beaver closer into the camp. "You think you can move 'round good enough to lend a hand, or are you just gonna lay there?" he asked.

"If you think this here little cut is gonna keep me down, you don't know me as well as you should, Samuel. I been shot, stabbed, sliced, beat, an' had more than one arrow punch holes in this hide of mine. An' I always managed to get the job done. This time ain't no different," I said as I got to my feet.

"I didn't mean nothin' by it, I was just wonderin,' that's all," he said defensively.

"I know," I said. "I ain't mad at you. I just wanna finish up this coffee afore you do," I said with a grin.

"You an' your coffee," he said, shaking his head. "We better get twice as much this year, the way you go through it."

"Quit your whinin' an' start gettin' them plews lashed into packs," I replied.

Chapter 38

At sunrise the next morning, we pulled out. Not wanting to head directly west towards the Arapaho village I knew was there somewhere, we decided to go south for a ways first. Then we would swing west and go to Bear Lake.

The rains started to fall on us the second day out, a light drizzle. By the middle of the day, it turned into a steady downpour, soaking all of us to the skin.

"Head for them trees," I told Samuel. I was letting him lead us so he could get a feel for the land. I was riding near the middle of the packhorse string, checking our back trail in case we were followed. Buffalo Boy and the two women were in between Samuel and me.

"You think this is gonna let up anytime soon?" Samuel asked as we entered the tree line.

"Hard tellin.' Probably not, an' that's why I wanna camp early. I'm soaked to the skin an' cold."

"You just want some coffee, I know," he said.

"No, we ain't gonna have a fire. I gotta funny feelin' we're bein' followed, an' there ain't no sense in givin' our position away."

"Then how we gonna dry out an' warm up?"

"We'll wrap up in our sleepin' robes to try an' stay warm,

but we're just gonna have to stay wet. At least until we know for sure if we are bein' followed."

"How long we gonna be stayin' here?"

"Till tomorrow," I replied. "Then we'll move on again."

As we covered ourselves with our sleeping robes, I was hoping we weren't being followed. My back wound was giving me some pain from twisting around in the saddle all day, watching our back trail. I wasn't in shape for a fight, and I knew it.

Shortly before sundown, at least as much of one as we were going to get, I heard my mule stomping her foot. That was a sure indication that she smelled something that didn't belong.

Cocking my rifle, I parted the buffalo robe covering my head just enough to peek out. Looking to my mule, I saw her head swiveled in the direction we had come from.

"Samuel," I whispered, "we got company comin.'"

"Where? I can't see nothin' with all this rain," he whispered back.

"Watch my mule."

I heard the muffled cocking of guns from under the buffalo robes, realizing we were all awake. I had made sure everyone had at least one rifle each and that they were all ready before we had covered up to wait out the night.

I couldn't see anybody, but I trusted my mule. If she smelled something, than something was definitely around. And as I watched our trail, I saw them start across the small meadow we had crossed.

There were seven in all, and it looked like they were trying to make it to the trees on the opposite side of the meadow, away from us. Either they knew we were somewhere close, or else they were just lucky.

We watched in horror as they started making their camp, not over four hundred yards from us. I hoped it was far enough away for the horses not to smell each other. That would surely give our hiding place away.

As we sat there watching them build a fire, I thought about trying to slip away in the night. We needed to put as much distance between them and us as possible. Chances were, they had been following our trail, only moving into the trees for the night because of the coming darkness. And in the morning, they would pick up the trail again, if the rain didn't wash out all our tracks.

Not trusting the horses to be quiet if we tried to escape in the night, I realized the only other thing we could do was attack them tonight. Try to scatter their horses and shake their confidence. Maybe even kill a few of them.

When it was full dark, I scooted closer to Samuel so we could try and figure a way out of this one.

"How we gonna play this?" he asked.

"Only thing I can think of is to creep on into their camp an' kill as many of 'em as we can," I whispered.

"What 'bout the women an' Buffalo Boy?"

"You're gonna stay here with 'em while I go in," I told him. "That way, if anythin' happens to me, you can lead 'em out of here."

"I don't like it," he replied. "Why don't we just wait till mornin,' then they'll move on. The rain should wash out our tracks tonight, an' when they don't find 'em, they'll keep goin' on the way they're headed."

"I don't wanna chance that, Samuel. By mornin,' they'll be able to see our horses. No, I gotta go in an' whittle 'em down some."

"So what do you want us to do?"

"Just sit here an' wait for the ruckus to start. Then get on out of here. I'll catch up as soon as I can."

"Where you want us to go?"

"Head due west. There's a big valley 'bout a half a days ride from here. A third of the way up the valley, strike north. Once you get up in the hills a ways, find a good place to sit an' watch for me. Or them," I added.

"How long do we wait?" he wanted to know.

"I should be there no later than dark. If I'm not, you'll know I went under."

"Don't talk like that, Razor. You sound like you already know you ain't gonna make it."

I was under no illusion about what could happen. There was every chance they would kill me, or worse yet, capture me. In that case, I would wish I was dead. But it had to be done, no matter the cost to me. Autumn Sky and Little Rabbit were going to have babies, and they, along with Buffalo Boy and Samuel, deserved every chance I could give them.

"I'll be alright," I told him, grasping his hand.

Sliding back over to Autumn Sky and Buffalo Boy, I quickly told them what I was going to do. Both of them started to protest, but I held up my hand, stopping them.

"It must be this way," I told them. "Listen to Arrow Catcher and do exactly as he says. I will catch up to you tomorrow night, so do not be worried," I added. I was worried about it, but didn't want them to know it.

Giving both of them a quick hug, I slipped through the trees, heading for the Arapaho camp. I wished I wasn't so wet. My buckskins were heavy with water, forcing me to use up more energy than I wanted, and they were starting to chafe me in all the wrong places.

Circling downwind from their horses so they wouldn't smell me, I moved in closer, a little at a time. I needed a closer look at how they were set up before I could know just what I was going to do. There was no snow down this low, so I didn't have to worry about a reflection alerting them to my presence or crunching underfoot. Likewise, the rain had softened the forest debris on the ground, making it less likely that I would snap a branch and alert them to my presence.

Edging closer and closer, I found a good spot to observe the camp. After making sure I was well hidden, I watched the camp, trying to get an idea of who was their leader. He was the first one who had to go.

After watching for several minutes, I suddenly realized there were only five of them in camp. I was sure I had counted seven as they crossed the meadow. That meant they had posted two guards, one of which I was sure was with the horses. I needed to find the guards first so I knew where they would be coming from when the shooting started.

Not wanting to move around too much, I decided to wait here until they changed the guards. While I was waiting, I realized I was dog-tired. Tired of traveling, tired of fighting the Arapaho, tired of it all. But there was no way I was going to go back to the settlements. I could live with the Ute for the rest of my days, raising my family and trapping when I wanted.

While I was pondering all this, two of those in camp got up and left. Changing of the guards, just what I had been waiting for. One headed for the horses, as I suspected, and the other one moved off in the opposite direction. Shortly, the other two came back to the fire.

Judging from the time the second Arapaho brave had headed out away from the horses, until the one he relieved came back, I knew he wasn't very far from the camp. When I started shooting, he would more than likely come rushing back. Good, I thought. I won't have to go find him.

Waiting for the two guards to settle in, I watched the others. These braves were not young boys. They were hardened warriors, tried and true. Looked like I might have bit off more than I could chew this time. But I had to follow through with it in order to give my wife and the others time to escape.

Checking the charge on my rifle again, I made sure the powder was dry, adding a little bit more to the pan. Leaning it against the deadfall in front of me, I drew both pistols from my belt. After making sure both of them were charged and ready to go, I took one more look at the camp.

Going over the actions in my mind that I was going to make, I was suddenly brought up short. That brave by the fire. He was much larger than the others, and I noticed for the first time that he carried a rifle. His back was to me, but the more I watched his movements, the more sure I became.

This was a white man.

Chapter 39

What was a white man, a trapper from the looks of him, doing with these stinking Arapaho dogs? Somewhat in shock, I slid down behind the downfall I was using as a rest. There was something going on here that I didn't understand, and I knew I had to get to the bottom of it.

Who was this trapper? What was he doing with these Arapaho braves? There were too many questions and not any answers. Maybe if I could see his face, I might have a better understanding.

Turning back to face the camp, I poked my head above the downed tree. The braves were getting ready to bed down for the night, each one of them pulling a robe from their packs. What I needed to do was to get this white man all by himself so I could talk to him.

As he drew his robes from his pack, he turned just enough for me to see his face. It was covered with whiskers, but I knew I had seen him before. But then, after all the years I had spent up here trapping, I had seen just about every trapper at one time or another. Now it was a matter of putting a name to the face.

Poking my face a little higher, I waved my arm, hoping to draw his attention. He suddenly stood very still but only for a few seconds. He had seen me, I knew.

Saying something to the others, he walked away from the fire, but not directly towards me. Stuffing my pistols back into my belt, I started creeping in his direction. When I figured I was close to where he was, I stopped. There was no sound from the camp, and when the branch snapped, it was not ten feet from me.

"Lucky for you nobody else saw that wave," came a deep voice from the darkness.

"What, in all that's holy, is a white man doin' with a 'Rapaho war party?" I asked the voice.

"Lookin' for you," came the reply. "That is if you're the one they call 'Round-Ball.'"

"An' who might you be? I seen your face afore, but I can't pin a name on it."

"Harris. Moses Harris be my handle. Are you the one we been lookin' for?"

"Yea, that be me. But I don't understand what you're doin' with these murderin' dogs, Harris. What gives here?"

"These boys been sent to find you. Not to kill you, mind tell. They're bringin' you a message from their chief, Blue Calf. An' when I heard they was lookin' for a white man, I figured I better come along, in case you don't understand the lingo of these here 'Rapaho."

"That's mighty kind of you, Harris," I said. I didn't trust him, not by a long shot. I couldn't trust anybody that ran with an Arapaho war party.

"So what's this here message you been sent to tell me?" I asked.

"Seems you been goin' 'round killin' 'Rapaho warriors, an' their gettin' kind of—"

"I only kill 'em when they attack me first, Harris. They tell you that too?" I asked. I was starting to get a funny feeling in the pit of my stomach.

"Just hold on, Round-Ball. They did tell me 'bout that.

They also told me you spent a winter doin' nothin' but killin' their braves every chance you got."

"Yea, I did do that. But they had it comin' for somethin' they done to me first," I added.

"Your wife an' partner. They told me that too. But things is different with 'em now. They got 'em a new chief. An' he don't want you killin' anymore of his braves. You know how many you killed in the last few years?"

"No, I ain't one to keep track of such things. Why?"

"You've killed twenty-eight of 'em since they killed your wife an' partner. That's a lot of warriors they've lost to you. An' you're only one man," he added. I detected a little admiration in his voice, but I brushed it aside.

"How they know it was me that killed all them warriors?" I asked.

"You're the only one who strips 'em an' hangs 'em upside down in the trees. So they know it's you."

"What am I suppose to do when they attack me, Harris? Let 'em put me under? I don't think so. An' if them, or you, think I ain't gonna defend myself when I'm attacked, then you're all off the deep end."

"We been sent here to ask you to stop killin.' You fulfilled your blood vengeance, many times over, for what happened. Blue Calf wants to offer peace between you an' them."

"I don't buy it, Harris. That don't sound like no 'Rapaho, talkin' peace. I been up here a long time, an' I never been offered peace afore."

"Well, it's true. Blue Calf really wants peace between you an' him."

"How do I know this ain't no trick?" I asked.

"Blue Calf has sent you his personal guarantee, in the form of his very own war shield. We're supposed to give it to you, to hang up in your camp. That way, any 'Rapaho that come across you will see it and know that you're protected. And," he added, "he's also told all his warriors that if any of 'em don't abide by the peace he's offered you, he's gonna personally kill 'em. That is if you don't kill 'em first."

"An' I'm suppose to take your word on this?" I asked.

"I'll do you even one better. We'll pull out in the mornin' an' head back the way we come. I'll leave the shield behind for you, hangin' in the trees. That way you know I been tellin' you true."

"What 'bout the rest of my party, them that are with me now? This cover them too?"

"Yea, it covers 'em. Anybody in your camp's covered by the shield."

"An' I can still trap up there, in the Parks? 'Cause if I can't, then there ain't no point in takin' this offer."

"You can trap wherever you want to. He just wants you to stop killin' his braves an' hangin' 'em upside down in the trees, that's all."

"I don't know if I trust him. Or you," I added. "What kind of man would I be if I believed everythin' I was told? I'll tell you. I would be a dead man, that's what kind.

"Now let me think on this a minute. You say you ain't here with these 'Rapaho to kill us, right? An' this new chief of theirs, he wants peace between him an' me. All I gotta do is hang his personal war shield up whenever I camp, an' they're gonna leave us be. That sound 'bout right, Harris?"

"Yea, 'cept the part 'bout you stoppin' killin' 'Rapaho warriors. You kind of left that one out, didn't you?"

"Well, I can't agree to that, at least till I get me some proof they're gonna do as he says. An' if they attack me first, then I'm gonna defend myself an' the rest of 'em with me. Show me you mean what you say, an' I'll agree to this truce with the 'Rapaho," I told him.

"I'll do just what I said. Tomorrow mornin,' we'll pull out, headin' back north to our village. But I'll leave the shield behind for you. How's that for proof?"

"How I know you ain't gonna double back an' kill us anyway?"

"You just gotta trust me on this, Round-Ball. But you better make up your mind mighty fast. I been gone too long already, an' they're gonna come lookin' for me anytime. Just take the deal. You won't be sorry you did."

"Alright, you got a deal. But I give you fair warnin,' Harris. I find out you lied to me, an' I'll make sure you regret it, right up till the time I light you on fire in front of the whole Ute nation. You understand me, boy?"

"Yea, I got you. Now get out of here, afore they come lookin' for me."

"If they ain't suppose to kill me, why you so worried 'bout it? But I see the point you're tryin' to make, Harris. If you an' these 'Rapaho try anythin' when you leave, I'm gonna kill ever' one of you."

Turning around, I made fast tracks out of there, but not directly back to the others. I still didn't know if I trusted Harris or not, and I wasn't about to stake the lives of Autumn Sky and Buffalo Boy on it. He might just decide to try and bring my head in. That would be a big coup for him.

Hiding behind a tree, I watched as Harris went back to the fire. Well, at least he wasn't coming after me tonight. I would just have to wait for the sun to come up in the morning to see if he was telling me the truth or not.

Samuel and the others would be worried by now, not hearing anything from the Arapaho camp. I thought I better get back over there, and let them know what was happening. Harris had seemed like he was telling the truth, but only time would tell.

"You think he's tellin' the truth?" Samuel asked when I told him of finding Harris in the Arapaho camp and then of my talk with him. He was just a skeptical as I was, and I was glad I wasn't the only one.

"No tellin,' but I told him I would wait for the sun to come up before I made up my mind. It sure would be nice, huh? Not havin' to worry 'bout them murderin' dogs sneakin' up on us while we're trappin.'"

"Yea, that would be nice," he agreed.

"You wanna watch while I get some sleep? Wake me in a couple of hours, then I'll wake everyone afore it's light so we can get ready for 'em, in case they change their minds."

But they didn't change their minds. It was just as Harris had said. We waited a good hour after they pulled out before I went back to their camp. After making a full circle around the place they had camped, I knew they were gone.

The decorated war shield was hanging in a tree, just like I had been told. Taking it down, I was surprised at the intricate painting covering its surface. It was about as big as one of the beaver plews stretched into a willow hoop frame, the whole surface covered with designs.

In the very center, there was a lone buffalo calf, painted blue. It was surrounded by many lodges in a circle. There was a river cutting across one side, and I made out the meat drying racks, heavy with meat, beside it. On one side there were four eagle feathers tied to the shield, and on the other was a piece of what I took to be a patch of buffalo hide, the hair painted blue.

This shield belonged to a very important man, I knew from the workmanship alone. I was starting to think Harris had told the truth, and this chief, Blue Calf, really wanted peace. Well, as long as they kept their end of this deal, then I would too.

Chapter 40

When we finally got to the rendezvous, the traders had already been there for close to a week. Lucky for us, though, most of the trappers were still trading in their winter's take of furs for whiskey. I wanted to get our furs traded off in a hurry and trade for what we needed before they ran out of goods.

Samuel wanted to get good and drunk, and I had to admit he had it coming after all he had been through with me in the past year. I didn't take to drinking whiskey myself, but there were some that did. Mostly, they did it to help them forget all the troubles they had seen and survived for the past year. So I figured to let Samuel have his drunk, if that's what he wanted. He would find out that after a year of being dry, it wasn't going to take much to get the job done.

After unloading all our plews on the traders, we got everything I wanted to get, except for the rifle for Buffalo Boy. Try as I might, there just wasn't one short enough for him. Autumn Sky was pleased about it, but both Buffalo Boy and me, we were sorely disappointed. Maybe I could do some trading with another trapper for one, I thought.

"Who you got there, Round-Ball?" asked my old friend, Daniel Potts.

We were headed back to our camp, and as we were passing a bunch of high-spirited trappers, all engaged in competition with throwing knives, Daniel spotted us.

"This here's my son, Buffalo Boy, Daniel," I told him. "We just come from the trader's tent, an' he ain't too happy right now."

"What seems to be the problem?" he asked.

"Well, I promised him his first rifle this year, an' he earned it this spring. Lashed my pelts into hoops, then fleshed an' grained 'em. You know how hard that gets at times. Anyway, I promised him a rifle this year, but I ain't been able to find one short enough for him. That's why he has such a long face," I explained.

"Might be, I could help you out. That is, if you got somethin' left to trade with," Daniel said.

"You watchin this here knife throwin,' or are you playin'?" I asked him, my interest showing through.

"Naw, I'm just watchin.' But I do need to read a letter for a friend in a little while. You gonna be at your camp later?" he asked.

"Yea, we'll be there. We're camped over by them trees," I said, pointing towards our camp.

"Come on over when you're done. You can meet my wife, an' we might be able to talk her into cookin' us somethin' to eat. She's fixin' to have a baby in 'nother couple of moons, an' she don't get around like she used to, but we'll figure somethin' out when you get there."

"Sounds right fine to me. I'll be there as soon as I can. An' I'll bring the rifle with me so we can size it up on him. Anythin' else he's needin' for it?"

"Naw, not right away. He made a deal with my brother for some other things, an' we'll wait to see how it fits him 'fore we get the rest. But if you got a mold for it, bring it along too. I'd rather see you get my hard earned money than them traders," I added.

As Buffalo Boy and I were headed back to our camp, I told him what Daniel and I had talked about. He had been trying to follow along as we spoke English, but he couldn't keep up. When I mentioned the rifle, he became his old self, full of excitement.

"But we still need to wait and see if this is the right gun for you. It may not work out, so do not get too excited yet," I told him in Ute.

When we reached camp, I was surprised to see Samuel up and about. He had sat around the fire last night, slowly getting drunk, just like he wanted to do. The rest of us were there as well, but we left him alone. At times, I saw tears running down his cheeks but didn't say anything. I suppose he was remembering his father and all they had been through in the short time they had been together.

Autumn Sky and Little Rabbit were nowhere in sight when we got there. When I asked Samuel about it, he shrugged his shoulders.

"I been up for a while now, but they was gone already. I figured they went with you to the traders' tent," he said.

"No, they didn't go with us. Makes me a little worried, though. Neither one of 'em knows that much English. I think we better go look for 'em. What do you think?" I asked him.

"I think you're right. As drunk as these boys get, there ain't no tellin' what might happen. Let me get my rifle, an' I'll be ready."

Thinking on that, I figured I better get my rifle too. We were supposed to meet Daniel here in awhile, but this was more important. I'm sure he would understand if I wasn't here and he got here before we returned.

"I know they ain't over towards the traders' tent. We just came from there. An' they ain't down by the knife throwin,' either. Why don't you head over towards that stream, an' me an' Rowdy will walk through some of the camps. If you ain't found 'em in 'bout half an hour, meet up back here."

Nodding his head, Samuel went one way, me and Buffalo Boy going the other. Those trappers nearest to us knew who the women were, but some of the others didn't, and I was starting to get real worried.

There were a lot of different Indian tribes here, but for the most part, they knew this was neutral ground. There was an unwritten law that everyone left their differences behind when they were here. But there were some, red and white both, that if given the chance, would take advantage of two Indian women alone.

We hadn't gone far when we heard Samuel bellow in rage, followed by a shot. We were only a few hundred yards from camp, and Buffalo Boy and I turned around, sprinting towards the sound.

Crashing through the brush along the stream, we found Samuel and the two women. Samuel was reloading as fast as he could, and as I looked, I saw two Indian braves running as fast as they could.

Throwing my rifle to my shoulder, I shot the closest one, just as Samuel finished reloading. As he lined up for his shot, I spotted something moving in the brush by the stream. Pulling my pistol from my belt, I advanced towards it.

As Samuel's gun went off, I heard the sound of running feet. Lots of them, all headed this way. Knowing they were trappers, I parted the brush with my rifle, the pistol in my other hand, ready for a quick shot. But this brave wasn't going anywhere. He was bleeding from his left side, and then I saw the bone sticking out of his leg.

Leaving him there, I went back to where Samuel was telling the other trappers what had happened.

"These three was tryin' to rape our wives," he said. I could hear the anger and pain in his voice as I went to Autumn Sky.

She was still lying there, her face pale. Beside her, Little Rabbit was starting to get to her feet.

Kneeling beside my wife, I reached for her as she was starting to get up. She flinched at my touch and started to crawl away before she realized it was me. When it dawned on her who I was, she flew into my arms, sobbing great tears.

Buffalo Boy had come up to see how his mother was doing, and as I watched, his hands curled into fists. His whole body was starting to shake, and I knew what he was going to do before he did. As he started to turn away, I called out to him.

"No, son. Do not do it. We need to talk to him first. Then, you can do what you need to do."

I knew he was on his way to finish off the last brave, but we needed to see what tribe he was from first. The other two were already dead, and I wasn't sure if they had actually raped the women. The fact that they had even tried was enough to justify our actions, but I didn't want the last one dead yet.

Samuel was holding onto Little Rabbit as Autumn Sky and I joined them, standing there with the trappers who had come to see what was happening. One of the trappers was following Buffalo Boy over to the wounded Indian, and together, they dragged him over to us.

"What you want to do with 'em, Round-Ball?" a voice asked. I knew that voice! Scanning the group of trappers, I spotted him. Moses Harris.

As Buffalo Boy and the trapper dragged the wounded Indian into our midst, I saw he was an Arapaho. So much for the truce between us and them, I thought. But then I had another idea.

"Harris, you told me back in the mountains that if the 'Rapaho attacked me again, that Blue Calf would kill 'em if I didn't. Now's the chance for you to prove it. Right here an' now. So go get him, an' bring him here," I ordered.

"Sure, I'll go get him. But you better promise me no harm

is gonna come to him, once he gets here. Otherwise, I ain't gonna bring him."

"Depends on if he's gonna do like he said or not," I told him. My whole body was starting to shake with anger now, and I found myself clenching my hands and teeth, trying to hold back the urge to kill.

As Harris left to get Blue Calf, I took Autumn Sky to one side of the gathering of trappers. She was pretty shook up, I could tell, about being around so many white men. But I had to know if these Arapaho had done the deed or not.

"Are you doing well?" I asked her. When she nodded her head, I asked her to tell me what had happened.

"Little Rabbit and I were going to the stream to wash, when these three enemies saw us. We started to run back to our camp, but they were faster than us. When they caught us, they threw us down on the ground."

Here, she stopped her story, shaking her head. I was thinking the worst had happened to them. As I lifted my arms from her, she looked up at me.

"They did not have enough time to do what they were planning to do, though. Arrow Catcher arrived before they could do more than jeer and curse us. I tried to tell them about the truce between you and their chief, but they did not understand me.

"When Arrow Catcher came through the brush, he went crazy. Shooting and screaming at them, he ran them off. Then you arrived," she finished.

Hearing a commotion behind us, I turned to see Harris come riding up on his pony. With him was the man I knew had to be Blue Calf.

As they dismounted, I studied Blue Calf. He was tall for an Arapaho, a little taller than me, in fact. He wore a buckskin vest that was decorated with fancy quillwork and a simple breechclout. His face was unpainted, his black braids framing his almost square face. He carried a war shield, exactly like the one I had been given.

As Blue Calf strode up to his downed brave, I saw the muscles in his arms ripple with the movement. Unless I missed my guess, this man was very strong, physically. It was no wonder he had been chosen for their chief.

When he reached the brave, he squatted down by his side. After a quick exchange of words I didn't understand, he stood back up. Moses Harris came over to me, motioning for Blue Calf to follow.

"This here is Blue Calf, chief of the 'Rapaho. When I told him what happened, he was anxious to meet the man who has killed so many of his warriors," Harris told me.

As Harris told Blue Calf who I was, I saw he was looking me over real good. Probably surprised him I wasn't the giant of a man he had been told I was.

"He thought you were gonna be bigger," Harris said with a slight smile.

"Never mind 'bout me. Ask him what he's gonna do with this brave of his. He broke the truce we had by tryin' to rape my wife, an' he said he would kill any of 'em what tangled with me an' mine. Is he gonna be true to his word?"

Harris turned back to Blue Calf, and they talked back and forth for a few minutes. When they were finished, Blue Calf went back over to his wounded warrior.

"Well, I guess he meant what he said last spring, Round-Ball. He's tellin' his brave that he broke the truce an' that he knew what would happen if he did," Harris said.

Then, with everyone watching, Blue Calf drew his knife from his sheath. Walking around behind the doomed man, Blue Calf lifted his eyes to mine. Saying something in Arapaho, he slit the man's throat, the blood spraying out in a great arc.

Chapter 41

Nobody was more surprised than me at what Blue Calf had just done. As the trappers milling around started to wander off, I gathered my small party up, and headed back towards camp. Looking up, I saw Daniel Potts heading towards us, a confused look on his face.

"What happened?" he asked.

"Tell you later, Daniel. I need to get these women back to camp, an' away from all these folks that want to talk 'bout it. They don't need to keep hearin' it."

Nodding his head, Daniel followed us back to our camp. When we got there, he added some wood to the dying fire as Samuel and I got the two women settled back into the brush bowers we had made. Making sure they were as comfortable as they could be, Samuel and me went to the fire.

Looking around, I didn't see Buffalo Boy. When I asked Daniel if he had seen him, he told me he saw him head back the way we had come, back towards the scene we had just left. Not liking the sound of that, I grabbed up my rifle and started after him. But just as I was on the outskirts of camp, I saw him coming up, holding something in his hands. Then I noticed the blood.

"Son," I said as he came up to me. "Please tell me you did not scalp them." I knew he had, but I couldn't help but ask.

"Yes, father, I scalped those enemies," he said with a crooked grin. "The Arapaho chief left, so I returned to count coup on them for what they did to my mother and her sister." He said it proudly, acting like he had been doing this kind of thing all his life. And then I realized that he had been, from that first time when he was five years old. But this could cause some serious problems for us, scalping them Arapaho right in front of everyone.

As we walked up to the fire, I saw the worried look on Daniel's face. We both knew this was going to destroy the truce I had with the Arapaho. Squatting down beside my son, I took the scalps from him and laid them on the ground.

"Rowdy, do you know what you just did?" I asked him.

"I did what I have been taught to do. I scalped the enemies of my people."

"Yes, you sure did do that," I said, nodding my head at the fresh scalps.

"But you also destroyed the truce we had between the Arapaho and our family. Now, we must fight them all the time again," I told him in Ute. I wanted him to understand the consequences of what he had done very clearly.

But it was lost on him.

"There is not an Arapaho dog ever born that you cannot kill, father. I am proud of what I have done. And when the rest of the Arapaho dogs see how I cut up their warriors, they will think about it before they try to attack us again."

"You cut them up and scalped them?" Samuel asked in shock.

"Yes, Uncle," he replied.

"We better think 'bout gettin' out of here, Razor," Samuel stated. "When them 'Rapaho go back to get them bodies, there's gonna be nothin' but trouble for us."

I had been thinking the same thing. Nodding my head at him, I told him he was right.

"Best you an' Rowdy start packin' up all our plunder. I still got some business with Daniel, but soon as I'm done, I'll lend a hand."

As Samuel and Buffalo Boy got up to start the packing, Daniel passed me the rifle.

It was a .36 caliber flintlock, a little smaller than I wanted, but it was about the right size for Buffalo Boy. After checking the stock over for cracks, I looked at the lock for signs of stress. Not finding any, I cocked it and released the hammer several times to check the condition of the springs. Everything was in good working order with that, so I looked down the barrel. There was no pitting that I could see, only a very light coating of oil.

Nodding my head at Daniel, I asked when was the last time it was fired.

"It's been awhile," he replied. "It's a little small for me to shoot, so I didn't use it that often. Only during those times when I needed an extra round, if you know what I mean," he said.

"You got a mold for it?"

"Yea, an' I also got a couple of jags an' some other things I thought I'd throw in. That is if you're interested in tradin' for it."

"I'm interested in it," I told him. "But what's it gonna cost me?"

"Well, you said somethin' 'bout a meal earlier. How 'bout you feed me some of your wife's cookin,' an' we'll call it even."

"That don't seem like much for a rifle, Daniel," I said.

"It may not seem like much to you, but for a man that's been eatin' his own cookin' for as long as I have, it's enough. 'Sides, I'm tired of packin' it around with me," he said with a grin.

"Then it's a deal."

Chapter 42

It was close to dusk by the time we had everything loaded on the horses and were ready to leave. There were a few things I had wanted to do before leaving the rendezvous, but the safety of my family was more important. Besides, I told myself, there was always next year. That is if I managed to make it through another one.

Daniel Potts had agreed to run interference for me with the Arapaho and Moses Harris, if they came looking for blood. And I had no doubt that they would. It might not be right away, but sooner or later, they would catch up to us. Right now, all I wanted to do was put some distance between them and us.

"Where we headed, little brother?" Samuel asked after we had put an hour behind us.

"Not sure yet. But I been doin' some thinkin' on it. It's still way too early for the fall hunt, and with the women in this condition, I think we better just find a place to hole up for a few moons."

"And then?" he asked.

"I got me an idea 'bout that too, but we best take on one thing at a time. We'll see what the next few moons bring, and then we'll all make the decision," I told him.

"You think them 'Rapaho are gonna follow us?"

"I 'spect so. They'll send out some of the hotheaded youngsters after us, an' see how they do. But I don't look for 'em to follow us tonight. They'll wait till sunup 'fore they head out. Maybe Daniel can talk 'em out of it, but I doubt it. They're gonna follow. An' when they do, I wanna be a long way from here."

At daybreak, we stopped long enough to make some coffee and cook up a small meal. Then it was back in the saddle for another day of moving on. I wasn't going to make it easy for those that were sure to be following us. We twisted back on our own trail a time or two, confusing the tracks as much as we could without spending a lot of time doing it.

About mid-day, we stopped again for a short rest. We might need these horses to move in a hurry, and I wanted them ready for that burst of speed. We were all dog-tired, and it was starting to show on the women. Pulling Samuel to one side, I told him of my plan.

"You an' the rest are gonna go on from here, an' I'll stay behind you to cover your back. Unless I miss my guess, they're behind us even now. Them tricks we pulled won't slow 'em down long," I said.

"Where you want us to go?" Samuel asked.

"Head for that saddle towards the west, there," I said, pointing the way. "You should be able to make it at least part way to the top 'fore dark. I'll stay behind you for a day or two, so don't be lookin' for me."

Buffalo Boy had been following our talk, and when he heard that, he rushed over to us.

"Father, I want to stay with you," he said. "I know I am the cause of all this trouble and I want to help to make it right. If it were not for me, we would not be running away."

Kneeling in front of him, I took him by the shoulders.

"Yes, this is partly your fault, son. But I am to blame for some of it too. I have not let you be a child. I have treated you like an adult, and you were only doing what an adult Ute warrior would do. But I need to do this on my own."

Seeing the hurt and confused look on his face was almost too much to bear. I pulled him to me in a fierce embrace, not wanting to let go.

Finally releasing him, I held him at arms length. His head was hanging low, and I could see the tracks of his tears running down his face in a silent cry. Lifting his chin, I tried to give him courage.

"I need you to go with your Uncle, now. If something happens to me, he will need you to help him defend your mother and her sister. Can you do this thing for me?" I asked him.

Not wanting to, he nodded his head yes, dragging his sleeve across his face.

"Good boy," I told him. "I need you to go get me an extra rifle and another powder horn from the packs. I need to tell your mother what is happening."

As Buffalo Boy turned away, I walked over to where the two women were dozing against the side of a downed tree. Hearing my footsteps, Autumn Sky opened her eyes.

"Is it time to leave already?" she asked.

"Yes, it is time for you to go. I will be staying behind you for a few days to take care of anyone following us. Arrow Catcher knows where to go," I told her.

Helping her to her feet, I led her to her pony and helped her mount.

"You will be careful, husband?" she asked.

"Am I not always careful?" I asked in mock hurt.

Smiling, she shook her head no.

Buffalo Boy handed me the extra rifle and powder horn, and I was lashing it to my saddle as Samuel rode over to me.

"Anythin' else you want me to know?" he asked.

"Yea, there is one more thing. Keep a sharp eye on Rowdy.

I wouldn't put it past him to sneak off an' come back to help me. I need you to keep him away from here. If he comes sneakin' back here, I may not realize it's him in time. An' you better stand watch till you see this ugly face of mine again. If I can't stop 'em, they'll keep followin' you," I added.

"You sure you know what you're doin,' Razor? I don't like leavin' you behind by yourself. They might be sendin' out a whole passel after us. I just don't like it," he added.

"Right or wrong, Samuel, this is the way it's gotta be. Just take care of my family for me."

Turning away from him before he could object further, I went to my mule. After tightening the cinch up a bit, I mounted up and started back the way we had come. There was a place about two miles back that would make an excellent ambush. I wanted to get there while I still had the time and the daylight to study it some more.

Turning back in the saddle, I was just in time to see the last packhorse go around the corner. Samuel would take care of them, I knew. My only thought was to try to slow the Arapaho warriors down long enough to confuse them.

I figured they would send some of the younger warriors after me, and I hoped they would. They would be more apt to cut and run with their tails between their legs when I made it too hot for them. If I could take out the leader and a few of the other key warriors, then the rest would blame it on bad medicine.

But there was always the chance that this would be the last fight for me. I didn't have any special power or anything like that; I was just lucky. Might be my luck was about to run out.

Chapter 43

I reached the meadow about an hour before sundown, giving me plenty of time to come up with a plan for my one-man ambush. The way this small clearing was made, there was only one way in and one way out, and that was straight through the middle. The whole thing was surrounded by blown down trees and deadfalls, except the game trail we had followed.

I circled off to the left side, following the edge of the clearing, until I was more than half way. There, I dismounted and led the mule carefully back into the brush and deadfalls for about fifty feet. Tying her securely to a tree, I pulled both rifles loose, and headed back to the exit side of the trail.

I wanted to completely block it off so there was nowhere for them to go, except back the way they had come. Dragging some dead brush and broken trees over, I piled them up, trying to make my barrier look as natural as I could. It was almost dark by the time I was satisfied with the way it looked, and I headed back to where I had tied my mule.

Singing softly, so as not to spook the mule, I made my way to her. I hadn't taken the saddle off before, but now I did, giving her a well deserved break from the weight. I knew she was wanting a roll to scrape off the sweat and grime from the past two days, so I let her wander loose for a short time. I wasn't too worried about her running off in the dark.

Along about daybreak, I was wishing for some coffee, but I wasn't about to start a fire to give my position away. So I settled for some jerked buffalo instead, moving the mule to a new patch of grass as I ate. Not wanting to be caught off guard when the time to run came, I decided to saddle up now so I was ready.

Then I settled down to wait. I didn't have any idea how long it would be, but I guessed it would be before too long. I had leaned Pepper's rifle, the one I always took as my extra, against a tree about thirty feet or so from where I was sitting. I could get to it without too much trouble when the time came.

By the time the sun was half way across the sky, I was starting to have doubts. Maybe they didn't send anyone after us, I thought. Might be, I was just too jumpy in my old age. Always expecting the worse, at least when it came to the Arapaho, had become second nature to me. I had fought them too many times to take them lightly. But I just might be wrong this time. Maybe their chief, Blue Calf, had decided that his warriors had it coming for what they did back at rendezvous and didn't send anybody after us.

Such was my thinking when my mule suddenly blew, scaring the devil out of me. Cocking the rifle and the two pistols in front of me, I looked towards the lower end of the meadow. At first, I didn't see any movement, but then I caught a red flash of war paint.

They were expecting an ambush, I realized. They were on foot, cautiously checking the meadow out. Hoping they wouldn't go all the way through, I decided to wait and see what they were going to do. Maybe I could get a count of what I was up against while they tried to sneak up.

I counted six of them sneaking through the grass in the clearing. I figured they would've sent more, knowing how much they wanted me dead. Six wasn't going to be too much trouble, I told myself.

The leader suddenly stood up in plain view and said something I couldn't understand. I was tempted to shoot him right then, but something made me hold my fire. And it's a good thing I did, for as I watched, five more warriors came out into the clearing, leading the horses of those on foot.

Something caught my eye at the back of the group, and I realized in an instant what it was. Buckskins. All the rest of the warriors were dressed in simple breechclouts, but that one had on a buckskin shirt. Even before he turned so I could see his face, I knew who it was.

"Moses Harris," I muttered. What was he doing here? Then I noticed his face was painted like the rest of them and I knew. He was sent to make sure I didn't make it this time.

There are some things a man can take and some he can't. A white man siding with Arapaho was one thing I couldn't take. He was the first one I was going to kill. Let the others that survived take that message back to Blue Calf. Red man or white, when they came up against me and mine, color didn't make no difference.

After they were all mounted again, they started across the meadow, walking their horses in single file. When the leader was about fifty yards from the end of the clearing, I shot Moses Harris.

The .54 caliber ball took him just below the throat, throwing him backwards off his horse. As the other horses and riders started to panic, about half of them kept going forewords, only to be stopped by the logs and brush I had put in the way. The rest of them turned and ran back the way they had come.

Scooping up both pistols, I ran towards the other rifle. They had no idea where I was, at least not yet, and I wanted to take a few more down before they found me.

As I reached the second rifle, I pulled up the pistol in my left hand and squeezed the trigger, just as a warrior streaked past. I saw the bullet hit him low down in the back, and knew it was a good kill shot, even though he would suffer for a while.

Dropping the empty pistol, I drew a bead on another warrior as he spotted me in the trees. With a shout, he charged his horse towards me, only to be blown out of his makeshift saddle when the pistol went off. I wasn't sure if it was a hit or not, only that the others now knew where I was.

Picking up Pepper's rifle, I sighted down the barrel at the warrior I had seen in the lead. Leading him slightly, I squeezed off the shot, immediately dropping the rifle and pulling the knife and tomahawk from the back of my belt. Dropping down into a crouch to make less of a target, I felt the hiss of an arrow as it flew by me.

Panting heavily from the running and the excitement, I was glad when the remaining seven braves pulled off. By no means were they done, this I knew from past fights with the Arapaho. They were regrouping, trying to decide if I was alone or not. They knew there were five of us when we left, but it wouldn't take them long to figure out I was alone. Then they would rush me.

Taking the time to reload both rifles and both pistols, I was ready when they charged in on me. Instead of coming at me in a line, they attacked in a wide arc, spread out in front of me. I managed to get off one shot with my rifle, tearing the face off one on them. Then I felt the blood gush from a head wound.

Falling to the ground, I tried to find a pistol, anything that I could use as a weapon, but the blood was pouring down my face like a waterfall. I wiped at it several times, but all I managed to do was smear it around more.

Pulling and tearing at my shirt, I managed to get it off

and wipe some of the blood from my eyes. And then I wished I hadn't. The last thing I saw was a grotesquely painted face coming at me with a buffalo lance in his hands. With no way to defend myself, I threw the shirt at him as he thrust the blade into me.

Epilogue

The plodding footsteps of the mule slowly brought me back to consciousness. Opening the one eye I could, I saw it was dark. I had no idea where I was or where I was going. I only felt the pain of my wounded head and side. Then I passed out again. I remember waking up to the sun shining on my face, and then it was dark again. Somewhere along the way I had managed to tie my hands to the saddle horn. Or did someone do it for me? I couldn't remember.

The next time I woke, it was daylight. I had no idea where I was, but the mule must have known where she was going from the steady pace she was walking. My whole body felt as if it was on fire, and I was thinking about finding someplace to get a drink of water, when the mule stopped, her ears standing straight up in the air. That's when I realized just how helpless I was.

e|LIVE

listen|imagine|view|experience

AUDIO BOOK DOWNLOAD INCLUDED WITH THIS BOOK!

In your hands you hold a complete digital entertainment package. Besides purchasing the paper version of this book, this book includes a free download of the audio version of this book. Simply use the code listed below when visiting our website. Once downloaded to your computer, you can listen to the book through your computer's speakers, burn it to an audio CD or save the file to your portable music device (such as Apple's popular iPod) and listen on the go!

How to get your free audio book digital download:

1. Visit www.tatepublishing.com and click on the e|LIVE logo on the home page.
2. Enter the following coupon code:
   6ed8-9d85-5ea1-dad 0-7ff5-c370-94c6-9280
3. Download the audio book from your e|LIVE digital locker and begin enjoying your new digital entertainment package today!